OTHER VISIONS
OF
HEAVEN AND HELL

Jessica Palmer

Parallel Universe Publications

First Published in the UK in 2016
Copyright © 2016 Jessica Palmer
Front and back cover: Frans Francken the Younger

LAST LAUGH was first published in *Weirdbook* #28 Autumn 1993, edited by W. Paul Ganley
CINDERELLA REVISITED was first published in *Weirdbook* #29 Autumn 1995, edited by W. Paul Ganley
WHAT THE DICKENS was first published in *Substance* Sept. 1995

ISBN: 978-0-9935742-1-4
Parallel Universe Publications, 130 Union Road,
Oswaldtwistle, Lancashire, BB5 3DR, UK

CONTENTS

DEVIL'S DUE

On the seventh day, He rested.

A big mistake.

For idle hands are the devil's playground, but God couldn't possibly know that yet, for the world was young and so was He, comparatively speaking.

Lucifer had been an angel then. The Angel of Light. And the position of devil hadn't even been invented yet, much less filled. The daemon hadn't been demoted – by the simple expedient of removing a single letter in their names (and a few rungs on the evolutionary ladder). Thus the daemon became the demon, and the divinities of old were transformed – Astoreth becoming Astoroth and Baal, Bael.

And a friend, a fiend.

A god by any other name…

The Almighty sniggered.

Never underestimate the power of THE WORD.

At that time, though, a week hadn't even passed, for the week also hadn't been invented yet. Jehovah hadn't got around to that until day thirty when He came up with the idea for a month. Unfortunately, He didn't bother to sit down and figure out the maths on it until He devised the concept of a year. By then it was too late, and there was no way He could correct the calculations without fiddling them.

A quarter of a day here, a quarter of a day there, and every four years, Bob's your uncle.

Time.

God grunted as he slipped into yet another veil.

Now that was a bit of a botched job. In other universes, He'd dispensed with the formality as extraneous. For with time came mortality and where fatality existed desperation soon followed.

But God only understood this later, much later, after He had the opportunity to ruminate upon some obvious design flaws. He had made quite a few. He'd already had to give up on giants as too cumbersome and large lizards as too clumsy – and not particularly bright. After those first abortive attempts at creation,

God had wiped the slate clean.

Except for the angels, of course. It had been the angels and not man who had been made in His image and likeness. They were immortals like Himself, and He was stuck with them as they were with Him.

Sometimes He wondered if angels had been a mistake also. They were something He'd whipped up one boring afternoon – long before day one – when the sky was grey with the nothingness of void and he had wanted someone to talk to.

Still, God thought He'd corrected the basic angelic faults when he upgraded to man. First, He'd eliminated a lot of the frivolities and fripperies. No flaming wheels of fire, no multiple tongues or thick covering of hair — each with a myriad of mouths and a multiplicity of eyes. No halos of radiant light that forced Him to squint.

Nothing flash.

No wings either. They were much too ostentatious. The daemon and angels spent hours preening them, and comparing them. ("I got sixteen-thousand and you got only four.") That was when God had discovered the sins of vanity and pride.

Wings weren't necessary for land bound creatures. So man became simple streamlined versions of the original.

Never let it be said that God didn't learn from His mistakes. He knew now that He should never have given the angels the knowledge of good and evil. With that He'd given them the ability to reason, to think and to judge others — even him the Supreme Being. In so doing He'd opened the door to contention and debate.

But in those days God had been young and idealistic, believing in individual rights. Little had He known that with this single act He'd spawned an eternity of discord and dissent.

There would to be no such nonsense with His new children — man. Without partaking of the fruit from the Tree of Knowledge, they would remain innocent. Humanity couldn't possibly grasp anything abstract, like death. Knowing neither bad nor good, they would remain ignorant of avarice and greed.

Yes, God had learned His lessons well.

By the seventh day, Jehovah had been tired in an Almighty way. Even the Supreme Being needed a break now and then. He designated that day as a holiday, a day of rest. But He forgot to tell man which day it was. Man, as usual got it all muddled; thus, the correct day for the celebration of the Sabbath became a ready cause for religious dispute.

Jehovah would have been better off if He'd planned some sort of festivities for this first heavenly holiday. The angels had used their leisure time for reflection. Always dangerous. Let's face it, the angels weren't all that old either and this thinking thing was new to them too.

Left to his own devices Lucifer — one of the more erudite of His corp of elite — pondered the purpose of creation which seemed as yet incomplete.

Oh, Lucifer agreed with some of the changes. Like the elimination of wings — the skyways were crowded enough as it was — and he approved of the simplified design. But Lucifer lamented the loss of intelligence in beings that were his mortal mirror. The angel suffered to see God's scions scrabbling naked in the dirt, digging for tubers and rooting among dead leaves for rotted fruit, just because they were too stupid to pluck it ripe from the tree.

It was undignified. Unseemly.

In the week that followed the first, while God was putting the finishing touches on the universe, Lucifer questioned Him, casting his blasted light on the dark corners of creation.

Who, Lucifer asked, wanted the adulation of creatures which were the intellectual equivalent to cattle?

Jehovah was not amused.

The Supreme Being could already see the plan that was forming inside the archangel's fevered skull. Lucifer wished to remedy what he was sure must've been God's oversight.

Halos, the Lord shook His head in dismay, another bad idea. All that brilliance tended to burn out the brain.

God needed a bit of a think, so the Lord on High declared a second holiday (thereby instituting a tradition which employers everywhere would come to rue, Bank Holiday Monday).

He didn't pay particular attention when the Heavenly Host — Michael, Lucifer and the boys — went down to the garden. For he had made paradise to be enjoyed by all, and it was a pretty spot.

Although by unspoken agreement the archangels avoided the area known as Eden. God should have forbidden access to Eve, but it would have made the temptation too great, and, as far as God was concerned, the instruction had been implicit.

Adam, Lord knew, could not be swayed. Adam was much too interested in his genitals to think of anything else. Another lesson: never leave the genitalia in direct line of vision. God should have learned this with chimpanzees, but things had been a bit hectic that day. The basic blueprint worked well enough with four-legged creatures — when God finally got around to designing the male of each species — but not so with the two-legged. Because the first thing man saw when he stood upright was his reproductive organs and, with the male, sexual consider-ations took precedence over everything else.

Of course, God had told them to be fruitful and multiply. Only He hadn't told them how, thought they would figure it out for themselves.

But with her genitals nicely hidden, Eve wasn't copulating — or co-operating. She couldn't be persuaded to participate, developing nature's first headache. And God had to admit that her lack of interest had presented something of a dilemma to the be fruitful and multiply bit.

The solution when it came was a stroke of genius — even if He said so Himself. The Angel of Light had already decided to take matters into his own hands — pre-empting Him — and God let him, although He decided He must be seen to be angry or He'd have angels revolting all over the place.

The rest was history. After the act, God spoke without thinking, forcing Lucifer to adopt his guise of a snake whenever he entered the Divine Presence.

That was when the Supreme Being learned about phobic reactions. Repelled by the serpent form, a right old ruckus broke out between Michael and the insolent Lucifer. The universe had almost been destroyed, and God had been compelled to hurl Satan from heaven in order to keep the peace.

Since then, many millennia had passed and now another was drawing to a close. Time for Lucifer's millennial appeal.

"Sixty-nine-thousand-nine-hundred-ninety-nine."

He counted the veil as the Almighty wrestled into yet another of his judicial robes and wondered why the Moslem had saddled him with such ungainly garb as seventy-thousand veils of light and darkness.

Only one more to go. By this time, though, His movements were savage. The buttons of this last celestial gown came off in His hands.

"DAMN!" He cursed and somewhere on earth someone's life went hopelessly awry — and that of his children and his children's children unto the seventh generation.

"Velcro," God thought, "that's the ticket."

Not all technological inventions were the devil's work. He snapped His fingers and Velcro strips were snatched from the nether regions and neatly installed on every heavenly gown. On earth, people's shoes fell off mid-step and their rucksacks self-destructed on their backs. Southern California trembled, slipping a little bit closer to the sea, and somewhere out in space, galaxies collided.

*

"Well, I'm pleased with the judges." Confined to his serpentine form, Satan swivelled his sinewy neck to peer at his solicitor. "God has been truly generous."

"Yes, I'm rather worried about that," said Belial, perdition's master of rhetoric and law and Satan's chosen representative. "It's not like him."

The names panel read like a Who's Who of Hades: Leviathan, Bael, Forcas, Astoroth, Behemoth. The Supreme Being had even been lenient in the matter of the superior judge, selecting Mary Magdalene — who had had seven demons cast from her person, and, therefore, had an intimate acquaintance with the devil — as magistrate instead of the more severe Solomon.

Something was up.

God's clemency seemed to have stopped there, for he'd appointed St Francis as prosecuting attorney who, having ascended to Lucifer's throne after the fall, had a vested interest in maintaining his holy seat.

*

"Here ye, here ye, the..." — and the bailiff Jeremiah rattled off a number so long that even the gleeful demons sitting in the flaming maw of the serpent started to snooze — "...Appellate

9

Court is about to begin. The Honourable Magistrate Mary Magdalene presiding. All rise."

The Lady emerged from the celestial chambers and ducked her head in regal acknowledgement. Then she lowered herself into her chair.

Jeremiah bowed to the magistrate and waited until she had settled before recounting the charges.

"The appeal of Lucifer versus the Holy Estate, against the charges of acting contrary to the public weal, defying a Divine command, ignoring a Holy day, defacing Holy ground with his unholy person and general wreaking of havoc."

Mary nodded at the bailiff and then turned to the councillors. "You may make your opening remarks."

Belial stopped his agitated pacing to take his place before the judges. Satan's representative was in fine fettle. In the powdered wig of the barrister and the black dovetail coat, he cut an impressive figure. The demon had opted for the mask of common man. Something that was bound to appeal to Mary's more human eye. Only the leering face of an imp that occasionally peered out from betwixt the tails of his coat marred the almost mortal image, and then only when Belial turned his back to her. This he avoided doing at all costs, prancing backwards rather than turn tail upon the judge.

"Long ago, my client was indicted for several counts of defiance to Divine ordinance and insubordination to an indirect imperative. He was found guilty and sentenced to servitude for a period of not less than one thousand years. As part of his punishment, he and his followers were cast from the Divine Presence.

"In accordance with Omnipresent edict, as noted in Revelations, my client has the right of appeal at the end of each millennium. As the second millennium, B, eh, er — " Belial's mouth contorted as if the second letter was difficult to spit out " — thingy, er, C draws to a close, we would like to exercise that right of appeal, your..." Speaking in the many tongues of Babel, the Devil's Advocate launched into the list of all God's names, in a thousand different universes, a thousand different worlds.

From behind His seventy-thousand veils of light and dark, God interrupted. "ENOUGH. I KNOW MY NAME(S)."

Belial flinched away from the curtained alcove, where God

10

hid His holy person. God always talked like that. Upper Case, in a voice so booming that even the parenthesis were audible. "Sah-sah-sorry."

"I AM ALSO AWARE OF THE ORIGINAL EDICT — AFTER ALL, I MADE IT — AND THE RIGHT OF APPEAL. DO GET ON WITH IT. CALL YOUR FIRST WITNESS!"

"The defence would like to call, the Archangel Phanuel."

"ARE YOU SURE?"

"Yes, sir," Belial said.

Surrounded by whirlwinds, thunder and radiant light, Phanuel advanced across the great court and took his place in the dock. He folded his magnificent wings primly about him, as Jeremiah — with the assistance of Ezekial, Joel, David, Joshua, Amos and Obadiah — strove to lift the celestial text which is the true word of God, a much more weighty tome than any mortal Bible. Magnanimously, the angel leaned forward and placed his hand on the book. The prophets' knees trembled under them.

"Repeat after me," the bailiff said.

"Repeat after me," Phanuel responded dutifully. The prosecuting attorney St Francis of Assisi hissed and the panel of judges broke into twitters.

Doggedly, Jeremiah carried on. "I — state your name — do... wheeze... promise to tell the truth the whole truth and nothing but the truth so help you Him?"

"I state my name do... gasp... promise to tell the truth the whole truth and nothing but the truth so help me Him."

"Excuse me, your honour, I believe that was a wheeze and not a gasp," Belial said.

"WHETHER IT WAS A WHEEZE OR A GASP IS IRRELEVANT."

"And his name. He didn't state his name."

"COME NOW, YOU ARE JUST STALLING. WE ALL KNOW PHANUEL."

"He could be an impostor."

"HE WOULDN'T DARE."

"Ah, yes, well. Right." Belial concentrated on Phanuel. "For sake of reference you are Phanuel, known to some as Uriel. Now will you please tell the court the position you hold in the Holy Hierarchy?"

"I am in charge of repentance, or repentant souls."

"Repentance of sinners, I presume." He walked over to the gallery. A saint hawked a wad on his powdered wig. "As in Original Sin?"

"Of course, what else?"

"Just checking to see if we were agreed on terms. Let me ask you this. Could there be repentance from Original Sin, without Original Sin?"

"Objection," Francis thundered. A flock of pigeons squawked and began flying around the court.

"Your honour, how can my learned colleague object to a something that is already a matter of public record?"

"Overruled," Mary said. "You may answer the question."

"Could you repeat it again please?"

"Could there be repentance from Original Sin without Original Sin?"

"Well, no, I suppose not."

"In other words, man couldn't find grace in God's sight if there had been no Original Sin." Belial extended his arms.

"You said it, I didn't."

"Has it also been said that God is a hidden treasure; so he created the world that he might be known?"

"Yes, I believe Mohammed said that."

"And with the gift of the apple, isn't Satan attributed with giving humanity their sense of self? In essence Satan gave man an identity so that he knows himself to be something separate from God?" Belial forged on. "And could it not be said in giving humankind their separate identity, Lucifer enabled them to worship the Divine?"

"Ah, er — "

"Therefore it could not be assumed that in creating this individuality, which permitted humanity to venerate the divine, Satan was doing God's work?"

The prosecuting attorney was on his feet. "Objection! My learned colleague is calling for conclusions on the part of the witness," Francis said, muttering under his breath, "Always a mistake with Phanuel."

"Sustained." Mary turned to Belial. "Pray continue."

"I'd rather not pray, your honor," said the demon.

Her brow creased and she frowned. "Just continue then."

"We have no more questions of this witness, your honor."

Mary Magdalene looked expectantly at St Francis. "Cross examination?"

The saint grunted. "I have no questions at this time, but I reserve the right to recall the first witness if necessary."

"The defence would like to call the archangel Azrael," Belial said.

"Azrael," bellowed the bailiff, "calling the archangel Azrael to the stand."

Belial examined his fingernails as the formalities were repeated. He approached the witness box. "Will you please state your current occupation for the record?"

Azrael looked affronted. "You know who I am."

"Ah," Belial said, "humour me."

"I am the Angel of Death. My job is to sever the immortal soul from the mortal body."

"And how do you define 'soul'?"

"That's simple. Everybody knows that. It's the spiritual and immaterial part of man, that which survives death."

"Very good, sir," Belial nodded in agreement. "I believe that's the Oxford's English Dictionary definition."

"Is it? I wouldn't know."

"If I may be permitted to read the next portion of the OED text. It further defines soul as the 'moral and emotional part of man'. Tell me, Azrael, would you agree with the content of this particular meaning?"

"Well, yes, I suppose," Azrael said reluctantly. "I don't see anything wrong with it."

"The moral part of man." Belial stressed the word moral. "That would mean that the soul, which it is your duty to amputate from corporeal flesh, is the portion of man capable of distinguishing right from wrong. Correct?"

"Well, ah, er," Azrael stuttered.

"Now I ask you, wasn't this the very gift Satan presented to Eve in the Garden of Eden? The ability to distinguish right from wrong? Would there even be a moral part of man without Lucifer?"

"Well, ah…"

"In other words it could be said that it was Lucifer and not God who gave man his soul."

The entire courtroom erupted into chaos.

"Blasphemy!"

"Sacrilege."

"Order, order in the court!"

Belial continued as if nothing happened. "Certainly without this knowledge humanity would remain ignorant of the concept of morality. And without morality, man would be without soul as defined by Oxford's English Dictionary and approved by this court. More importantly," he paused significantly, "you, Azrael, would be out of a job. Is that a correct assessment?"

"Well, yes." Azrael fluttered nervously. The gallery erupted again.

The angel shouted them down. "That's the real problem. He made work for all of us. Thanks to Satan, we got souls to sever, sinners to repent and what — not. Worse," he said indignantly, "because man has the ability to reason, we in the divine hierarchy are questioned, expected to give just cause for what we do."

"I have no more questions," Belial said.

Francis rose to address the court and they fell silent to listen to his rebuttal. "My learned colleague has raised some interesting points about soul. Azrael, I would like to redirect your attention to the first definition given."

"Uh, what was that again? I forgot."

"That the soul is the spiritual and immaterial part of man. Do you remember saying that the soul is that which survives death?"

"Yes."

"That which survives death." Francis repeated the words. "Put another way, it can be said that soul is that which provides the spark of life and animates the outer shell of man. Correct?"

Confused, Azrael considered this. "Sounds, uh, good to me."

"And is it not this spark of life, or spirit, that Lord Jehovah breathed into man during the act of creation?"

"Yes." The angel sounded relieved.

"And if this is the case, then soul is neither knowledge nor the ability to distinguish right from wrong, but something else again, something innate."

"Yes!"

"Thus the soul could only have been given to man by God."

"YO!"

"Thank you, Azrael, the prosecutor has no further questions at this time."

"Next, I would like to call Gabriel to the stand." Belial rose and took his place next to the witness box. "State your name and occupation."

"I am Gabriel, messenger of God."

"Messenger of God, very good," said Belial, "which, I suppose in modern parlance, would be called his publicity agent."

"Humph," Gabriel ruffled, "nothing so mundane."

"All right, then, perhaps you could elaborate on your the duties What precisely do you do?"

"As I said, I'm His messenger. I carry His Word to man. It is my position to explain God's mandates and His decrees."

"Explanations, which according to Azrael, Lucifer made necessary."

"Yes." The angel folded his arms across his chest. "Indeed."

"Therefore, you would also be out of work if it hadn't been for Satan, correct?"

"I object to this line of questioning," said Gabriel.

"I'm sorry, you're in no position to object. Please answer the question, yes or no."

"Yes, I suppose so."

"So you agree that without Lucifer you would be unemployed or, at least, underemployed because if it wasn't for Satan humanity would have the mental agility of a peanut and be unable to grasp God's missives?"

"Ai — yee — yes."

"Is that a bad thing that God can converse with man and be understood? Remember God created man so that He may be known by them."

"Ah, er, no, I don't know."

Belial changed the subject. "I believe in your job as messenger of God you coined the phrase: `the Lord moves in mysterious ways', did you not?"

"Yes, I did." Gabriel preened. "I'm rather proud of that one."

"You are? May I ask why?"

"Well, it gets us off the hook, don't it? God being ineffable and all."

"Yes, ineffable. Inexplicable would be another way of putting that. Yes, that is a nice catch — all, isn't it?" Belial stared hard at the witness. "Thus, God does not have to explain what He does, How convenient."

"Now wait a second..."

Belial shrugged. "Do you agree that if it hadn't been for Lucifer, mankind would be too stupid to comprehend the import of your messages and there'd be no reason to deliver them?"

"Well..."

"Answer the question, yes or no."

"Yes."

"Not only you but Uriel, Chamuel, Zadkiel and Japhiel would all be unemployed. There would be no need for a courier, no need for severer of souls. No need for repentance. No need to sway souls for good or for ill."

"Probably not," the angel conceded.

"No need for saints. The Fourteen Holy would be redundant, for what need then to comfort man with God's goodness at the time of his demise? What need to spread His joyous word? Francis would become just a very nice man with an affinity for birds..."

*

The next witness, Michael, approached dock bench wearing his most horrific visage, that of the Islamic Mika'il. Hairs of saffron sprouted all over his face, arms and chest. Each hair had a million faces, a million eyes, each crying tiny tears, and million tongues that repeated each statement.

"Have you not been quoted saying 'the absolute cannot be contemplated in its absoluteness'?" asked Belial.

"Yes," Mika'il shrugged, with a single shoulder and the nonchalant flap of feathered pinions. "It sounds like something I might say to a passing prophet or a saint."

"The absolute? By this you mean, the complete, the perfect, the pure?"

Mika'il pulled himself up to full height and unfurled his great wings of green topaz. His pectorals rippled. "Absolutely."

"As perfection, the absolute is incapable of making a mistake, correct?"

"Of course." But the intimidating visage of Mika'il dissolved

16

to the more congenial image of Michael, reflecting his uncertainty.

Belial continued: "And since it cannot be contemplated, it cannot be comprehended. In your estimation, can the absolute be questioned?"

On firmer ground, Michael relaxed visibly. "Who are we to challenge the Divine? The flawless model of He who made us."

"Quite right," the advocate agreed affably. "As perfection can make no mistakes, it is reasonable to assume that all that has occurred must have a purpose. Would you agree?"

"Such is the way of absoluteness."

"Therefore, you would contend that the fight, the casting of Lucifer from Heaven's gates was part of a plan."

In his curtained alcove, Jehovah's veils shook. Whether in ire or discomfort Belial did not know, but he gulped audibly and waited to be blasted to Kingdom come.

A little less secure now, Michael sensed the trap in the making. He hesitated, rubbing his chin to cover his indecision. "Well, like I said before, the absolute cannot be comprehended in its…"

"… absoluteness, yes, we know. Just answer the question, yes or no. Do you believe perfection has a plan?"

"Uh… huh." Michael wrapped a wing over his mouth, muffling his reply.

"What was that? Yes or No?"

"Yes!"

"And if perfection always has a plan, then it must be presumed that the releasing of knowledge to humankind must have been part of that plan. And if it was part of a plan, then why should Lucifer be punished?"

Michael opened his mouth to protest but Belial hastened on. "Would you agree that the Inestimable in creating us gave us the very natures we possess?"

"Yes."

"Thus, the Almighty made Lucifer the Angel of Light."

"Of course, everybody knows that."

"And as the Angel of Light, he would also be considered the keeper of Divine illumination."

"Yes!" Michael snapped. "Get to your point."

"I'm working on it. As the Angel of Light, it would be part of

17

his very, God-given nature to share this illumination with others. Would it not?"

"I suppose."

"Then in keeping with his nature, Lucifer would have no other choice than to give this Light to mankind. Therefore Lucifer did no wrong, could do no wrong, in acting as he did since it was integral part of his personality, his make-up, his God-given nature!

"And if Lucifer acted according to Divine nature, one must assume that it must have been according to the Divine plan."

"Huh? Was that a question?"

The devil's advocate swung dramatically toward the bench. "I rest my case."

*

"Gentlemen and fair lady. The matter before us is almost as old as time itself. I ask you to consider: How long must one pay for one act of insubordination? Assuming, of course, that it was an act of insubordination.

"It has been recorded in the scriptures that God told Adam not to partake of the fruit of the tree, but did the Almighty ever tell Lucifer not to offer it?

"And what of this deed which is called Original Sin? This sharing of knowledge, an act that was made with the best of intentions, and in the final analysis, an act which has been advantageous for all of us. Not least of which was man. Surely, Lucifer's heart was in the right place, for from this deed, man derived the thinking part of himself. The moral part, which according to some definitions is the part of man that is called the immortal soul.

"Never forget that through this act, Lucifer gave angels continuous employment. Pause to consider what afterlife would be like right now without Lucifer? There would have been no need for heaven" – the collective angels and saints in the gallery gasped, even the blazing balls of ophanim wavered – "or hell. No need for salvation or damnation. Punishment and retribution would have no meaning without an awareness of right and wrong, for without this knowledge how could man know sin?

"Without Original Sin, there would be no death and then

what good would Azrael's mighty sword be without souls to sever? What need would there be for the saints? Consider Saint Catherine who, with the end of the noble profession of spinsters, had no other work than to comfort mortal man at the time of his passing. What would she do if it hadn't been for Satan's selflessness? How boring would eternity be with no other occupations than holy harmonics and creative pin — dancing? How much poorer man, without Satan's act of compassion?

"And how else could Lucifer behave — except according to his nature? For is he not the Angel of Light? And what is light but the torch of wisdom which chases away the shadows of ignorance? Could Lucifer be expected to acquit himself in any other way? He is, and he acted, as he was created to be, by the absolute.

"The alternative would be to presume that perfection erred. That purity blundered. That the Supreme Being made a mistake in creating Lucifer." Belial's voice rose a notch in incredulity. His arms outstretched in an imitation of Christ on the cross. "Nay, I think not. Personally, I would not dare to imply that God diddled when he made any one of us. And if God created an emissary to carry His light, then what else could His herald do except carry it? In bearing light to man, Satan only fulfilled his Divine role.

"He did his bit, and yet he is cast into the abyss. Don't you think this a bit excessive?

"I exhort you, if you believe in the power and perfection of the absolute, then Lucifer's nature, his inclinations, were no accident, but part of a plan. Therefore, the responsibility for Original Sin lies not with Lucifer, but issues from a higher source." Belial concluded: "I'd say it's time we gave the devil his due and overturn the previous verdict."

*

Francis got up from his table, shook the birds off his shoulders and scratched his chin. "My esteemed colleague would have you believe that Satan is the one wronged. That God, and later Michael, grievously and unjustly injured him.

"The devil's advocate attributes good to Satan. Lucifer! Who is ego; who is the self incarnate. Think of the millennia spent

19

punishing evildoers, winnowing the wheat from the chaff, and consider the alternative, had he not acted. Had he stayed away from Eve, Eden would remain, and God's children would live idyllically. Instead of all this to-ing and fro-ing carrying messages of revelation and retribution. No lives to weigh in the balance, no souls to sway.

"My adversary says that we would remain unemployed. What he means, in fact, is that Lucifer has made work for us. Hard work.

"Even the Almighty Jehovah has been indirectly affected by his temerity, for with this knowledge, man in his all-too-finite wisdom has learned to question Him, expecting rationale and explanations from the ineffable. Imagine God expected to justify his actions.

"Who is to pay for the ages of hard labour? God? Or he who caused our travail? Satan. The case is not about guilt or innocence — that was decided long ago — but the duration of the punishment inflicted for this guilt.

"I would also implore you to ask yourselves this question: Do you" – his finger halted upon a demon — "or you" — the finger swooped to stop at another demonic face — "or you, for that matter, want to return to the right hand of God? For this is the question you must decide."

*

His servant, Belial, had made several good points, but asserting that Lucifer's act was according to God's prearranged plan was a stroke of genius. Belial was getting better at his work all the time.

Lucifer would have to keep an eye on him.

"Why? Why did you rule the way you did."

Still in the serpentine form of a dragon, Lucifer whirled upon his minions and roared, spewing fountains of fire from his many mouths. A few disintegrated, while other took themselves to healthier climes, pleading urgent matters of state. Those who were trapped by the evil eye examined their nails, their toes, anything but Satan.

"Foreman!" the devil bawled, and the pitiful creature dropped to his knees before his master. "Explain your verdict."

"Well think of it, master, the prosecutor was right when he

said the question was whether or not we wanted to return to the right hand of God."

Lucifer pulled back slightly and began to shrink into a more human form. "Yes?"

"We do that and we just become part of the rank and file. No status. No power to act. No authority. It'd be just like before and we'd be just like them." The demon shivered. "With nothing better to do than flit and fly, hanging around all day long singing His praises."

Lucifer nodded tersely.

"If things went back to the way they were, with mankind little brighter than cattle, where would we be? Without man to transgress, then we wouldn't even have sinners to convert. So in the long run, it'd be worse than before because we'd know what we were missing. Quite frankly, sir, we think it would be boring."

*

Rrrip! The Lord Jehovah divested himself of the first of the seventy-thousand robes, with a flick of a wrist.

This Velcro was neat stuff.

RIP! The second fell to the floor.

He moved over to the mirror to observe, not his own regal reflection, but the gates of hell where his servant Lucifer berated his demons for their decision. It had been touch and go for a moment there, particularly when they started talking about perfection's plan.

"But why?" Satan asked, turning on them with eyes of fire.

RRRIP! Several of His many veils fluttered to the floor simultaneously.

"Quite frankly, sir, it would be boring..."

God grinned. He had been right to assign demons as judges.

RRRRRRIIIIIPPP and a thousand veils cascaded to the ground.

God inclined his head in satisfaction.

Despite His reputation, the Lord Jehovah was not punitive by nature. Oh, God admitted to being a little lazy — He delegated authority whenever He could — and a trifle sloppy when rushed. But who wasn't?

RRIPPPPP! Another five thousand robes were flung to the floor.

Jehovah had just got a lot of bad press, that's all. The tribe of Levi, He decided long ago, had a lot to answer for. The Lord was always being misquoted.

Take Leviticus for instance. Moses was a very nice man, and all. He may have meant well, but he had the memory of a sieve. God was glad He had written the Commandments down, and even then the clumsy ox had dropped more than half the tablets. There'd been a lot more of them in the original draft. Hence the need for Leviticus to amend the list. It hadn't helped matters any that Moses' cousin was an out-of-work butcher, so Kosher was born.

Jehovah added, get a new press agent, to His mental list of things-to-do in the next millennium, and he clasped the last veils and tore them from His back.

YES! He scratched His sides as He studied the diabolic visage. The thing was: the system worked. One thing an eternity of experimentation taught Him was: if it's not broke, don't fix it. By careful honing and moulding through the ages, Lucifer was the smartest of the lot. And after centuries of experience, Lucifer was quite obviously the best man for the job.

His demons dismissed. Satan clacked across the room to his desk and sat, fingers drumming. Then he shrugged and pulled a piece of paper toward him with the names of wayward souls.

God sighed.

All was as it should be.

He waved a holy sigil over the mirror. The diabolic visage faded to be replaced by His holy reflection, magnified a hundred-fold. The figure that stood before the glass, though, was tiny. For without the embellishment of his many gowns, Jehovah stood at about three-foot-six. He'd reconciled himself to his size a long time ago, after the Jurassic period.

He'd learned then that bigger wasn't necessarily better.

THE FAITHFUL

"Mr Bakker, I've been sent to meet you." The man extended a hand.

Jim Bakker blinked, blinded by the suit. It was a stark white in what appeared to be leather.

"Nuggle-hyde."

"Huh?"

"Manufactured, faux fake."

"Oh."

Bakker glanced down at the proffered hand.

The cloth outfit was garish. The sleeves tapered at the wrist; they were attached to the back of the garment by a red material made of the same stuff, and fringe that flowed to the cloud beneath his feet. Like wings.

Shining sequins of glitter and gold ran down his chest, wide at the top like a yoke, narrow at the bottom that formed a V that pointed at his host's groin. At his shoulders, there were Epaulets that seemed to work the wings, and he looked like... Elvis.

"Elvis?"

The man looked pleased. He pirouetted and struck a pose, finger pointed at the sky. "No, but others have mentioned the resemblance. Except the hair, of course."

Bakker examined the fiery red hair. "No, not the hair."

Phalec again offered his hand.

Reluctantly, the preacher took it and shook it. The hand felt wet, limp and at bit slimy to the touch. Bakker dropped it and repress the impulse to wipe his palm on his shirt. "Where am I?"

"The afterlife," the mellifluous voice purred.

He studied the suit again. "Oh, well. That explains it."

"Explains what?"

"Your, uh, attire."

"Well, we try to keep up with the times, and we always put on the dog, so to speak, when such an important personage as yourself arrives."

"This is heaven?" Bakker brushed away a wisp of candy floss that had escaped from the cloud and was trying to enter his nose.

23

"Or its facsimile," Phalec said.

"What?"

"We have a special place set aside just for true believers like yourself." He set out down an eternally long hall with the minister scuttling after him.

Bakker nodded as if he expected no more than his due. The ground, cloud, or whatever you might call it, lurched forward underneath his feet. He fell.

Phalec offered his hand to help the preacher up. Bakker almost grabbed it, and remembering the clammy feel, waved it away.

"The Lord helps those who help themselves," he said.

"Oh, very good, sir. You certainly knew how to take advantage of that expression to the fullest, didn't you?"

Bakker scrambled to his feet. "Pardon?"

His host examined his suit, plucking off the strings of sugary floss. Rooms, doors, windows, fluffy bits of cloud swept passed.

The angel clasped the preacher's shoulder to steady him as what must have been an unseen conveyer screeched to a halt.

"We are here, sir."

"Here?"

"Here, the special place reserved for those who have seen the light, the born again," the sparkling daemon replied.

"Oh, yes, right, yes, of course. So where does everyone else go? Hell?"

"Metaphysically speaking?"

"Never mind," said Bakker as he attempted to squeeze past Phalec to get to the door beyond.

"Not so fast, sir. We have an extra special place for the holies of holy, the speakers of a generation. Let me show you." Phalec draped his arm over Bakker's shoulder and drew him over to the window.

"Is it pretty?" Bakker asked. "With brilliant blue skies, green grass and flowers in bloom with eternal spring."

"You could say that."

Bakker peered through the glass. A large field spread out before him, with people compressed shoulder-to-shoulder, standing in straggling, wobbly lines as a commandant barked at them. The men, women and children were dressed in para-military garb, complete with helmets. The costumes were a bit ad

24

hoc, with khakis mixed with olive drab and camous — both desert and jungle — but all the basic elements were there, right down to the netting on their war bonnets, for bonnets they were. Some of the women had adorned theirs with flowers and the kids had toys dangling from theirs or woven into the netting.

In the background he saw a beautiful garden completely ignored by the rigid population. Next to this a lion ripped a lamb to shreds. In a far corner he noted a series of tables set up in what appeared to be a stone hall.

Bakker turned to face his host. "What is this?"

"The home of the faithful."

"But why this?"

"This is the home they imagined where they all moved as one, motivated by the righteous hand of God, nothing... ah, er... disturbing, where they could defend their faith. To the death if need be."

Bakker heard a distant voice bellow: "Hut, two, three, four. Hut, two, three, four. Hut —"

He returned to the window. "I never knew there were so many."

"Faithful? Oh, yes, you should be proud," the angel chirped.

"Hut, two, three, four. About face."

The faithful spun in unison, some right, some left, and stumbled into each other.

The angel chuckled. "Of such stuff, holy wars are made.

The commander roared. "Halt. Pay attention. Eyes to me. Would you fight for the Heavenly Host? Would you die for them?"

"Yes!"

"Will you defend the righteous?"

"YES!"

"Defend the one true faith?"

"YESSSSSS!"

"Good. Now straighten up. Let's try it again. Hut!"

The many faithful clapped their left arms again their sides and stood at attention.

Only then did Jim Bakker notice the rifles they had propped against their shoulders.

"Good God, man, they're armed." He stared at his host. "The children? Surely, those must be toys."

Phalec shook his head.

"What did you expect?"

"Oh, I don't know. The lion laying next to the lamb, maybe?"

"I'm sorry, that's passé."

"The lion is eating the lamb!" Bakker fixed his host with an accusatory glare.

"He's got to eat. Besides, it is the image they conjured. Not a peaceful frolicking lamb in a field somewhere. Don't worry; the sheep come back."

"I never spoke about bloody sheep, I can assure you."

"Are you sure?" said the angel. "You may not realize this yet, but you started the entire revolution when you told people they could buy their way into heaven. Not an original idea, admittedly, the Catholics got there first with dispensations; but you, sir, did it so much better using the mass media, getting millions of viewers to 'reach right down into their pockets', isn't that what you said?"

"But I renounced that," Bakker insisted.

"A bit late, I'm afraid."

Bakker tapped the glass. "What do I have to do with this, this," he stuttered, "this blasphemy? This travesty? This abomination? This parody of heaven?"

"Are not the ministers of the faithful calling the people to arms using mass media, as you did. Only now they have the internet and not-so-social websites. Screaming against imagined threats, against the perceived infidel?"

Bakker gaped at his host. His jaw unhinged and then clapped shut. He said nothing.

"This is what Christianity has become. Damn those you don't like, don't understand. Attribute their perceived faults to acts of Satan. Hate those who have different faiths, those who genuflect with two fingers rather than three. Hate those who have lifestyles unlike your own. Hate homosexual."

Bakker interrupted his host. "As is right and proper. It's unnatural. It's against God's edicts."

Phalec tapped his forefinger against his pearly white teeth. "Funny, I don't seem to recall a scripture about that and, believe me, I've read them all. Some, even, that you have not seen."

"There's Onanism," Bakker piped up. "Spilling one's seed upon the soil."

"Yes, well, we'd considered making man as vegetative matter, sort of an intelligent plant, then such precepts would be unnecessary. In fact, seed spilling would be imperative for the procreation of the species, and Onan would be a hero." The angel tugged at his ear. "It might have worked out better. A damage limitation sort of thing. The only reason that seed spilling made it into the Bible is because Management were worried about whether humanity would ever catch on preservation of the species, and it seems you still haven't got the hang of it or you wouldn't have wars."

"About face!" The disembodied voice penetrated the wall, and Bakker cupped his hands around his face to blot out the glare of the harsh light so he could have a better view of the faithful.

"No, no, no, NO!"

"Wait a second," Bakker exclaimed. "Isn't that Hitler?" His voice rose on the name.

Phalec rubbed his nose. "No, it's his cousin Sid, a look-alike. Adolph had, um, a previous engagement with Lucifer, but that's okay, Sid preaches the same schtick and he fits right in."

"Doesn't anyone ask any questions?"

"No, that's the thing about the faithful, the chosen; they don't ask questions," said Phalec. "The creed remains the same, exclude anyone who doesn't hold the same views, hunt them and eliminate them if necessary, Moslems, Catholics, Jews." He shrugged. "Of course, it's not a new concept. The Catholic Church had the Inquisition and the Crusades, but the faithful have advantages. The Crusades took their cue from feudalism. Fighters were restricted to a privileged few, the knights. The modern day is much more egalitarian. Everyone has guns, and everyone wants in on the act."

The angel grinned; it was not a reassuring smile. "However, you should not worry about the rank and file. Your place is among the exalted. We have reserved a seat for you at the table."

The preacher's gaze went to the far corner.

Phalec added: "With the money lenders"

"The money lenders? No," Bakker barked.

"Oh, that's right, you don't lend money, do you? You take it, bankrupting the faithful, and then you steal what is given. I do recall a commandment against theft," Phalec commented.

"I acknowledge that I am a miserable sinner who succumbed to temptation."

"I'll say."

"But I did my time, and I have always prayed in Jesus' name. I should be shriven."

"Actually, I think he has a bone to pick with you. You took his name in vain, so he asked that you be placed with the money lenders who extorted money from the flock."

"Is that an exit?" Bakker tapped on the glass. "That hall."

"More of an entrance. It leads from the field, beyond the Garden of Eden, the lion and the lamb, and circles back to the temple. Let me tell you, real estate is a precious commodity in the afterlife," Phalec said. He clapped the man on his back. "You should be honoured to be whipped daily by Jesus."

"Jesus?"

"Or his facsimile. Usually, he is a busy with so many prayers calling upon him, although I think you may be visited by him occasionally. Otherwise, we send a copy." His host brightened. "Replica or not, it still hurts the same. You won't be able to tell the difference."

Suddenly there was sound of gun fire.

The startled Bakker jumped into the arms of the gaudy angel. "What is going on?"

His host set the minister down, pausing momentarily to polish his bangles. Bakker pressed his nose against the glass. Outside – or within – the Christian faithful shot at something, something red. It flew like a bird, staying aloft. As the melee continued the target shattered and split into smaller pieces which reformed to become more of the same.

Bang, bang, bang. Pop. Pop!

Phalec fiddled with his creases, rearranging the folds of his wings. "That, sir, is the highlight of the day. When they get a chance to hone their skills until such time when the holy war begins."

"What are they shooting at?" Bakker yelled over the noise of gunfire.

"A Starbucks cup."

AND NOW, A WORD FROM OUR SPONSOR

The Lord Most High, Host of Hosts and King of Kings, whirled into yet another shape, shifting from the frog form of the goddess Herd to the many-armed Shiva. He performed the dance of death before the mirror. The necklace of skulls rattled and clacked, coming to rest around his neck as he struck a pose and admired his reflection.

Jehovah smiled at himself. As a loving, giving God, a God who wanted all men to know Him, to love him, He was ready to appear in any of the million manifestations His creations had made for Him, and He had learned a long time ago it paid to practice.

With a snap of fingers, He transformed again to the white-bearded patriarchal image of Zeus. One never knew what might come back into fashion. With that thought in mind, He took on the horned figure of ancient myth, the Green Man. Very popular nowadays with the fantasy crowd. He squatted, testing the backward-hinged joints. They popped, and He winced.

Stretching his legs, the Lord adopted the less physically taxing Buddhist image. He glowered at the swirling mist of nirvana, although it more closely approximated the intent of his true form, that which men sometimes called the Holy Ghost, it gave nothing much to revere or adore aesthetically and artistically speaking. And God had discovered if He wasn't careful He got distracted, losing pieces of Himself to the cosmos. As if to confirm this thought part of the whirling vapour detached itself from the mass and went slinking away.

Then in rapid succession: He became the feathered serpent Quetzacoatl; He preened; the curvaceous, female form of Astarte, He spun, pranced and admired his breasts as they bounced; the toad god of some aboriginal tribe with a name that gave tongue-twisting a whole new meaning; lastly Freya; He sneezed. The woman always smelled like something reminiscent of goat.

Enough of humankind, God thought, and He began with the

infinite variations of Himself that could be found in the other planets, galaxies and universes.

Crackle!

And God was caught between two forms — one of which had sixteen heads — when the intercom interrupted him. The likeness dissolved into a miscellany of muddled parts.

"Father!"

"JESUS!" One of the sixteen heads glared at his right hand. The boy was a nuisance. "I THOUGHT I TOLD YOU NOT TO DISTURB ME WHILE I WAS IN THE OFFICE."

"There's a prayer coming in."

"PRAYERS'RE COMING IN ALL THE TIME." The shape from the QZ)C*:@V#%!~&~:X universe melted, and the Lord Jehovah was Himself again fleetingly.

He cocked an ear and tuned into the on-going universal communications link.

"… if you want anchovies, press hash…"

He shook his head. Wrong line. He scanned the infinite until he zeroed in on the right line.

"… Hello, welcome to the prayerline, internet to the divine… If you are Moslem, press…"

His noble brow furrowed as He concentrated on the hiss of requests — coming to him in a thousand different languages on a thousand different frequencies like so much psycho-babble.

"I want… gimme… donnez moi… please… help… I am unworthy…"

Sounded pretty much like business as usual. God chuffed as He tuned it out. The words of old blues tune came to mind.

"… won't you buy me a Mercedes Benz…"

Ah, Janis. God sighed.

An unlikely candidate for heaven, He agreed. Some of the archangels had strenuously objected to her admittance into the heavenly host, but God had not relented, granting her special dispensation. She at least spoke truth — and he was glad he had given her a place here. Her presence had livened things up.

"Er-hem!"

"OH, YES, SON, YOU WERE SAYING?"

"The prayer, sir."

"WHAT'S SO SPECIAL ABOUT THIS ONE?" The Lord on High swirled into another manifestation. The Polynesian god,

Tinirau, was half-man, half-fish, not split fore and aft as one might expect, but left and right. Jehovah tottered a bit on foot and fin.

Untidy that. Maybe He'd reveal Himself to someone so that they would change the concept. God mused. A message about balance would be ideal.

The voice intruded on His heavenly reverie. "It's about the end of the universe, sir."

God fell over, flopping around... well, like a fish! With an impatient gesture he righted himself.

"OH," He sputtered, "WELL, THAT IS A DIFFERENT KETTLE OF KIPPERS, ISN'T IT? WHICH UNIVERSE?"

Jesus listed it by number. God scowled. A cumbersome means of identification when there were an infinite number of parallel, converging and endlessly changing universes.

"COME ON, JUNIOR, DON'T BE COY. IT'S YOUR WORLD, ISN'T IT?"

"Well, uh, yes."

"YOU KNOW AS WELL AS I DO THAT THE END OF THE UNIVERSE IS NOT SCHEDULED FOR..."

The disembodied voice broke in before He could complete his sentence. "It seems man has been hurrying things along a little bit."

"HUMANITY HAS ALWAYS BEEN IMPATIENT."

"Yes, but it's starting to have a tangible impact."

"OF COURSE, THAT'S WHAT WE HAVE FREE WILL FOR, SO PEOPLES' ACTIONS INFLUENCE THEIR FUTURES. HOW ELSE CAN WE TEACH RESPONSIBILITY?"

"Well..." Jesus waffled.

"LOOK, SON, WE HAVE HAD SPATES OF THIS IN THE PAST, AND THIS IS THE END OF MILLENNIUM. MANKIND ALWAYS LOOKS FOR OMENS, PORTENDS AND SIGNS AT SUCH A TIME. ANY REASON TO BELIEVE THAT THIS EXPECTATION OF IMMINENT DESTRUCTION IS MORE SUBSTANTIAL THAN, SAY, IT WAS THE FOURTEENTH CENTURY?"

"Well, there are nuclear weapons now, sir."

"MUST I REMIND YOU THAT THE LONG BOW CAUSED TERRIBLE DESTRUCTION AND LOSS OF LIFE AT AGINCOURT."

"But wars rage across the Baltic, Middle East, Africa, Asia, South America..." the voice droned on. "It is now estimated that about ten to twenty-five percent of the earth surface is at war at any given moment."

"SO WHAT ELSE IS NEW?" God, bored with the transformations, returned to His preferred form. He had to stand on tip toes to see his reflection now. He was going to have to get that mirror fixed.

"EVER HEARD OF THE 100 YEARS WAR, BOY? OR HOW ABOUT THE WAR OF SPANISH SUCCESSION? THE FIRST TRULY GLOBAL CONFLICT." God wandered over to another part of the room.

"There's Aids, father. It is becoming endemic."

"WELL, THEY HAD THE BLACK DEATH IN 348, 49, 6. DO I REALLY HAVE TO LIST THE YEARS FOR YOU, SON?"

God turned away from the mirror. On the opposite side of the room a miniature golf course materialized — complete with pseudo windmills, plastic flamingos and neon lights. All part of Jehovah's attempt to keep up with the entertainment of the masses.

Humanity, He decided, could best be understood through their fancies.

"IN FACT," God said as He leaned nonchalantly on His putter, "IN THE FOURTEENTH CENTURY, THEY HAD WAR, FAMINE, FLOOD AND DISEASE THAT DESTROYED BETWEEN FORTY AND FIFTY PERCENT OF THE POPULATION. SORRY, UNLESS YOU CAN COME UP WITH SOMETHING NOVEL, I'M AFRAID I JUST DON'T SEE THE URGENCY OF THIS PARTICULAR REQUEST."

"There's the greenhouse effect."

"GETTING THEIR FEET A LITTLE WET, HUH? WELL, YOU CAN'T SAY THAT THEY HAVEN'T BEEN WARNED. WHY DO THEY THINK I GAVE THEM SCIENTISTS?"

"But... but..."

He switched off the intercom with a simple frown.

After testing the weight of his putter with a great waving of arms, he aimed and struck. The ball shot forward, ricocheted around the room a few times to bounce into, and back out of, the cup.

Lights flashed and bells rang.

God pulled a wry face. Sometimes, He didn't know his own strength. He plucked another ball from the bucket.

Quite honestly, the Lord on High couldn't understand the appeal of the game. He preferred mystery plays Himself.

The still-open celestial prayer-line resounded with a distant chuckle.

Lucifer!

Startled, Jehovah sliced his next shot, sending the rainbow-coloured ball through a stain-glass window, as Satan whispered in the hallowed ear: "You would, old man, you would."

HEAVENLY BODIES

"Mary?"

A melodious voice intruded upon the symphonic landscape of her dream becoming incorporated into it.

"Mary?"

The twelve-year-old girl twisted upon her bed. Gabriel grimaced. A little young for the task laid before her, he thought. He could just see the headlines in the *National Enquirer* now, but he needed a virgin named Mary. And this one had been hard enough to find.

"Mary?"

Finally, Mary realized that the voice that interrupted her slumber was coming from outside the comfy confines of the duvet. She dragged the sheets across her face.

"Just a few more minutes, Mum."

"Mary!" The voice was brisk, sharp and... definitely male.

The knuckles on the sheets turned white, and the body under the covers trembled.

The voice came again, soft, muted, gentling her. "Come on, Mary, I know you're awake."

She sneezed.

"Oh hark, oh hark, I bring you news of great tidings and joy."

Mary screwed up her courage. The sheets spoke with more bravado than they felt. "Right, pervert. Who are you and what are you doing in my bedroom?"

"Great tidings, indeed. Rejoice, rejoice, Mary, for you have been chosen."

Mary eyed the enormous figure — an equivocal outline in the cotton cloth — but the girl sensed no immediate peril. She relaxed slightly. The shape continued talking. "You of all people have been selected to bear the daughter of God."

"Right! Don't tell me, let me guess. You're God," the sheets spoke with real confidence.

"Well, no, of course, not. Don't be silly," the figure sniffed and rustled disquietly beyond the cloth, "God doesn't come down and talk to the... rabble Himself. He works through emissaries like me."

All fear evaporated. This was a real nutter here. Not even smart enough to claim to be God. Definitely, not someone to be afraid of.

"Look, perv, if you don't go away. I'll scream real loud. I'll… I'll…" She thought of the worst threat she could imagine. "I'll call my mum!" The knuckles tightened their grip upon the hem and lowered the sheet slowly. Mary steeled herself to hazard a peek at the creep. "And she'll call the cops."

A single eye peeped from behind its veil of white. It opened and closed rapidly. Mary blinked. For standing there before her was a creature from her worst images of hell. It had wings, but more than the normal complement for, say, either a butterfly or a bat, and it was completely covered with fur. There must've been a million-zillion eyes extending from each hair. And when it uttered its next syllables, they issued from at least a trillion mouths.

And it was huge!

Then her mind focused on his words.

"No, your mother won't be waking up. I made sure of that…"

And Mary didn't wait any longer; she threw off the covers and ran screaming from the room.

"…I granted her blessed sleep and sweet dreams. I… I… Mary? Mary? Are you there, Mary?"

Gabriel shifted under the weight of his wings. "Well, I say! The cheek of the maid!"

Then the nightmare faded from the room.

*

"HOW DID IT GO, GABRIEL?"

"She was, ah, less than thrilled, boss," said Gabriel.

"OF COURSE, THE FIRST ONE NEEDED A LITTLE PERSUASION, IF I REMEMBER CORRECTLY."

"I'll say. That clumsy oaf," roared Mary above the Heavenly Hosts.

"QUIET, MOTHER, I NEED TO HEAR THIS. SO WHAT HAPPENED, GABRIEL?"

Gabriel fussed with his robes and fluffed his wings. "She, uh, ran away."

35

"SHE WHAT? SHE RAN AWAY? FOR GOODNESS SAKE, WHY?"

"I don't know; I don't understand it. I mean I wore my most magnificent demeanour."

"AND JUST EXACTLY HOW DID YOU APPEAR?"

Gabriel shrugged. "Oh, you know, all covered in nice fur, lots of wings, eyes, and mouths spitting fire. The usual. You said to wear my best."

The Heavenly Father slapped his forehead. "JESUS CHRIST. YOU IDIOT!"

"Yes, Father? How have I offended You?"

"NOT YOU, JUNIOR. IT'S JUST AN EXPRESSION. WHY DON'T YOU RUN ALONG AND DO A GOOD DEED SOMEWHERE?"

He turned his attention back to Gabriel. "OF COURSE, SHE RAN AWAY. HOW MANY TIMES DO I HAVE TO TELL YOU? YOUR SUNDAY BEST, NOT YOUR FRIDAY BEST. THAT'S ISLAMIC TRADITION. FOR CATHOLICS AND SUCH LIKE, YOU APPEAR PRETTY MUCH AS YOU APPEAR NOW. WHITE ROBES, GOLDEN HAIR, HALO. MAYBE A HARP. YOU PROBABLY SCARED THE BEJESUS OUT OF HER. GREAT, NOW WE'RE GOING TO HAVE TO FIND ANOTHER VIRGIN."

Gabriel groaned and dug his toe under a portion of the cloud, lifting it to see if he could find any dirt.

"JUNIOR?"

"Yes, Father?"

"WHY DON'T YOU TAKE OUR FRIEND HERE AND GIVE HIM A CRASH COURSE ON THE MANY MANIFESTATIONS OF THE DIVINE?"

"Mumble, mumble, mumble, morph!" said Jesus.

"WHAT WAS THAT, JUNIOR?"

"I said, 'oh Father, let this cup pass from me'."

"NO SUCH LUCK."

"Grumble, mutter, grrr... Come on, Gabriel... mumble, mumble, mumble... never get any respect..."

ON THE WINGS OF A PRAYER

"No, no, no, no, no!" said noted scientist Carl Sagan as he pushed the bundle back at the confused clerk. "I don't believe it."

He stood at a nondescript counter — a counter that could have been any institutional counter, anywhere — featureless, white, almost too white.

The clerk opposite just shoved the pile of what looked like laundry toward Sagan again. Laundry. Someone else's laundry, mind you — albeit clean — but Sagan didn't go in for the white-robed look.

Or the wings.

"No, I'm sorry, I can't accept these. They are not mine. They can't be. I wouldn't be caught dead in them."

The clerk interrupted. "We've been through that already. Of course, these are yours. Whose else would they be?" He inched the bundle a little closer to Sagan. "They're your size. Trust me. Try 'em on; see if they fit."

"So, what's this?" The scientist plucked at a wing.

"Yours too. Standard issue."

"I don't believe it. What is this for? Some kind of fancy dress party?"

"We've discussed that. You've —" he gave a little cough "— ahem, passed over. As it were. Figuratively speaking."

Sagan raised a quizzical brow.

"All right, literally speaking, then. You're dead, sir. Dead."

"I don't believe it."

"Oh, rest assured, you're dead, sir. Living people don't usually make it this far." The clerk pulled a wry face. "Except for an occasional medium who gets lost every now and then."

"Nope, I still don't believe it. I don't believe any of it. Not heaven. Not hell. If this is heaven," he flicked the radiant white robe with his finger, "where is it? It's not above the earth. We've explored it. Neither for that matter is hell buried deep beneath the planet surface either."

"No, you're absolutely right. Good to find someone so enlightened. They are metaphysically speaking right next door."

"Pardon?"

"It's a little difficult to explain to someone who is used to linear time. You wouldn't understand."

"Well, you don't seem to understand either. I don't believe in Heaven or Hell, at all! Therefore, I cannot be here — wherever here is — even if I am dead. Presuming you do believe in the Christian ethos, which I don't, then by its own tenants, I shouldn't be here." He tapped the counter for emphasis. "As an unbeliever, I should be..." Some still small, primeval part of his brain clamoured to be heard, and it said you shouldn't tempt fate, "in some existentialist nothingness somewhere. And you," Sagan jabbed a finger at the clerk, "don't exist."

The gentleman opposite him looked nonplussed.

They'd said this one might be a problem. His fingers scrabbled along the underside of the counter until he had located the button and pressed it.

"If this is Heaven and you're an angel, where's your wings, eh?" Sagan looped his hands across his chest and defied the clerk to poke holes in his reasoning.

"Oh no, you wouldn't wear them to work, man." The clerk motioned at the vast expanse of counters backed by rows and rows of shelves, the long lines of humanity and the scurrying clerical workers. "It would be impractical. You'd be getting tangled up all the time."

"Wait a second. That man," he pointed, "is getting a different uniform."

"Of course, different socio-ethnic background, different ideas about God and the afterlife." The clerk leaned forward and whispered conspiratorially. "And if you're smart, you'll stay away from Valhalla. That is if you value your head."

"If I'm already dead, why should it matter? It's not as if cutting off my head would kill me."

The clerk sniffed. "Believe me, if you ever lost your head you'd know what I'm talking about." He spied the massive security guard and abandoned all pretence of affability. "Sir, you're holding up the queue. Please, take your bundle and go. If you have a complaint, take it up with the Complaints Department."

"What! Complaints Department? You mean to tell me Heaven has a Complaints Department?"

The clerk blinked, nodding at something over Sagan's shoulder. "Who do you think handles all the prayers? Unless, of course, you call the twenty-four-hour prayer hotline."

Someone grasped Sagan's elbow. He turned to regard a huge winged guard.

"Come along now, sir; mustn't cause a ruckus."

The clerk sneered at Sagan and said to the guard: "I believe, this gentleman would like to talk to someone in Complaints."

The guard's eyes widened and he backed two steps away from Sagan. "Oh no, you don't really, sir, do you? You don't want to talk to the Complaints Department."

Sagan pulled his back upright — he was not about to be intimidated by some idiot wearing wings — and succeeded in looking straight into the massive pectorals.

"I think I might have a few things to discuss." Sagan tugged at one of the guard's wings. "Take these, for instance. They're aerodynamically unsound. Poor design. Do you realize that in order to fly with wings such as these the average human would have to have a rib cage that extended four-feet from his spine, and the musculature to match, just to support the mass. Oh yes and legs like stilts in order make up for the additional weight."

The guard's eyes darted nervously about, beneath his golden helm. "I'm not exactly sure what that has to do with anything?"

"It means you can't fly. Neither can I. It's impossible with this ridiculous get up."

The guard waved the scientist to silence, glancing over his shoulder at the waiting crowd. "Shush, sir."

The person behind Sagan stabbed at his ribs. "Move along. I ain't got all day."

Sagan laughed at the ferret-faced man. "But you do, sir, you do. If this is Heaven you have not only today and tomorrow, but an eternity of waiting before you."

Before the other man had a chance to retort, the guard seized Sagan's arm and dragged him away. The scientist let himself by manhandled through the throng.

"Whew!" said his angelic host. "That was close."

"What was close?"

"You've got understand, sir. We didn't have geometry and such-like when wings were invented. Just some rather vague and fuzzy images in the backs of men's minds."

Sagan snorted.

"Why don't we go to the dressing rooms?" suggested the guard, hopefully, "I'm sure you'll feel much better once you've tried on your new togs. You won't even worry about aerodynamics. I mean, it doesn't bother the bees, so why should it bother you?"

Sagan halted. "No! I said I wanted to go to the Complaints Department."

"No, you don't. Trust me, you don't want to go to the Complaints Department."

A second security officer moved up behind the mutinous scientist.

"Why?" Sagan demanded, "What's wrong with the Complaints Department?"

"I can't explain," said the first officer. "All I can say is you don't want to go to the Complaints Department."

"Oh, this is a place I just got to see. Which way?" Sagan demanded.

The guard looked every which way, but one. Sagan immediately headed in the blatantly disregarded direction. The second guard caught up with Sagan in three strides.

"Can you explain it to him?" asked the first.

The second winged guard shrugged.

"Whose working the desk?" said the first, trying to make idle conversation above Sagan's head.

"Valentine," replied the second.

"Still? The poor bastard."

Sagan balked. "Valentine, as in Saint Valentine?"

"Yes, poor sod, it's not his fault he had a holiday named after him. I mean he's a martyr, just like most the saints."

"Decapitated he was," the second, more taciturn guard informed the scientist.

"Now there's a man who has lost his head," twittered Sagan, feeling suddenly that he was becoming unglued. If this was the afterlife, he didn't like it.

The first continued. "He shouldn't be held accountable for the fact that some greeting card company picked his name out of a hat, do you think?"

"You mean, you get sent to the Complaints Department as a punishment?" Sagan bleated. "Why?"

Both towering guards studied some imaginary spot on their robes. The first whistled.

The scientist considered the new data. "Maybe I don't want to make a complaint."

"Very good, sir." The first guard brightened visibly, shining with a confident golden glow. "Shall we take you to your assigned cloud?"

"What? Leave me in a collection of vapour of water and ice with wings that are so badly designed that they're guaranteed to send me plummeting to earth if I attempt to use them for flight? No, sir," Sagan countered. "I didn't say I didn't want to go to the Complaints Department, just that it might be a bit premature to make a complaint."

His angelic host scowled. "Suit yourself."

"So what's wrong with this place?"

"It's just some place we prefer to avoid. You never know when you might catch the Divine Eye and be sent to work there."

Both angels shuddered.

"You'll see," admonished the first.

By this time they had left the counter and its queues far behind. As a unit they swung left, proceeding down a long empty corridor that terminated in three closed doors.

"Here we are," said the first guard.

"Hey, that was fast."

"Time and space can be tricky things up here."

The trio hesitated outside the first door.

"Are you sure about this?" said the guard.

"What can it hurt to sneak a peek?"

The less talkative of the two shook his head. Then he opened the door and stepped aside to let Sagan enter. Cautiously, the scientist stuck his head inside the room and beheld — nothing, complete and utter blackness.

"Hey, it's dark," complained Sagan. "I can't see a thing."

"That's right. Pressure-sensitive lighting. No point in wasting energy, even up here. You'll have to step inside the room if you want to see anything." The celestial eyes glinted in challenge.

Sagan blanched. His gaze shifted anxiously between his heavenly hosts and the door. He was starting to get a bad feeling about this. And he was caught in an internal debate between scientific logic and his own dark subconscious.

41

Reason reasserted itself. He placed a foot just inside the door so that he stood one foot in the corridor, the other in the room. The ceiling, the walls, even the floor beneath his foot began to glow with a feeble light.

And he discovered a room void of adornment, except for the box-like desk at its centre. He shifted his weight until everything was bathed a tenuous silver. The multiple sources warped the silhouettes, so that the figure seated behind the desk appeared somehow abbreviated.

Sagan swallowed, hard. His Adam's apple bobbed up and down in his throat. For it was no illusion, for the head had been severed from the neck, and it sat, or leaned, jauntily in the in-basket.

The scientist's eyes bulged from their sockets. He lifted his foot from the floor. The room was plunged into darkness.

Beside him, the second guard chuckled and said: "Decapitated."

Right. He'd been warned. Sagan stomped down hard on the floor, and the light flared. He released some of the pressure and then paused to examine the slumping figure and sleeping face. For the head, at least, was sleeping, the mouth slack, drool dribbled down the chin, and he snored — or the mouth did — as the shoulders rose and fell in time with the sound.

The man was old, or the head was, with straggly hair a silver-grey. The body was an undecipherable. Sagan's gaze moved to the elaborate web that was draped between head and neck, connecting the two of them. The spider spun happily, evidently undisturbed for ages.

Gathering his courage, Sagan took another step into the room, and he realized, upon closer examination, that dust coloured the head grey. By this time, Sagan had reached the half-way point. He faltered. To penetrate further into this realm was to risk detection by the sleeping occupant, and as if the divine mind had read his, the eyes opened, revealing an all-too-human hunger in their depths. The lids fluttered, blinded temporarily by the sudden light.

"Is someone there?" the head shouted. "Someone for me to talk to? It's been years." Fingers tapped against the wood as the Saint counted. "Centuries!"

Sagan's feet carried him back toward the door.

The head wobbled in the basket as it tried to turn of its own volition to get a better view of the fleeing scientist.

"Oh my, and look at me. I'm must look a sight." Busy hands fluttered across the desktop.

"No point in calling to it," the head explained. "No ears to hear with, you see."

The creeping fingers stopped when they felt lips, a mouth, and a nose. They clasped the ears like handles and attempted to reseat the head on the neck.

The scientist leapt from the room, grabbed the door and shut it firmly behind him. Then just to make sure, he leaned against it.

He heard a faint: "Hello? Hello? Is someone there?"

"The poor bastard," Sagan said.

"See what I mean?" said the first angel.

"Well, yes, and no, I must confess I was expecting something... a bit more spectacular. Fire and brimstone maybe?"

"Completely different division, under separate management."

"So this is it? This is what you're afraid of? An optical illusion that can be easily created by any Hollywood studio? A poor decrepit old man who — if he is to be believed — deserves our pity rather than our horror? If this is the best you can come up with, I'm afraid I'm not impressed. I can understand why you don't get many complaints. People would be bored to death here."

Sagan cradled his chin in his hands and thought for a moment. "Wait, if I remember correctly, the clerk said that the complaints department is where human prayers are heard. I know ours is a materialistic age, but there are thousands of believers. Millions. Born-again Christians. Catholics. I didn't see anything in there that might resemble a prayer."

The duo stirred uncomfortably.

"We-ell," the first drawled, "this door here is specifically for us, the Immortals. Pretty small department, not many complaints. The Mortal Complaints Department, though, requires a much bigger staff."

Sagan levered himself away from the door. "Then I want to see it. I want to see where people's prayers go."

The first guard put his hands out in front of him. "Oh, no. Oh no. Not that."

"Come on, let's go. Where is it?"

"The second door, of course," the guard indicated the door at the end of the hall.

"Okay." He marched for the second door.

Moving as fast as lightning the first guard interposed himself between Sagan and the door, arm outstretched, fingers splayed. "Are you crazy?"

Sagan sniggered. "I've been reliably informed that I'm dead already. How many times can one man die?"

"Plenty," mumbled the second guard, "what with reincarnation, parallel universes and what-not."

The scientist relented. His eyes narrowed as he examined the guards' faces. The fear was genuine enough.

"All right." Sagan put his hands on his hips. "Can it kill me? I mean what's so harmful? It's just prayers."

The first guard covered his mouth with his hand and began to twitter, while the other exploded in belly-clenching guffaws. It took a few minutes, but the two winged guards sobered a bit.

Wiping the tears from his eyes, the first turned to Sagan. "No, most likely not. They won't kill you."

Sagan touched the knob; the first angel placed a restraining hand on Sagan's arm.

"Here," he said, "at least protect yourself."

The guard surveyed the sterile hall, spied an empty dust bin, upended it and crammed it over Sagan's head. "They always go for the eyes. Mirror to the soul, don't you know."

Then, before Sagan could remove the ridiculous appurtenance, the two swung into action. The second guard seized the scientist from behind as the first hurled open the door. Then the second flung Sagan into the room, and the first slammed the door shut behind him.

Instinctively Sagan flattened himself against a wall. He was trapped inside a huge, auditorium-sized room. No, bigger than that. Remember, he told himself, size is deceptive, here, and he realized the lines of desks stretched as far as the eye could see.

Each was manned, or more appropriately hidden behind, by someone dodging for his life from strange bat-like creatures. Sagan just had enough time to assimilate this information when he too was besieged. He ducked to avoid the scratching claws.

The creature's eyes flared red as the bat went for Sagan's face a second time. He beat it back — noting that, despite the fact that the creatures were bat-winged, the body appeared human, or humanish, covered as it was with a fine down of grey fur.

It spat at Sagan, and bellowed from a swollen chest: "How could you? How could you!"

"Get away from me, you fiend! I can't help you. You want the Complaints Department." Sagan gestured at the nearest desk where the woman flailed, trying to fend off several of the creatures at one time. Her arms ran red with blood.

The bat sped away, carrying its message: "Oh, God, how could you?"

Then Sagan detected underneath the tumult of thousands, the murmur of single prayers. Each one of the bat-like creatures conveyed some brief snatch of human entreaty.

"...I want... gimme... why me..? Aren't I deserving..? No, not me... please... How could you... haven't I been a good person?"

An occasional butterfly flitted into the room — "Oh Father in heaven, thank you" — but they did not last long among the bats.

Sagan clasped the door handle and twisted it. It slipped in his fist, and for a panic-stricken instant he thought the others had locked him in. Then it spun in his grasp. He threw his weight against it, just as a second 'prayer' had discovered his presence and attacked.

"Why should I be punished so?" it shrieked at Sagan as he reeled through the door and pressed himself against the outside wall.

The first angel moved in swiftly to shut the door behind him before the creature could escape.

"That's awful," Sagan panted. "Who would've thought?"

"Told you," scolded the first.

"Much more impressive than the first." Sagan straightened and nonchalantly brushed his rumpled clothes. "But nothing in there that a Hollywood director with a good FX manager couldn't devise. In fact, I think I remember the creatures from some movie. Unfortunately, I can't remember which one."

He examined the final door. "Where does that go?"

The guards exchanged glances and rolled their eyes towards the ceiling. He wouldn't learn.

"You know."

"No, I don't," said Sagan. "We've got the Immortal Com-

45

plaint Department, and one for the Mortals. I think that just about covers it."

The first cleared his throat. "You can figure it out. Process of elimination."

Sagan sauntered over to the door.

"So what's behind it, a stairway leading straight down, a lift?"

The others avoided his gaze.

"Come on, fellows, let's say I'm a believer now."

"It's a bit late," murmured the second. He stooped and whispered something in his partner's ear.

The first guard shook his head, abruptly and belligerently, no. "Can't interfere," he hissed.

"Maybe it won't open," said the second.

Sagan ignored them. "I guess, I'm going to have to see for myself."

This time the door retracted seamlessly into the wall with a soft whoosh.

"How high tech!" teased Sagan.

Like the first this room was small, but tastefully decorated in a mixture of bright scarlets, ruddy browns and burnished oranges.

"Oh nice," Sagan muttered. "Great colour scheme."

His commentary was quickly arrested and his jaw became unhinged when he saw who — or what — sat behind the desk. Satan himself — or a damned good facsimile — complete with cloven hooves, flaming red skin, goatee and curved horns.

The catlike eyes settled on Sagan, and the demon smiled. The scientist began feeling for the opening that should have been directly behind him.

A forked tongue lapped out from between scaly lips and licked them.

He spun and ran into the wall. The door, if there had ever been one, had vanished without a trace. The scientist began to shake in spite of his professed scepticism as the demon leaned eagerly over the desk toward him.

"Yes, young man," he said, "I understand that you've got a complaint."

FALLEN ANGEL

"Did you hear what he said?" said the next man in the queue.

"What?" replied the man following the third.

"Angels can't fly. Aerodynamically speaking, that is."

"Says who?" the second man sniffed.

"That man, that man they're hauling away."

"It looks more to me like the others are having trouble keeping up with him."

"That's Carl Sagan, the scientist," said one of the women in the line.

"Him?" The second man's eyes widened. "I saw him on the telly once. Pretty famous."

The first shook his head. "If that's Carl Sagan, he ought to know."

The woman spun on the person behind her and hissed. "Don't trust the wings," she whispered out of the corner of her mouth. "Angels can't fly. Take it from me. I heard it from a reliable source. Pass it on."

The next woman dutifully turned and relayed the message.

An hour later the queue ground to a halt, the exit clogged, as those already serviced and changed into their designated regalia refused to move from the cloud. Security was called, and each newcomer was flown on to the next destination. Until angels — the experienced, those who had flown for decades, centuries, millennia even — began dropping from the skies.

The rumour spread like wildfire across the cosmos, as rumours often do. Proving just how boring a place heaven can be — with nothing to do all day long but sing the Lord's praises.

Of course, you could always slip across the border to another celestial section. Celebrate the afterlife in the Egyptian Field of Reeds, for instance. However, such excursions were not without their hazards, for with one wrong turn in Duat, you could easily find yourself a part of the digestive processes of the dragon Apep. And exit from this bilious prison was almost as tortuous as entry was.

One trip through Apep, the reconstitutor, or a single junket into Valhalla was pretty much all that it took before people decided to stay at home where it was safe. Hence, the heaven's denizens were always ready for the next bit of juicy gossip that came up from down below. The rumour that God was dead had really taken hold in the sixties, and Jehovah had been forced to put in a personal appearance at church one Sunday. There'd been big changes in the service after that.

"Angels can't fly; pass it on."

The words floated across the ether net, darting from cloud to cloud. The single murmur replaced the songs of praise, for even the seraphims' voices trembled at the content of the message.

"... can't fly... can't fly... can't..."

"What?"

"Who?"

"Carl Sagan!"

"You don't say."

"Can't fly!"

Until even the biggest and the best plummeted down to earth like stones.

*

The presenter's facial muscles twitched as she reviewed the text for that day's lead story, and she had to repress a laugh.

She slammed down the report. "What the hell is this? Somebody's idea of a joke?"

"No joke," said the producer. "Haven't you been listening to the news?"

"No, I just drove in from the Cotswolds, and I listened to CDs all the way rather than the radio. It was my holiday, and I didn't want to start work one moment too soon."

She scanned the text a second time. "Look, I am not reading this. This is crazy. Next thing you know you'll have me talking about little green men."

The title music died away. The control room cued her. This was no time for debate; the program had begun. She stared at the glowing red light on the camera and gulped.

"Reports have been coming in all day long of people dropping out of the skies. Meanwhile there have been confirmed sightings of Mother Teresa, Princess Diana and Elvis..."

A STITCH IN TIME

"Well, I'll be damned."

"Too late," the assistant grumbled to himself, "you already are,

The sudden appearance of his boss had caused Fleurety's finger to flex, inadvertently launching one of his missiles. A space ship, his space ship, exploded in flaming Technicolor.

"Something wrong, sir?" The aide peered at his superior through the thick glass of the VR headset. The lenses magnified his eyes. Laser projected images danced across his retinas, casting shadows that distorted his features and augmented the prominence of the already deep-set orbital ridges.

"Wrong? No, nothing wrong." His boss leered him and pointed at the ceiling above their heads. "He fell for it, the Big Man, himself."

"Oh, very good, sir," said Fleurety. His skin glowed greenly, reflecting the radiance of the Virtual Reality grid.

"Yes, so far so good." The boss rubbed his hands together. "But we have to make sure that it stays that way." He swung on his assistant. "He's a tricky little devil, you know that. Remember what he did with that Job deal? 'A bet,' he says. 'A simple little wager,' he says." Fleurety's superior stormed around the room, and somewhere in the multidimensional universe a fight erupted which would have fatal consequences for all combatants.

Grimacing, Fleurety turned off the game.

"I should've known better to get involved in a gentlemanly wager with the Big Man, and I'll be DAMNED if I lose again." Lucifer glared at Fleurety, daring his adjutant to challenge him. Fleurety withered in his chair.

"Uh..."

"Uh? UH WHAT!

Fleurety disintegrated into a gelatinous heap. His voice, a high-pitched squeak, came from the dark recesses of the chair. "Well, boss, you know you can't trust Him — the man upstairs, I mean. He just don't play fair."

"True." Lucifer ducked his head magnanimously at the

demon.

"How soon is he expected, sir?" Fleurety said as he slipped the gloves from his hands and the plastic helmet from his head.

Lucifer turned to the wide bank of screens. "Soon."

"Won't we need some time to prepare?"

"We shouldn't, not if you've got the videos?"

The aide counted the tapes for the hundredth time. "They're all here."

"And the books?"

"Yep." Fleurety pointed at the pile.

"Great!"

"Are you sure he'll fall for it?"

"Have you fast-forwarded the videos beyond the credits?"

"To the places you indicated, sir," Fleurety said.

"He should then. You know how he feels about technology."

"Not all technology, sir. Remember what he did with Velcro," Fleurety reminded his master.

Satan sneered. "He can have it. Velcro never was one our better inventions. Man actually liked it."

*

"Freeze!"

Lucifer hit the stop button with his tail, and everything in the crowded courtyard halted.

God stared at the television set, where the guards poised, with one foot in the air. Gesticulating hands stopped mid-gesture — arms flung wide in the course of a swing. People seized in the act of turning, canted precariously off balance. Even the wind sloughing through the trees ceased — the boughs bent under its caress, the grasses caught in an undulating roll. While a peregrine falcon was suspended in a sky of a crystal blue — its wings outstretched in a graceful arch.

"Trouble in paradise?" Satan said as he slithered from his seat and went to peer over Jehovah's shoulder.

"Get off, serpent." God brushed him away. "You once were the trouble in Paradise."

"As you wish." Satan spoke mildly as he coiled next to Jehovah's chair.

"Unctuous snake, I know what you're thinking."

"Do you? Do you, indeed?" The massive serpentine head swung to Fleurety and winked.

"This one," said God, his nose only inches from the screen, "looks familiar." He squinted at the affable features of Bing Crosby. "I seem to remember those ears."

Rather than looking at Jehovah, Lucifer prodded the nobs on the control panel with his nose.

"You said that this is a live transmission?" God tapped the screen. "Why then is it in black and white?"

"Something's wrong with the camera. You know how unreliable technology is," Lucifer purred.

God snorted, and a volcano erupted somewhere in the Pacific.

"We could run it through the computer and colourize it for you," Satan offered congenially.

"How do I know you wouldn't tamper with it?"

Lucifer lifted a single shoulder in an indifferent shrug, a difficult manoeuvre for a snake. "I thought you might say that, that's why I left it alone."

God made a rude noise and straightened. "I don't understand if these —" He pointed from one screen to another "— are all real-time, then how come they're not all the same? Or for that matter how come they're not all in black and white?"

"That's what I was trying to explain. Thanks to man's fascination with this era, time's been diddled. Look at this," Satan hissed at Fleurety who addressed himself to the buttons. Bing Crosby disappeared and was replaced by a space ship that hovered over another version of King Arthur's court. The word "NASA" was plainly emblazoned on its side.

"I warned you that it was only a matter of time," Lucifer chuckled at the pun, "before man mastered time travel, and once they did to what other period would they most likely be drawn?"

God climbed down from his chair. The demons giggled. Then the Lord Jehovah toddled over to another of the many view screens and stared in amazement as a young black girl bounced, with the best of African rhythms before a group of women in medieval dress. The fair Guinivere mimicked the child's movements — hips undulating and arms swinging in time to a rock and roll tune.

"Who's this?"

Satan nosed the cassette case from its hiding place and glanced at the credits. "Keisha Knight Pullam."

"What on earth is she doing?" asked God.

"The Funky Chicken?" said Fleurety helpfully.

Lucifer glowered at his aide.

"The boogaloo?"

No one was listening.

"This is wrong, all wrong." Jehovah strode back and forth before the panel.

Fleurety muttered, "I bet Samuel Clements isn't particularly pleased, either."

Satan silenced him with a murderous look, and the demon died, or did a fiendish corollary by shrivelling into a ball.

On the screen, the panorama spun dizzily from scene to scene, and the girl demonstrated a karate kick for the ladies of the court.

"That's what I was trying to tell you." Lucifer slithered forward, keeping pace with his master. "You see the problem? One camera, three simultaneous transmissions, yet three different scenes. Time has got scrambled somewhere."

"Funny." God peered from one picture to another. "I don't remember the Dark Ages being quite so tidy. I mean, look. No rushes on the floor. No dogs fighting over scraps of food. No chickens scratching in the dirt. And, most of these people look like they've taken a bath sometime in the last six months!"

Satan interrupted Jehovah's thoughts before he could reach any conclusions. "Obviously this trend must not be allowed to continue. Who knows how many visitors will arrive eventually, and how they will affect the course of history? If this goes on unchecked, the world as we know it will cease to exist."

The Supreme Being raised himself to his tip-toes and studied the three images.

"Wait a second!" God held a single finger in the air. "Something's wrong with this. The castle! That's it. The castle is different!"

All three tellies went blank simultaneously.

"Call it back!" He commanded.

Fleurety unrolled from his quivering ball and rose. He moved over to the console. His fingers flew over the keyboard. The screens remained black.

"Sorry," he said, "no can do?"

"You and your technology. Hah! Never works when you need it to. Probably mankind's biggest afflictions, leads more people to temptation than sex…"

"We try, sir." Satan bowed and then, returning to the topic, said, "You know how dodgy this time thing is. Who better than you who created it?"

God frowned at the reminder.

"Surely, you must see that we risk creating a time warp. A loop like you find in software," Lucifer explained, relishing the puzzled expression that rippled across the Supreme Being's face. "Where all times converge on each other and all end in single place. Forming a circle. If that happens, then nothing will ever reach beyond this point.

"Look at this." Lucifer slunk over to a table heaped high with stacks of books. "All purported histories of the period. Each with a different set of characters and different scenarios." He spun. "Certainly, they can't all be right."

"Yes, you know how shaky mortal memory is."

"Ah, but I fear it may already be too late. If you look closely at these volumes you will discover many claim to be written by visitors who got through to King Arthur's court precisely because the fabric of reality that separates one era from the next has worn thin."

Satan slid forward and whispered in God's ear. "We must do something. You know as well as I do, this time thing is not my field of expertise."

"Back, serpent." Jehovah stuck His pinky in His ear and jiggled it violently around in a circle. "That tickles."

"By now, the whole epoch has been contaminated by modern man." Satan rasped. "I told you that you were investing too much into a single era. I don't know why you were so enamoured of this period. I mean, look at Lancelot the flower of mankind. Look at Guinevere. They have flaunted your values…"

"That's your fault."

"That's my job, sir," Lucifer corrected Him.

"Yes, I suppose you're right." God sighed.

"What do you propose to do now?"

"Me? Why me? Why not you?"

"You know. You made the rules." Lucifer stabbed at a digital clock with his nose. "In matters like this, I cannot act. Not alone."

"Well, what do you recommend?" God snapped.

"Lift Camelot from the time-space continuum, leaving no clues behind for archaeologists to find. Maybe modern man will stop looking for it then."

"I hate to admit it, but I suppose you're right," God conceded. "Too bad, some of my best work was there."

"Mine too. People like Mordred don't grow on trees, you know."

God inclined His head in assent. "Morgana's a pretty piece of work, too."

"Thank you," Lucifer said. "I was rather proud of her."

"I had hoped that they might find the grail for me," God said. "I hate to lose something that valuable." He slapped at the control panel and feedback reverberated throughout the nether regions. "Irresponsible boy, I never should have let him play with it."

Satan made soothing sounds at his maker.

"Okay, I'll do it."

The Lord mimed plucking something from the air. "Erase all traces of the kingdom. Every brick, every stone, so that no evidence remains that can be unearthed during excavations or archaeological digs... but..." and God cast a sly glance at Lucifer... "leave the memory... the ideal... to give humanity something for which it can strive."

The atmosphere around them began to thicken, shimmering as one exited molecule collided with another.

"Well." God clapped His hands. "That ought to do it. Anything else?" He said to Satan.

The devil looked worried. "Ah, no, like you said: 'that ought to do it.'"

"Aha, got you there, didn't I? You didn't think I'd leave the memory behind, did you?"

God vanished.

"DO NOT," the disembodied voice echoed around them, "BOTHER ME AGAIN UNTIL THE NEXT MILLENNIA!"

Lucifer's serpent form began to shift. His face split with a great rending noise, and Satan leapt from the skin.

"All right! Lucifer jumped up, clicking his heels together. "Yes!"

He grabbed Fleurety's hands and jigged around in a circle. "He did it! He did it!"

"Yes, sir, he did at that, but does he know what he's done?"

"I doubt it. He's never been much on the physical sciences."

"But I thought he made them."

"Oh, he's aware of natural laws in a subliminal sort of way. He must be since he created them — on a Tuesday, I believe — but he doesn't bother to obey them. Too busy to worry about the tedious extrapolations of science." Lucifer cackled gleefully. "Inexorable, that's what he is. Above that sort of thing. Much more interested in the grandiose, miracles, special effects, anything that's flash."

"A pity," said the demon.

"Isn't it, though?" Lucifer's eyes gleamed hotly.

"So he doesn't realize that he's created a parabolic loop under the British Isles."

"Nope."

"Ah, er, can you explain it to me. I'm a little unclear about this time thing myself," Fleurety said.

"Everybody is," Satan paused, "except Himself, and as you can see he's confused too."

Fleurety looked bemused.

"It's very simple, really. What God's done is the very thing he was trying to prevent, creating a fracture — a complete break, mind you — in what's supposed to be the fluctuating time-space continuum. By lifting the physical Camelot he's produced a metaphysical rift — concentrating all the energy that should have been there in its opposite pole, the place of most density, London."

"Which means?"

"A warp has been created under England and because of this it takes as long to get from one side of London to another as it does to Birmingham."

"And that's good, huh?"

"Of course. Think of the practical applications. The frustration factor. I can hear souls crumbling even as we speak."

The devil stopped dancing and placed a hand against a pointed ear. Released from Lucifer's grip, Fleurety spun to the side of the chamber. Both paused to consider the cacophony of honking horns and people swearing.

"Such sweet music to my ears."

"Diabolical!"

"Why thank you." Lucifer gave an elaborate bow. "What else would you expect?"

He moved to the video recorder and ejected a tape marked, *Connecticut Yankee in King Arthur's Court*.

"Now, Fleurety, how are we doing on the global warming project?"

INFINITY

Carl Sagan awoke to grey. Unrelenting terminal grey. Not black or white, just grey, like the grey of a cloudy day. As far as the eye to could see.

That was assuming Sagan had opened his eyes, for he could find no way of differentiating whether they were open or shut. No change in the immediate environment. He couldn't even tell if he was breathing.

Sagan shifted positions, or at least, he thought he did, but he couldn't have said for sure.

Drifting in the gloom, the scientist had no sense of position. No sense of feeling or touch. No sense of movement, or confinement for that matter, although his body did not seem to be restricted in any way.

Sagan cast his mind back to the last thing he could recollect — a fiery face, a snaking tongue — and he blotted out the fanciful image. It must have been a dream.

Then he remembered an infernally long line, stretching throughout infinity, and his fateful words as an idiot clerk tried to give him someone else's laundry. The scientist slapped his temple at his arrogance and monumental stupidity, but no reassuring sting fired synapses into the brain.

The words came back to taunt him. "An unbeliever, I should be in some existentialist nothingness somewhere."

The scientist squeezed his eyes closed and opened them again, or tried, hoping for some change, but there was no variation in his perception of grey — dismal, dreary, depressing grey.

No sight. No sound.

Nothing. Nothing at all.

He spoke: "Hey, wait as second. I didn't mean..."

The void swallowed the sound.

Sagan began to scream silently, and the once great mind crumbled into madness.

Ideally, I would like to use the symbol for this, the over-turned 8, but my software does not have that capacity.

NO GOOD TURN

Alec Fowler awoke to a mouth made of cotton. It tasted like hell. He exhaled, stopping when his breath wafted back at him. It smelled worse, like the worst effluence the underworld could create. And his tongue was two-sizes too big for his mouth.

He'd really tied one on last night.

The producer smacked his lips and groaned, or he tried to, for his mouth actually was stuffed with cotton. Fresh off of a multi-million dollar shoot in the Middle-East, thoughts of terrorists, kidnap and hostages slithered across his mind.

His eyes popped open and he perceived that they were likewise covered with gauze.

"Son of a bitch," he said. Only it came out: "Sssmmfbish."

Warily, Alec rearranged his hands underneath him and was pleased to discover that they were untied. Maybe this wasn't a "hostage situation" after all. Slowly he lifted his head above what appeared to be a thin layer of cloud to gaze at what must be a set, and he wondered when he'd started a new film.

Something Biblical, Fowler thought, eyeing the huge gates before him. They were fantastical. Whorls and whorls of silver — aluminium foil most likely — inlaid with pseudo mother of pearl. A bit over the top to his mind. Alec decided he must've taken leave of his senses if he'd signed on to do a religious saga.

Alec sat up and thought wearily that they'd better finish this scene before all the dry ice melted. Then he dug around in his mouth, plucking white stringy stuff from between his teeth. What appeared to be the same fibrous material of which the fake clouds were made.

"Jesus," he said.

"No, Peter," a sonorous voice intoned overhead.

Alec spun to view a kindly looking gentleman, with long flowing beard and equally long and flowing robes.

"Christ," Alec said, rolling his eyes toward the heavens.

This had to be some kind of a joke. Yes, that was it. He'd got drunk last night, and he'd passed out. Kirby and Bob had done this to him, taken him and dumped in a set for a grade-b religious flick.

"Okay, very funny, ha, ha! Now what's going on?" Alec yelled at the shimmering backdrop, ignoring the actor that fluttered around him full of solicitation and concern. "Kirby? Bob?" Alec bellowed. "Anybody? Come out, come out wherever you are."

Fowler's lips dipped into a scowl as he tried to remember, which studio, if any, had scheduled a religious flick. It would help him figure out precisely where he was.

"You may talk to him if you'd like," the man said through an all-too-fake white beard.

"Who? Kirby?"

"No, Christ," the man said very patiently, "but first you have to sign in, go through orientation, that sort of thing."

"Right," Alec huffed loud. "And when do I get to pick up my wings?"

"Well, first we must discover if you belong here. Not often, but every once in a while someone tries to sneak through." Peter looked at a large clipboard, a mundane affair made of pressed sawdust, and the hoax was revealed. Couldn't they have at least spray painted it the appropriate sparkling silver or glossy white?

"Name?"

"All right, I'll play along," Alec said, standing up and dusting pieces of stringy cloud from his slacks. "Alec Fowler."

An almost luminescent finger skimmed down a list. Then the too-white teeth of an actor flashed within the beard. "Yes, here it is right on the list. "Fowler, Norman Alec."

Alec winced. No one knew his first name. He'd dropped it in high school. Not even his driver's license gave his complete name.

"Right on schedule. Welcome." The actor ducked his head in greeting. "If you could just sign here…"

The man proffered a huge quill, but Alec's outstretched hand reached beyond the pen to clasp the beard and pull, hard. It remained firmly rooted to the man's face.

The mild expression clouded, and for an instant Alec thought he saw what people called the wrath of gods. "You know I get really tired of that. It's not like I am some department store Santa Claus, you know."

"Ah, sorry." Alec took the quill and shook it at him.

59

"Impressive. And where did the boys in props get this?"

"It is, alas, a feather of the long-extinct dodo," he said.

The producer snorted. "Sure."

Saint Peter, or whomever the fuck he was, gestured at a table that Alec hadn't noticed before. Like the gates, it is a fanciful filigree of silver and pearl.

"Look I don't belong here," Alec said, "I wasn't any saint." The actor looked offended, tucking his chin to his chest like an affronted pelican. "You know what I mean," Alec said. "I drank; I chased enough women when I was single, even had an affair once. Although it didn't last long."

"The list doesn't lie," Peter said, showing him a computer print-out, ferchrissakes, and pointing to his name, along with a few vital statistics — like his age. His real age. He'd subtracted a few years from his official age after he'd had plastic surgery.

Alec gulped.

"Come on, come on," the actor urged, "Mustn't dally and dither. The next one will be along any second now."

Alec signed the book.

His pious demeanour tarnished slightly by his frown, Peter herded him through the pearly gates.

"Wait a second," Alec shouted, "where do I go now?"

"Someone will be along to meet you shortly," Peter said, "Before I forget, I loved your version of *Samson and Delilah*."

And Alex cringed, head between his ears. The movie to which the actor referred was one of the first films Fowler had ever directed, back when he was young and didn't have any options or choice. It was a picture Alec preferred to forget.

Alec expected to walk beyond the glittering and ornate facade into the dark shadowy world of backstage. Where miles electrical cords coiled to cameras and spotlights. A place of ropes and pulleys, bare particle board and planks. The truth beyond the Hollywood lie.

Instead, Alec found more of the same. More fluffy white clouds and clinging filaments, which was neither smoke nor dry ice, but something semi-solid that adhered to his legs and tangled in the laces of his shoes. More blinding whites, dazzling golds, iridescent silvers and, of course, blue sky.

Other "clouds" like spun-candy confection were suspended in a blissful firmament which seemed to stretch on into eternity.

Lilting music of harp and choir surrounded him.

Alec fingered the stuff on this trousers. It was sticky.

"Yuck."

He stuck his finger in his mouth.

And sweet.

"All right, Kirby, Bob, you got me good. Now let me go home. I'm hung over, and I'd like to take a shower or a bath and maybe get a little more shut-eye."

"Ahem!"

The producer nearly jumped out of his skin as he pivoted to confront another actor garbed in white. Only this one didn't resemble Hollywood's typical caricature of sanctity.

Placing his hand over his heart, which was doing a fast rumba in his chest, Alec swore. "Goddammit, you almost gave me a coronary!"

The little weasel-faced 'angel' shrugged with a great flutter of wings. His head swung from side to side. "Tsk, tsk. Such, ah, er, language isn't tolerated here."

"Uh, uh, of course," Alec stammered.

"Are you Norman..."

"Alec," Alec corrected.

"...Fowler?"

"Yes."

"Come with me."

Falling into step beside him, Alec examined the other man. His face was scarred — or it was one helluva make-up job — and he was short, the top of his head coming only to Fowler's shoulder, and Alec wasn't exactly tall. When his escort moved, Alec detected the faint chink of metal, as though his guide wore armour under his robes.

The man noticed Alec's scrutiny, and he apologized. "Sorry about the scars, but there's only so much they can do for a man who's been scored by a dragon even up here."

"A dragon?" Alec parroted.

"Yes. My name's George, by the way," the man said.

"Saint George the Dragonslayer?" Alec squawked. "That's laying it on a little thick, don't you think?"

George sighed. "You are like many of your age. Suspicious, sceptical."

Alec sniggered.

"Fewer and fewer of you come up here any more. It's a sad sign of the times, I'd say." He gestured into a room of crystal and gold. "Here, we are."

The producer's step faltered. Maybe now he'd pass beyond the pretence to a hot Sunday afternoon in California or Tunisia, or wherever this shoot was.

"Don't worry, you'll get used to it eventually."

Reluctantly, Alec shuffled through the door to take his place in a queue which recalled the days of his induction into the army before he'd been sent to Nam. More reminiscent of the worst hell earth had to offer than heaven as Alec envisioned it.

"Size?" The person at the head of the line mumbled something in a language Alec didn't understand. And the gentleman behind the counter, suitably garbed in the uniform of snowy white, handed over identical robes to the other man who sauntered away, pulled along by what Alec presumed was his 'guardian angel'.

"Size?" the man barked at the next person in line, and the next, each of whom responded in French, in English.

The men gathered in a tight little knot to compare robes. They were all the same size.

Alec nudged 'George'.

"Look," he said.

"Sh-sh-sh, not too loud. They're all the same. They shrink or expand to the cover the immortal form, but Gabriel doesn't know that. It gets pretty boring here, doing nothing but passing out gowns eternally. It makes him feel important, giving him something to occupy his time."

It was Alec's turn next.

"Size?"

The producer glanced down at his round belly. "Small."

Gabriel peered at him critically. "No, I'd say you take a large."

"Do you have something a little bit more colourful? Something in a mauve or a hot pink would be nice," Alec quipped.

Shoving the robes at Alec, Gabriel turned to the next in line. "Size?"

"No one ever told me that you lose your sense of humour coming up here," Fowler muttered as he unfurled the gown.

"Oh, Velcro, a nice touch."

George tugged at his sleeve.

Then Alec found himself in another queue, this one for halos. And finally the one for wings. The other men accepted these gifts, and Alec noted their expressions were just as bemused as his must have been.

"What if I don't want to change?" Alec whispered out of the corner of his mouth to George.

"I'm sorry. There's only one permissible costume here in heaven."

"And if I refuse?"

"You don't really have a choice," George said pointing at Alec's feet. The producer glanced down, and his jaw flopped uselessly upon the hinge of his mandible. His toes — the nails yellowed and ridged with age that no plastic surgeon could correct — protruded from white robes which he couldn't remember donning.

And the first chink in the chain mail of disbelief appeared. "But, but..."

"Now I take you to your own personal cloud, and then you are on your own. I have others to greet."

"Hey, George or whatever the fuck your name is," Alec said, or thought he said, but the words that issued from his lips were deferential. "George, great slayer of old."

The producer tugged at his lip and tried to peer at it over his nose.

"I told you that profanity wasn't allowed," George said.

"I want to talk somebody; I'm sick of dealing with dumb—f — —" his tongue tangled in his teeth, "f — —, f — —, actors. I want to talk to the person in charge of this charade."

The little man recoiled. "You mean Jehovah?"

"Yeah, God, if that's what you want to call him," he said.

"Nobody talks to God unless He summons you, and you'd better hope He doesn't because that means He's reconsidering His options about you and your presence here in the City of Eternal Light. Remember Satan was once an angel, cast from on high for his insolence. Trust me, you don't want to talk to Him, if you can help it." The man shooed him forward with a metallic clatter.

Alec shifted his shoulders, oppressed by the weight of his

wings. They moved on in silence until they stood on the edge of a great precipice with no ground in sight. It was a great special effect, too real to be tested by extending a foot or a toe beyond the cottony field.

Alec seized George's arm.

"Come along. Must hurry," the ancient Dragonslayer said.

"Wait, no, I can't. I'm afraid of heights." Fowler's knuckles paled with the strength of his grip upon the mailed arm.

"Not up here, you don't," George said, and he pushed the producer over the edge of the abyss.

The last vestiges of doubt were torn away. This was no artist's rendering of abyss, no effect of mirror reflecting the sky overhead.

Alec dropped like a stone. A scream ripped from his throat as he plummeted.

"The wings! The wings!" George hurled himself off the edge of the cloud and shot after Alec, his wings folded against his back. "Use the wings the good Lord gave you, Godda — it!" The saint clapped a hand over his mouth and cast a frightened glance over his shoulder.

Lightning flashed somewhere, and his pal George reeled, head over heels, until he was parallel with Alec. Then he straightened, unfurling his wings so they could act as break. The two of them landed softly in a fluffy cloud that looked like every other cloud in the place.

The interior was furnished with a single bed, a table and chairs — all white — and a... television set?

Seeing that, Alec threw his head back and guffawed.

"All right, that fall was a pretty good trick. Fantastic special effects, but you can stop now." He swung on George, saying, "You can stop pretending."

The 'angel' grimaced.

Some were harder to convince than others.

"Come off it," Alec said, noting the grim expression. "Television? In heaven?"

"What did you expect? We keep up with the times, even here in heaven." He picked up a video tape and waved it under Alec's nose. "This is the highlights of your life. What brought you up here instead sending you down to the other place." The saint shivered, a most unchivalrous gesture. "It gives you something to do if you don't feel like flitting about, polishing your halo, rearranging the folds of your robe, or participating in Holy Harmonics or dancing on the head of a pin. Which reminds me, do you play an instrument?"

"No," Alec said.

"Too bad. I guess that means, it's the harp for you then." George pointed at the corner of the circular room of woven white walls, and the instrument appeared with a muffled twang of strings.

"I told you I don't play the harp," Alec protested.

"You do now," George said as he lifted off in a flurry of wings.

"But —" Alec chased him to the end of the cloud.

"Don't worry, you'll get the hang of it. You've got an eternity to practice."

Alone at last, Alec wandered around the tiny cubicle with its stark white furnishings, which would have done justice to the most austere monastery.

Screw this, he thought, and Alec stripped the bed to look under the mattress, although he couldn't have said what he was searching for. Perhaps a label, something which said "Made in Japan, Mongolia, or Newark". He didn't care, as long as it gave some clue to his real location, but the mattress was a pristine white. Devoid of stripes, pattern or stain.

In desperation, he turned to the video tape that sat on top of the television set and studied it. Like everything else in this place, the cassette was white, with gilt edging — his name outlined in gold: "Norman Alec Fowler".

He slammed it back down upon the television and made another quick circuit of his room, with its walls of spun cotton. Like a padded cell.

"The rubber room at the Heavenly Hilton," he mumbled.

That took a total of two seconds and again Alec was back at the television.

He found himself wishing for a cigarette, a habit he'd given up years ago, and a pack materialized on top of the tape. Alec stepped quickly back almost tripping on his robes.

It said something about God's priorities that smoking was permissible, while swearing was not. But then what did lung cancer and heart disease matter up here? God probably owned stock in a tobacco company.

"Aw, hell," Alec said as he grabbed the tape and jammed it into the VCR. "Might as well watch it. I haven't got anything better to do. Wonder what kind of cheap-assed production this is."

Thunder rumbled somewhere and Alec glanced up at the dome-like ceiling.

"Ah, sorry," he said as he a lit a cigarette.

Exhaling a large cloud of smoke which immediately got absorbed into the walls, Alec fiddled with the knobs of the television and settled back on the chair, only to leap up as his wings got squashed against the rungs. His chin rested on his shoulder, Alec inspected them with difficulty because whenever he moved, they moved with him. He revolved, and they followed. He pivoted again and they whirled away from his scrutiny. Like a cat chasing its tail.

His fingers kneaded the cloth, trying to find the harness that surely must attach them to his back. The robe tore, and Alec noticed what had escaped him before. They sprouted from his shoulder blades. If the wings were fastened by any human means, then his friends had used Superglue to secure them directly to his flesh.

Just then heavenly music filled his room and, bewildered, Alec sat, his back held rigid, the wings wrapped carefully around him to prevent them snarling with the chair.

The credits scrolled, giving the same vital statistics that he had observed on the computer printout.

"Norman Alec Fowler (NAF)
Born: June 5th, 953
Died: February 4th, 994"

Today's date, or was it yesterday's?

The verbiage faded from the screen as the music climbed in crescendo to what he could only call celestial cacophony, and the next thing he saw was a pair of splayed legs, the pink buds of vulva spreading wide against the pressure of a black scalp. A shriek reverberated around his little cubicle room, and a head appeared over the 'v' of calf and thigh. His mother's face. And Alec realized he was watching his own birth. Pretty sickening really. He didn't like to think of popping from between his mother's legs, or any other portion of her anatomy for that matter. A wrinkled head erupted from the bloody vagina, and Alec had to look away, picking imaginary lint from his gown.

The music changed, and he chanced a peek at the screen. There, he was in all his glory, he recognized himself from his baby pictures. The features twisted in a ludicrous leer. A voice from off screen, his mother's, cooed.

"Look he's smiling."

"Gas," his father replied.

Trust dad to get to the heart of the issue, and Alec wondered if heaven bothered to record each individual case of flatulence. As though the heavenly producer had heard his thoughts, the next thing Fowler saw was himself perched upon his potty chair between to towering adult bodies. They were applauding the prodigious feat of his first successful crap in the potty, which was shaped like a duck.

Then the images speeded up, and he was releasing a lightening bug from a chubby fist rather than shoving it in the jar, with its punctured lid his mom had prepared for him. Or sharing some small something with his sister. Small kindnesses really.

Then a five-year-old version of himself, head hanging forlornly, confessing some small sin.

Dull stuff. Boring.

"Yup," he mumbled, "That's me, Alec Dull. That's why I'm up here. I'm so good I could just puke."

As the thought occurred to him, the montage of nameless faces and empty events slowed. The scene faded to black, and when it reappeared Alec saw himself offering a bunch of wilted flowers to his grandmother as she lay on her deathbed.

Alec's nose wrinkled as the stench of sickness and disease filled the room. The picture changed; the smell of his grandmother's sick room blended with that of dog.

Fur. The musky odour of dog and decay.

And suddenly all his senses got involved in the act.

Sight, scent, sound, and touch. His fingers twitched as he felt the silken flank of Woof, his one and only dog.

Talk about feelies! This was state of the art in virtual reality without the complications of cumbersome cap and bulky gloves.

An ephemeral wet tongue scraped his cheek and a sob lodged somewhere in his chest.

"No," Alec mewled. He didn't want to see this. Anything but this.

The child upon the screen lifted the fuzzy head. The eyes glittered blindly, and the boy pried the dog's jaws apart and drizzled water down the parched throat.

How long had he sat up with the dog? Believing he could fight the inevitability of extinction. It had been his first brush with death and futility. Woof had died in his arms. Alec never got another dog after that; he didn't want one. Nothing, no one could ever replace Woof.

Later a twenty-year-old Alec stared, ashen faced, upon a closed coffin which he recognized as his mother's. By now the scenes were more familiar. Being more recent, they were easily accessible in his memory. Alec watched this younger self, recalling all the things he meant to say to his mom before she died, and didn't. Never had time, or never took it.

A quick cut, and Alec was in a lush jungle, surrounded by the heady aroma of sickly sweet flowers in sticky, almost liquid air. Fowler buried his face in his hands, as the sounds of explosion filled the room and his small cloud shook violently. When he again lifted his head, a brilliant orange light flashed across the screen. More immediate, more real than any of Hollywood's best pyrotechnics.

Boom!

The muscles in his face spasmed against the pattering of dirt and shredded foliage. An Asian child, trailing flames, screeched past him. And the Alex wearing camou-fatigues leapt, tackling her and smothering the flames with his body. She died of her wounds, anyway. Then, the eyes of his best friend — some young buck from Arkansas, all freckles and good intentions and feckless luck — glazed in death. In the background, the rest of his platoon skulked by, ignoring Alec as he tried to replace the man's intestines in his abdominal cavity.

Just when Alec thought he could stomach no more. No more heroics. No more sacrifices, big or small, from a bunch of boys who would rather be home chasing some cheerleader. The vast panorama of green retreated. They airlifted him from the field, with the wound that would send him home. Back to the US of A to the jeers of pacifists, youngsters who didn't know how to live much less die.

Again the images and events passed in a blur. Nondescript. Mundane. Him refusing a shady deal; staying sober while others drank; turning aside propositions of young starlets — who offered their bodies along with their talents, just for a shot at the big time.

And Alec thought he knew where this was leading. His suspicions were confirmed as Alec viewed himself sitting naked on a hotel bed — elbows propped on his knees, back bowed and head lowered.

"I'm sorry," the television Alec said, while the Alec on the chair wings flapped in agitation. The woman, who sat Indian style next to him, was no starlet with silicone tits and collagen lips, but someone who worked in the cutting room. She had an intelligent face and serious eyes. And he'd fallen for her, a girl eighteen years his junior. Like all the bad jokes about mid-life crisis and aging actors, he'd pursued her relentlessly until she gave in.

His marriage had been getting pretty rocky of late. His son gone off to college and his wife bored out of her skull. And after he'd slept with the girl, Alec realized what he had done to himself and his wife. He'd said good-bye, pronto, but he'd still looked after the girl, seeing that she got a promotion from assistant to full editor. He'd even arranged for her to meet some nice young man, and let nature take its course. They'd announced their engagement on Valentine's Day, one reason why he'd thrown caution to the wind and allowed himself to drink and drive.

Alec twisted the tip of a wing between his hands.

"Ouch!"

Then he lifted a hand to his face, feeling tears upon his cheek.

Judging by the events, the tape must be getting pretty close to the end, he thought. So Alec was surprised when his wife's face peered at him over a man's bare shoulder, her fingers digging into the flesh. Her lips wet and parted, as were her legs, and she welcomed him into her, panting.

Alec rose to his feet. The chair clattered to the floor behind him.

Kirby?

Yes, Kirby. So that was it. All along it had been him. This whole goddamn thing — heaven, saints, clouds — was some horrendously bad joke to let Alec know that his best friend was screwing his wife.

How long had this been going on?

The next thing Alec knew, his wife was fully dressed wishing Kirby adieu with a passionate kiss, the like of which Alec hadn't seen in years.

"We have to tell him," Kirby said. "It's getting harder and harder to work with him."

She swallowed. "Just give it a few more weeks until Robert's out of school."

"It's been five years."

Five years! And Alec had felt guilty about what was roughly equivalent to a one-night-stand.

"The son of a bitch!" Alec didn't even notice the jagged streak of lightning that split the sky at his words, landing suspiciously close to his personal cloud. Instead, the producer strode about the room, looking for something upon which to vent he rage. He bumped into the harp. It chattered at him stridently. He punched it, cutting his hand on the strings.

Then he walked up to the VCR, ready to jab the eject button, but his movement was arrested — the extended index finger curled in upon itself as Alec gazed at the final scene.

His car appeared on the horizon. It pitched drunkenly on wet pavement. He was blinded by on-coming beams that shone out of the television, spotlighting his face in radiant light. The picture coalesced, and he saw now as he had seen then, in a final second of panic, the infant in its car-seat. His hand tore at the wheel, yanking it to the left. The action sent his car spinning over a cliff. His last living view, now that he remembered it, was the winking lights of Van Nuys.

The camera panned to the other side of the rode. The car pulled over, and a woman emerged shakily. Inside a baby screamed, perhaps catching some of its mother's frenzy.

And even as he watched, Alec breathed a sigh of relief. Mother and child were safe.

Final credits were superimposed over the glittering suburbs. The letters changed colours from white on black to black on bloody crimson as the car exploded, bleaching out the flickering lights of Van Nuys.

The words of the prayer Alec spoke echoed about the room as the car catapulted through space before catching on a boulder which sent it reeling end over end to the bottom of the canyon.

There was a click and a whir as the tape spun back to the beginning and started again.

"No!" he wailed and he ran out his room, quite forgetting about clouds and wings and other such things. And he plunged, down, down, down, down, down, down, down. Until he was sure he must have descended to Hades itself.

Suddenly his fall was arrested as he landed on someone else's cloud.

"Ooph!"

The man glanced up from his harp. "Ah, you're new here I see."

Alec sat up and picked cotton out of his mouth for the second time that day.

"Oh, yeah, how can you tell?"

The other fellow's gaze flitted up to the heavens above his head and made a whistling sound while his hands crossed, thumbs twined and flapped his fingers, ineffectually, then aped someone falling.

"Okay, okay, I get the picture," Alec said. "You're not some saint or another, are you?"

The man chortled. "Oi vay, I should hope not."

"You're Jewish! What are you doing here?"

"Who knows?" he spread his arms wide before him. "Learning the harp?" he said.

"Tell me, is this for real?"

The head moved up and down in assent.

"What am I doing here?"

"You, what about me? Imagine my surprise when I woke up in a Goya heaven. My poor mother's still whirling in her grave, I'm sure."

"Can't be, just can't," Alec mused aloud.

"Didn't they give you the tape?"

"I'll say. Horrible, watching my dog die, my mother, myself."

"Then you know more about what brought you," the man thumbed at the cloud below their feet, "here than I do."

"I don't believe it. This is it? This is heaven! Clouds of candy

71

floss and spun sugar, shapeless robes, and a video tape — a highlights of my personal hits," Alec spat the word disparagingly. "That is enough to drive a sane man around the twist. What a rip off!"

"You make do with what you have."

"Well, I won't watch that tape."

"When you get bored enough, you will," the other man said.

Disregarding the other, Alec grumbled to himself. "To spend the rest of eternity watching the saddest events of my life. No, this isn't heaven. It can't be." The producer jumped to his feet, grabbed the other man and shook him. "Tell me it isn't true. This is all a dream. It isn't heaven. It's hell, isn't it? It's hell. It's gotta be."

The other man extracted himself from Alec's grasp and unruffled his wings. He paused in his preening to regard the rookie with a certain measure pity before responding.

"Oh, no, friend, trust me, hell is much more interesting."

*

God reached over and selected a single cassette from a stack of three. A marvellous innovation this video thing... made His job a lot easier, and He wondered why He hadn't thought of them before.

He stared at the box. It said *A Connecticut Yankee in King Arthur's Court*.

"Hmm," He said, "Bing Crosby. I thought I knew that face."

*

Somewhere far, far away — or close depending upon how you chose to fold reality — Lucifer leapt to his feet.

"What!" he shouted at a cringing imp. "Wha'd'ya mean all the video monitors are out?"

LEAP OF FAITH

"What th–" The latter word was never completed, coming out instead as a gasp. Noah Isaacson's gaze took in the plain white room where white walls joined a white floor to a white ceiling. Without apparent door or even seams, it was more like a box than a room.

So much white, in fact, that one would have expected it to be austere, but it was not. It was dull, muted, as though the room had survived ages without the benefit of gentle swipe from either rag or cloth. Yet the walls were neither grey nor stained. They were featureless.

This was white in its purist pigmentary sense, the absence of colour, rather than the presence of light.

"Where am I?"

He grimaced, chagrined by the cliché.

"Brilliant, absolutely brilliant," he muttered as he stood up from his chair which was — he glimpsed behind him — white. Of course. What else had he expected? Someone had a lot to learn about interior decor.

Isaacson flitted impatiently around the room, noticing the paper slippers and drab, white gown for the first time. Definitely NHS issue. He relaxed.

Since he'd awakened — at least he assumed he'd been caught napping — Isaacson had been dreaming of plots and counterplots, espionage and counterespionage. Forget the fact that he'd given up on the military when he'd turned quantum and the information he had was probably dated anyway. As a former employee of the MOD, paranoia was part of the trade, and Isaacson did have any number of military secrets locked inside his brain for which many would pay good money. Even in this post-cold-war world, his knowledge had worth to any number of political groups and terrorist organizations.

He chuckled. He was just in for a physical. He walked around the room one more time and then reversed his direction. Isaacson didn't like waiting and it already seemed like he'd been there forever.

"Hello?" he shouted at the seamless white wall. His voice bounced back at him. "Hello... hellohello—lo—lo."

"NOAH?"

Isaacson jumped. The walls spoke! He scanned the room for hidden microphones, all his fears coming back at him.

"NOAH ISAACSON?"

The voice commanded all of his attention, seeming to emanate from the walls themselves. He stuck his finger in his ears.

"NOAH ISAACSON."

Loud, so loud that he didn't think he could've heard anything else, even a nuclear blast in the next room. His head thrummed with each cord.

"NO –"

Tentatively he responded, speaking aloud, anything to delay that resumption of that voice.

"Yes. Who are you? Where are you?" He swung around with a swish of cloth, firing his questions at the walls. "Where am I?" He corrected himself. "We?"

"NOAH ISAACSON, NUCLEAR PHYSICIST?"

"Oh, oh." Isaacson spun, trying to look everywhere at once. "Your information is a little out of date. I've gone quantum." He laughed. "A little shop humour."

"WHATEVER." The voice was disdainful, indifferent.

"There's a great deal of difference," the scientist sniffed.

"NOAH ISAACSON, PHYSICIST, LATE OF 3 ALBERT CLOSE, SON OF MURRAY AND CATHERINE ISAACSON."

"Wait a second, back up a bit. What do you mean, 'late'?"

"LATE AS IN FORMERLY."

"I don't recall moving," Isaacson said.

"YOU DIDN'T."

Isaacson tilted his head to one side, listening. Definitely contemptuous.

"NOAH ISAACSON, PHYSICIST, FORMERLY OF 3 ALBERT CLOSE, SON OF MURRAY AND CATHARINE..."

"Now hold on there. Where am I?"

"YOU ARE SUPPOSED TO BE A GENIUS. I WOULD HAVE THOUGHT THAT YOU'D'VE FIGURED THAT OUT BY NOW?"

"Well, I haven't." He kicked at a space on the floor and his white, paper slipper went flying.

Again the voice intoned: "NOAH ISAACSON, PHYSICIST, FORMERLY OF 3 ALBERT CLOSE, SON OF MURRY AND CATHERINE, LAPSED CATHOLIC."

"I am an atheist."

"WE ARE AWARE OF THAT."

"What's this we shit? Who are you?"

"METATRON, THE MOUTH PIECE OF GOD," it informed him with exaggerated patience.

"Right, and I'm Father Christmas."

"ARE YOU?"

"Do I look like him?"

"NO."

Isaacson glanced down at his scrawny arms. "Well, okay, let's just say I've been on a diet. Now will you quit joking around and tell me where I am?"

"WHERE WAS I..? oh, yes... LAPSED CATHOLIC."

"What does my religion have to do with anything?"

"IT HAS EVERYTHING TO DO WITH EVERYTHING."

"What do you mean?"

"WILL YOU ANSWER THE QUESTION PLEASE?"

"What question?"

"ARE YOU NOAH..?"

"Isaacson? Yes, yes, alright, already. I'm Noah Isaacson," he conceded.

"PHYSICIST, LATE OF ALBERT CLOSE?"

"Yes, I told you I was. Now you can answer a question of mine."

A pause, then a distrustful, "YES?"

"Where am I?"

"YOU HAVE NOT RECOGNIZED THIS PLACE YET?"

"No, of course not, should I?"

"IT IS PART OF YOUR COLLECTIVE UNCONSCIOUS."

"That's psychology — Jungian, I believe — not my subject."

The voice sounded sceptical. "REALLY? THE TWO GROUPS HAVE ARRIVED AT STARTLING SIMILAR CONCLUSIONS. I'D'VE THOUGHT YOU'D BE FAMILIAR WITH JUNG." It seemed to remember its original line of questioning and returned to its chant. "YOU ARE A LAPSED CATHOLIC, ARE YOU NOT?"

"My parents were."

75

"IT SEEMS TO BE QUITE A FAMILIAL TRAIT."

"What does?"

"LAPSING. NOTE: YOUR GREAT-GREAT-GREAT-GREAT-GREAT..."

"I'm familiar with the family history."

"... GRANDFATHER, THE ORIGINAL ISAAC WAS JEWISH."

"So what of it? Who are you to judge? If faced with option of burning at the stake or calling God by another name, which would you do? Besides, if there is a God — my emphasis on the if — then I don't believe he," he paused, considering, "or she, adheres to one faith. Do you?"

SILENCE. And Noah discovered that the voice was as loud and ominous in its absence, as it was in its presence.

Isaacson threw up his hands in disgust. "Where the hell am I?"

"NOT HELL, NOAH. PURGATORY."

"Screw this."

"TSK, TSK, YOUR ATTITUDE HAS BEEN NOTED."

"Look, I am agnostic."

"I THOUGHT YOU SAID YOU WERE ATHEIST."

"Agnostic. Atheist." He shrugged. "The point is what am I doing in, uh, purgatory?"

"YOU WERE CATHOLIC ONCE, CORRECT?"

"Yes, I was baptized."

"AND YOU WERE GOING THROUGH A CRISIS OF CONSCIENCE WHEN YOU PASSED OVER?"

"Passed over where?"

"COME NOW, THERE'S NO POINT IN BEING OBTUSE."

"Are you trying to tell me that I'm dead?"

"IT'S CONFIRMED, FOLKS. THE MAN'S A GENIUS." The walls shook with the sound of a vast sigh. "FOR A MAN WITH A RATED IQ OF MORE THAN 200 YOU'RE NOT VERY BRIGHT."

"Okay, so let's say I accept the fact that I'm dead. Why purgatory?"

There was a deep rumble like the clearing of an enormous throat. "THE CRISIS OF CONSCIENCE."

"I did come to question my previous work after I left the Ministry, but that's not exactly what I would call a crisis of conscience."

"WHAT WOULD YOU CALL IT THEN?"

"I don't know," Isaacson mumbled down at his slippers, "but not a crisis of conscience."

"YOUR ANCESTORS WERE JEWS, BUT YOU WERE RAISED A CATHOLIC; YOU BECAME AN ATHEIST. NOW YOU SAY YOU'RE AN AGNOSTIC. DO YOU MEAN TO TELL ME THAT HAVE YOU NOT COME TO QUESTION YOUR BELIEFS IN G0D JUST THE TEENIEST LITTLE BIT?"

He considered this statement and nodded. He'd concluded long ago that empiricists were really mystics by another name.

"Well, perhaps. I accept that there's been a transformation in my personal philosophy through the years. And my work with quantum theory has caused me to acknowledge that there might," he hesitated, "just might be room for the concept of a God within scientific thought." He thought for a moment and qualified his last observation. "Maybe... if said God is of a more Eastern flavour."

"THERE, YOU SEE," the voice was almost jubilant with relief, "YOU HAVE IT. A CRISIS OF CONSCIENCE."

Isaacson collapsed into the chair which scuttled along after him as he paced about the room.

Regaining some of its lost dignity, the Metatron thundered. "THIS ROOM IS AT THE CENTRE AT A GREAT MAZE. YOUR PURPOSE IS TO COMPLETE THE QUEST YOU BEGAN IN LIFE, FINDING YOUR WAY TO GOD."

"God? As in the supreme being?"

"THAT IS THE PURPOSE OF PURGATORY."

"You mean, God just happens to be lurking around here somewhere? You would think that he would have better things to do with his time," Isaacson murmured to no one in particular.

"HE DOES. HOWEVER GOD IS EVERYWHERE."

"If that is true, then I don't have to leave this room, do I?"

"IT IS ENTIRELY UP TO YOU. BE IT KNOWN, WHAT HAS BEEN DECREED. ON EARTH YOU LOST YOUR WAY. HERE YOU MUST FIND IT AGAIN OR SPEND YOUR ETERNITY HERE, IN THIS ROOM, LOOKING AT THESE FOUR WALLS."

The voice dropped conspiratorially, "AND LET ME TELL YOU, ETERNITY IS A VERY, VERY LONG TIME. HARD ENOUGH TO FILL AT THE BEST OF TIMES."

A subdued Isaacson bowed his head and waited.

"THIS MAZE WILL TEST YOU TO YOUR LIMITS, REQUIRING ALL YOUR FACULTIES AND THE USE OF ALL YOUR KNOWLEDGE OF SCIENCE AND SCIENTIFIC PRINCIPLES, BUT IT WILL TEST YOU BEYOND THAT. IT WILL REQUIRE —" SIGNIFICANT SILENCE "— A LEAP OF FAITH."

Isaacson snorted. "Of course."

"GOOD LUCK UPON YOUR QUEST." The voice faded and a door suddenly appeared in the heretofore nondescript walls.

Isaacson didn't start out immediately. First, he wasted a lot of time looking for speakers, wire or electrical conduit — anything that could explain how the voice had entered the room.

He found nowt. Then his fingers performed a minute examination of his face and scalp, searching for scars, hardened nodules, protrusion of any sort, anything that might suggest some sort of surgical implant.

After that the scientist dallied and dithered and then dawdled some more, waiting to see if the voice would return and exhort him to continue.

It didn't.

Still, Isaacson procrastinated. After all, he had all eternity, didn't he? To spend looking for God. Really!

He glared at the walls, willing them to speak. He was ready for a debate. His feet swung, kicking at empty air.

Finally boredom drove him from the room. The way he figured it, this was going to be a doddle. All mazes were built with the same basic design, maximizing the space allotted, which must, of necessity, be limited.

Or was it?

His step faltered and he stopped where he stood just outside the door of his room.

If this was the afterlife, then surely it must be crowded. It had to be. His mind boggled when he tried to imagine all the people who'd died since the beginning of time — from this universe, or any other parallel universe — who may possibly be crammed into this space.

The thought led immediately to another, and Noah paused to ponder the concept of soul. Did an individual, who may have an infinite number of splintered selves, have a single shared soul?

Or one each?

And what happened when one of them died? Did this self, or soul, have another self who was — even as he sat here — whooping it up at a scientific conference somewhere? And somewhere else, again, was a version of himself not dead or dying but recuperating in hospital? Or did all his selves cease in a single instant? If he had survived somewhere, was that self diminished by the loss of this one?

He tucked his chin into his chest in a moment of quantum revelation. That might explain the process of aging, the loss of self, as other lives died taking pieces of the soul with them.

Or was this 'Isaacson' the sum total of all his many lives? He shook his head. Didn't that refute the idea that individual choice sent lives spiralling off onto the analogous paths?

Better, Noah thought, to stick with the more immediate and physical problem. The maze. Isaacson couldn't possibly know how large the labyrinth was. The best he could do was guess at its total dimensions, its possible surface area and circumference. The amount of space allotted could be infinite. Noah quailed at the concept. The task suddenly became insurmountable, even before he had managed to start.

Of course, all this presupposed that the voice was telling the truth, and Isaacson had no way of knowing how much of what the voice said was reliable. As a man of science, he had a hard time swallowing a God who would go to elaborate lengths to convert Noah to His cause. Surely, God had bigger fish to fry than one lapsed Jew cum lapsed Catholic.

Too, basing his premise on infinite space, it was not only impractical, it was illogical. What of heaven? What of hell? He couldn't believe that all infinity had been reserved for the sole purpose of his edification.

So it seemed a safe assumption that, despite so-called divine intervention, the maze must be subject to some physical limitations — if for no other reason than overcrowding — and to physical laws, for even curved space had its rules. Admittedly, it was a shaky supposition when dealing with the sublime, but he had to have a starting place.

And there was only one way to test not only the veracity of the ghostly voice, but also his hypothesis. The longest journeys begin with a single step.

Cheered, Isaacson trotted down the long hall, noting the many doors, alleys and branching corridors. Some were immediate blinds, the hall ending within a few metres of its access point. He ignored them.

One thing was certain; the Metatron hadn't been lying when he said that this was a maze.

*

Hours later Noah stopped in a flurry of white cloth. The NHS issue robes split in a suitably embarrassing place. Although Isaacson no longer deluded himself that they were NHS, he was reasonably sure he knew where health professionals had got the design. Or had modern hospital gowns provided the inspiration? An interesting question.

Was man the initiator and God the imitator? He laughed. Might as well ask which came first the chicken or the egg?

The scientist picked at the robe. "You'd think He could've at least improved upon it. Add Velcro or something."

Somewhere he heard a mumbled curse and a sharp report like a thunder clap. Noah was so startled that he lost his balance and fell.

The chair did as it always did and materialized miraculously underneath him, saving him just before he hit the floor. The chair had become a permanent fixture, or a semi-permanent one, because it seemed to follow him — vanishing whenever he was on the move, only to reappear when he halted.

Evidently, the Management expected Isaacson to be here a while.

Something caught the scientist by the short hairs, quite literally. He tried to free himself, and Velcro scraped across his balls.

"Ouch! Ah, thank you," he said fastening the back of the gown.

The strip, more of a button really, was inconveniently located, right between the shoulder blades. Not much of an improvement. The salient bits still weren't covered.

He turned from the contemplation of his wearing apparel and studied the corridor.

When all was said and done, Purgatory wasn't a bad place. A

80

bit bland maybe. A bit tedious, perhaps, or rapidly becoming that way. And Isaacson no longer felt quite so confident about his progress, as he had when first starting this crusade.

He had known then — as he didn't know now — that there wasn't a puzzle he couldn't solve or a answer he couldn't find if he put his mind to it. He had faith in his abilities. It was an erroneous assumption, one of many.

At first, he'd tackled the problem scientifically. All mazes were laid out on the same principal. To make room for blinds and ruses, the through passages usually traced an outline of the perimeter, which was usually a square. So he walked down the main corridor until it ended, then retraced his steps and took the first right. He followed a similar procedure for the next two lefts and then the final right, which should have led to the end of the puzzle.

And he found himself back at his starting point.

Obviously, Noah had underestimated the complexity of the design. Perhaps the maze itself was not laid out in a square, but followed some other geometric shape. An octagon or a pentagon or... a circle.

He groaned.

Still the principals of layout and design should remain the same.

So he'd tried again, and again, and again, and he marvelled. If God had sat a mortal eternity, He could not have devised a task more likely to derange the scientific mind.

Nervous, Noah got up and began to walk again. The chair retracted to wherever retracting chairs must go.

He had no tools. Nothing that would allow him to mark where he'd been and no means by which he could measure how far he'd gone. Neither were there visual clues. Each hall looked identical to the one before. The very sameness of the place was daunting.

He'd tried counting off each pace as he took it. As a unit of measure the method was capricious at best, depending upon the length and vigour of his stride. Worse, though, he soon lost count.

He'd started over again. Eventually, he tired himself out, dropping from sheer exhaustion and falling immediately to sleep, curled uncomfortably on the magic disappearing/

reappearing chair.

Later he decided, as sedatives go, counting one's steps was much more effective than counting sheep.

The next — night? morning? day? — Noah tried marking his route, unravelling the hated gown, only to make the startling discovery that it too, like the chair, reappeared or replenished itself at will.

The process of reweaving began as soon as certain portions of his anatomy were exposed, so that the cloth always covered — or not quite covered — the appropriate parts.

Disheartened, Noah realized he could not calculate the distance covered by estimating the length of the thread used to make an entire gown. Not if it kept recreating itself as he went.

For a insane moment, he thought he might be able to measure the thread as he unravelled it by using the length of his arm, only marginally more reliable than paces, but he had no writing implements and no way to mark the thread as he measured it. And who's to say if he'd do any better keeping track of arm lengths than he had of paces.

He stared at the short length of cloth and wondered how long before it all grew back again.

One thing that Isaacson had learned, using this rather haphazard system of measurement, was that this maze didn't fit into any system of spatial relations, or follow any of the normal physical laws, that he knew. Otherwise, he should have crossed at least one of the former paths that he had marked by thread before now. He hadn't.

The maze could be three dimensional, branching up or down as well as laterally, but only if the gradient between levels was so negligible as to be imperceptible.

Or... this maze was quantum theory given substance, given flesh, as it were.

The scientist shrieked in frustration, grabbed a handful of hair and pulled. It had been all very well and good to deal with quantum theory in the abstract. To dabble in it. To speculate about it. The reality was quite different.

Despite his pretensions and high-flown conjecture, Isaacson must confess to having a three-dimensional mind, a mind that dealt with time as a single line. He understood now on a visceral level what he had only grasped on a superficial level before.

The infinite truly was beyond human comprehension. It was a symbol on a page, in a mathematic equation, a lop-sided eight. It was a place somewhere out in space where two parallel lines meet.

It was... impossible. He could not continue. Isaacson collapsed in a heap on the floor, or almost, for the chair rose up to meet him, hitting him squarely in the stomach.

"Oooh," he wheezed, and he passed out.

*

Isaacson halted in his mad dash up the hall. His demeanour had changed from what was once his typical countenance of quiet competence to a state of barely controlled panic. His eyes had taken on the hard gleam of madness. Muttering to himself, the physicist looked this way and that and saw more of the same.

White, white, everywhere, unendingly walls of dull, monotonous white.

"No," he moaned and took a weak swing at the wall, hurting his hand. He cradled his arm against his chest.

Long ago Noah had stopped marking his path. Why bother?

For the millionth time, the scientist folded, and for the millionth time, the little chair materialized from nowhere. A bit slower this time, as if it too tired of pursuit. It sighed under his weight.

Again Isaacson's head swung — right, left, forward and back. He scratched his beard.

Funny, growth and aging were not things he would have identified with the afterlife. He'd always figured, when he'd bothered to think about it at all, that he would be able to choose an age and stay there. Not get stuck with the one he'd had at the time of his demise and watch as his physical health deteriorated and declined.

He stared at his arms — they had grown wrinkled — and wondered how he had died.

Facial hair he expected, presuming that one's 'spirit' reflected one's earthly body. For it was well known that human hair and human nails continued to grow after death.

But age? Isaacson could see more grey in his beard than he had had in the past. And it had grown long, while he became stooped with age.

How long had he been wandering lost in this labyrinth?

Years?

Did years pass in purgatory?

Isaacson didn't know. In this artificial environment, there were no nights, no days, no seasons, nothing to indicate the passage of time except the facial hair.

He'd been there for a long, long time.

Forever...

He sobbed disconsolately.

Something inside his head snapped, and he knew, he KNEW, that he'd been going about it the wrong way.

All his knowledge, his theories were useless here. Everything he had learned in life was worthless. The solution was of the heart rather than the mind. It required a leap beyond logic, a leap of faith.

Just as this thought did a flittering dance inside his skull, a light began to flicker somewhere in the distance. Nothing more than a faint glimmer, but a disruption in the monochrome maze nonetheless.

It caught at his gaze and held it.

The hoary head shifted with an audible clacking as the vertebrae popped back into place, and he turned to stare down one hallway at the light.

Could it be?

Noah Isaacson stumbled to his feet. The chair vanished and he teetered in the direction of the disturbance. Slowly at first, he began picking up speed when he was sure that his eyes were not deceiving him.

The light winked at him. Like a star, a strobe or a beacon. It beckoned, urging him on.

Could it...

Faster and faster until his teetering walk had evolved into a loping run.

It was.

His arms stretched out before him, fingers snapping and grasping. His head outdistanced his feet and his body scarpered to keep up. Isaacson laughed; he cried, and he raced giddily down the hall, unmindful of the ancient limbs that protested the sudden velocity.

And he ran... and ran... and ran... and ran.

Still, the light was no closer.

Faster and faster until he was sure that his heart was going to explode inside his chest.

The next instant, Noah stepped on his beard, falling tit over tail to sprawl in the middle of the hall. He levered himself from the floor and peered into the distance. The light had taken on form and, yes, a discernible shape. A rectangle or a square. The scientist squinted.

Yes, it was... it was a gate!

Joy rocketed through his body. He struggled to his hands and knees and scrambled along on all fours. Until he didn't even have the strength for that and all he could manage was an unenthusiastic slither-crawl where he drew one leg after another to his chest and then shoved himself forward, inching along.

That's when his knee got tangled with his beard, and he went down, face first. He lay for a minute, staring at the blank white floor and wondering what it was made of. Finally, he tucked his limbs underneath him and tried to rise, but arms got snagged in his gown. The chair chose this inopportune moment to sprout from the floor. He lay, face down half on and half off the chair, flopping around like a fish.

He grabbed the back of the chair and dragged himself into an upright position. The light, or the door, was definitely closer now, and he could begin to make out some details.

Definitely a gate worthy of the name heavenly, it incorporated silver and gold in a fantastical filigree. The surface was shot throughout with pearl, or mother of pearl. Now that he was closer to it, it seemed smaller than he thought it should be, but then it was the back door after all.

He looped his beard over his arm and staggered to his feet. The gate wavered, and he lurched forward ready to give chase. Resolution rather than physical stamina provided the impetus as he shambled down the hall. Until even that wasn't enough to propel him forward.

Yet again Isaacson misjudged the distance between himself and his goal. The construction of the door itself defied human perspective and lent strength to the illusion of proximity. The floor and ceiling fell away and the hall widened the closer he came to the gate.

Finally he gave up the last vestige of dignity and knelt. He wept, begging for divine mercy, for holy intercession which would catapult him to the end of his quest. He prostrated himself, imploring, praying, pleading and beseeching, for the first time in his life, or more accurately his death.

The floor seemed to shift underneath him, surging forward. Suddenly, he was there. He lay before the pearly gates. Noah gave a cry that contained within its tones both triumph and defeat. He clambered to his feet, and then Noah Isaacson, the unbeliever, he threw himself at the door.

At last, he would look upon the face of God.

He pushed. The door didn't budge. He flung himself at it. The thud of impact was muffled, absorbed by the sheer mass of the structure.

Again. And again. And again. It didn't move. Still leaning against it, he sunk slowly to the floor. His cheek scraped against the rough inlay, drawing blood. The action dislodged a piece of aged parchment. The paper fluttered noiselessly to the floor.

His hand closed spasmodically around it, crumpling it into a ball, and he beat against the floor with his fist.

Nothing happened.

Belatedly he took note of the paper in his hands. Curious, he unfolded it and lifted the sheet close to his face so he could read it. For an instant he gaped at the message apathetically until the meaning started to register.

"No!" he wailed, glancing from the paper to the door and back to the note again. It said:

Out to lunch
Back by MMMCLXVIII

DIVINE COMEDY

Mmrph! Mmmrph! Mmrph!

Alec Fowler awoke to the sound of knocking.

Mmrph! Mmmrph! Mmrph!

The sound filtered through the snow-white domicile as a muffled thud, as if someone were pounding on a cotton-wrapped door which was, in essence, exactly what they were doing. Scientists might argue the point, stating that clouds were nothing but a collection of dust and water vapours, but Alec had learned that nothing up here in heaven was quite what it seemed.

A bell peeled loudly inside his head, and the surprised Fowler almost hit the ceiling as it coincided with the ever-more impatient knocking.

"Alec?"

Fowler recognized the voice of his nearest neighbour, the one who occupied the adjacent cumulus creation.

"Alec!" The voice sounded a bit panicky.

"Coming!"

Fowler traipsed through the fluff to the door. That was one thing that was nice about heaven — no dust, or dusting — because everything was covered in a fine, white fleece.

"Are you ready?" Lawrence Benjamin thrust his head through the portal until he took in the sleepy Fowler. "Good God, no. Come on, look lively. You've got to get dressed or we'll be late for church."

"Church? Shouldn't you being going to synagogue?"

"Synagogue, church, temple, *oi vay*, what's the difference? The only thing that's important is that attendance is mandatory."

"You mean to tell me, we have to go to church. Even here in heaven? You'd think we'd risen above that sort of thing."

"It's about the only thing that's mandatory here, except for the long-timers — saints, angels, archangels and such-like — each who have their respective job duties."

"I always hated church, and what about you? Your Sabbath is on a different day."

Benjamin shrugged. "Sunday, Friday, Saturday. Who's to say

what day it is besides the Big Man himself." He peered over his shoulder. "And the sermon is strictly non-sectarian, believe me. Now hurry up, get dressed. We mustn't be late."

Lawrence pushed Fowler toward the bed where an outfit had suddenly materialized.

Fowler put his hands on his hips. "What's this?"

For the ensemble consisted of a slinky dress, spike heels and the bizarre accoutrements usually required to paste the female form into position.

"Part of the package. By Divine Decree, the Robing Department picks the most uncomfortable attire from each era, which means women's wear in surprising number of cases. I think it's meant to insure that no one falls asleep during the sermon. Get dressed, and be glad you're not born Chinese."

"But look at you," said Fowler. "You're not kitted out like a five-dollar hooker."

The other man plucked at the white gown. "You haven't seen what I've got on under these robes."

"And if I refuse?"

"I wouldn't recommend it."

Fowler scowled. "This is going to take a while. I wouldn't even know how to put this stuff on."

"Just think it," said Benjamin. "And be quick about it."

"What?"

"Imagine what it's like to wear all that." He pointed at the bed.

Fowler grimaced, and the next instant he wobbled precariously on stiletto heels. He reached for a fluffy wall to steady himself and almost fell through.

"Good heavens," he gasped, "I can't breathe."

Lawrence Benjamin grabbed his hand. "No time to talk. Come on."

They flitted past, or through, clouds and Fowler noted that each one was an exact replica of his own. He choked and sputtered on bits of inhaled fluff.

They glided down to the steps of a large marble edifice. Fowler was caught in a fit of sneezing.

"You'll soon learn to hold your breath," said Lawrence.

The younger man stared at the fanciful structure in front of him. It was designed in such a way that it combined the worse elements of all religious architecture — golden Bhuddas next to huge stupas, minarets twinned with church bell towers. The entire thing was surrounded by a stone circle.

Benjamin followed his gaze. "I told you that it was non-sectarian."

A minister huddled at the top of the stair next to the door. He extended his hand in greeting.

Lawrence shook his head no, but Fowler, a creature of habit, reached out to take it despite the ominous nod.

ZAP!

"Ouch!"

"Sh-h-sh." Lawrence Benjamin grabbed Fowler's arm and towed him toward the open door. "I warned you."

The pews were full, but miraculously two appeared before them. The men — Fowler staggering in his heels and twitching at the pink dress as it found its way into the crack of his ass — took their places while the people, most dressed in drag, shuffled to accommodate the new arrivals.

A woman with shaggy hair and horsy features walked up to a microphone.

"Hey," Fowler exclaimed, "that's Janis Joplin."

Lawrence elbowed Alec sharply in the ribs, and he fell silent as Janis began to sing. "Oh Lord, won't you buy me a Mercedes Benz..."

When she'd finished, the deacon — or whatever — lumbered up to the microphone in full chain mail and a cod piece that must, judging by his gait, be several sizes too small.

"Now we will sing Hymn 06."

Fowler leafed through the hymnal, prodded Benjamin and exclaimed: "Hey, they're all the same song."

Lawrence cuffed Alec who nearly fell off his heels.

"Hush, unless you want to be struck by lightning, and believe me you don't. It leaves you with a headache that lasts for at least a week."

The organ wheezed, and the audience began to intone an off-key version of... "Oh Lord, won't you buy me a Mercedes Benz."

When they had finished the selection, the speaker indicated that the congregation could sit. Fowler lowered himself gingerly on to the pew.

S-s-s-blat! S-s-s-blat! S-s-s-blat!

Sometime later they stumbled out of church — most giving the minister with his outstretched hand a wide berth.

Fowler's ribs hurt from laughing, and he was almost glad he had had a girdle to brace them.

"Well, what did you think?" said Lawrence Benjamin.

"An experience to be sure."

"Ah, good, you're learning tact. What did you think of the sermon?"

"Funny. I laughed until I cried."

"Yes, I know your mascara ran."

Fowler turned and showed Benjamin his flank. "Split the side of my dress too. Was that really God up there?"

"No one knows for sure. Rumour suggests that He doesn't attend. He takes this day off. You know the seventh day, that sort of thing. Can't say that I blame Him. It must be ruddy awful to have to listen to the seraphim all the time. But I wouldn't dismiss His presence in the pulpit out of hand. As they say: the Lord moves in mysterious ways."

"Well, if it's him, then God bears a striking resemblance to Rodney Dangerfield."

Fowler tottered to a halt. "Why only one hymn?"

"Because He likes it."

"And why the hand buzzer?"

"Even the Lord Jehovah enjoys a little joke every now and then."

The newcomer and his friend stumbled across the courtyard — Fowler's heels getting tangled in the down of the cloud.

The younger man scratched his head, bewildered.

"The whoopee cushions on the pews are a bit much."

FORCE OF HABIT

Brother Dennis's eyes bugged out from his head as he took in the surplice, mantle, mitre and alb of the Holy Father of Rome. The figure was silhouetted in blinding light, and Dennis had only enough time to note the symbols of office, not the man himself, but his mind readily supplied the face that graced a million book jackets and CD covers.

The monk crossed himself, not as he should, but with his arms forming an X in front of his face. As if he would defend himself from the divine luminescence. Never in his wildest dreams had Dennis envisioned himself meeting the Pope.

He peeked timidly between his arms. The words "Sangue et sangue" were embroidered in red on the snowy white alb. Dennis gaped. Then suddenly aware of his strange posture, Brother Dennis dropped them, genuflected — as was fitting and proper — and sunk to his knees, head deferentially bent.

The heat struck him as soon as his shins touched the floor. Warmth radiated from the very stones of the papal palace — seeping through the rough-spun cloth of his habit.

What the hell am I doing here?

The thought rose unbidden, and Brother Dennis blushed, even though the Holy Father could not have possibly heard. While his hands seemed to take on a life of their own, acting without his direction or volition, to clamp firmly over his mouth.

Speak no evil.

Brother Dennis pulled his hands away from his face.

"Everybody asks that?"

The Pope had heard his thoughts?

Brother Dennis's embarrassment escalated into panic. Perspiration dotted his upper lip. The blistering heat was rapidly becoming as oppressive as the papal scrutiny.

The good brother assumed an attitude of calm that he did not feel as he waited to be either acknowledged or dismissed. The papal presence evoked all sorts of strange emotions in him. The Benedictine monk had never expected to be so, uh, blessed.

Sweat trickled down his sides. He could feel the papal gaze

boring into his skull. As his pulse rate steadied and his breathing grew less erratic his ears became attuned to the crackle of the fire, the faint clank of metal and the shuffling of a thousand feet.

"Ah-hem!" A throat cleared itself somewhere above his head.

Something was expected of the monk. He didn't know what. Dennis racked his brain for the proper procedures and protocols, etiquette and forms of address, for a meeting with the Holy Father of Rome. He must've learned them sometime during his novitiate. He drew a mental blank.

Dennis could recite the Rule, chapter and verse, but he was a little rusty on visiting dignitaries.

Wasn't there something about kissing the ring of office?

But his Eminence must offer his hand first. Dennis's eyes flicked nervously here and there. The papal appendage was nowhere in sight, just the scarlet hem of his surplice.

"Ah-hem!"

And Brother Dennis did the only thing he could think of doing. He threw himself flat on the floor, prostrating himself before the Pope, and kissed the pontifical skirts.

Above him, a deep purr of content resonated within the papal throat.

Brother Dennis's gaze, however, was riveted to the feet that shuffled with a decided limp toward him. The toes were knobbly and twisted with arthritis, the skin thickened and horny with age. Even the venerable toenails had calcified, having grown out in layers to form curved claw-like talons. Dennis swallowed his revulsion and closed his eyes.

"You may rise." The honeyed voice spoke into his ear, and Brother Dennis flinched. He hadn't realized the Pontiff was so near.

Gathering courage, the monk lifted his head from the stones and stared into the Holy face. His mouth dropped open, chin literally hitting the floor.

This was no Pope he knew. Yet the face was familiar in a vague and disquieting way.

The brother clambered to his knees and was nearly overcome with vertigo as the sweltering heat and suffocating tension took their toll. He sat back on his heels, and peered owlishly around him.

The Pontiff proffered his ring — the fingers flapping insistently beneath Dennis's nose. The monk glanced down at the stone. Instead of the expected amethyst, the stone was red like the surplice.

"We are waiting," The false Pope said.

Stalling for time, Brother Dennis considered his dilemma. What he should do? This man was not the Pope, or no pope he knew. Had a new pope been elected to office since... since... when?

Still, could Dennis hardly turn away from the man who wore those robes? Or spurn the hand that bore the papal ring? Didn't the office command respect, if not the man?

Dennis kissed the ring.

"Up, boy," the Pontiff said, "we haven't got all day."

The monk scrambled to his feet.

The Pope began to laugh. "Haven't got all day, get it?"

"Ah, er, no, father, I'm afraid I do not."

"You wouldn't, would you?"

"I guess not, your..." The monk foundered on the epithet, unsure what he should say or do as tried to put a name to the face.

"Oh, we're not much on formalities here. I am Clement, the seventh of that name, to be precise."

"Pope Clement?" Brother Dennis considered this for a moment. The next word came out as a squeak or a squawk as he realized to whom he spoke. "The seventh?"

The Pope looked him up and down. "Yes, no doubt you've heard of me."

"Well..."

Clement VII, the antipope, born Robert of Geneva, Pope's legate in Italy and the Cardinal that ordered the massacre at Cessna, the savagery of which set the stage for the schism that would follow. The slaughter of the 5000 townspeople, those who had surrendered in good faith, lasted for three days.

The monk stole an inquisitive glance at the Patriarch. He didn't look so nefarious or profligate, but the image seemed to fluctuate — the man appearing either fat or well-formed in the classical definition of the term. Mostly, though, the Pope looked old. Clement squinted back at him and leered.

The crack of a whip drew Dennis's attention away from the Pontiff to regard his surroundings. The walls were rough hewn.

The chamber itself was brightly and unnaturally lit — even the stones underneath his feet glowed with verdant light. An open grate graced the centre of the room where a bloated fire belched and popped queasily. The bright bank of coals bristled like a porcupine with the handles of many gleaming metal.

This was not the Papal Palace in Rome — unless it was the wine cellar, or the dungeon — and, he noted, it seemed to be lacking in wine bottles.

Suddenly, sounds previously masked by the noisome fire penetrated Brother Dennis's beleaguered brain — shrieks of pain and the rattle of chains. And the murmur of people. Thousands of them, tied to stakes or lashed to the rack.

Dennis blanched. The bristling fire, the instruments of torture evoked images of inquisition.

But that could not be. It was the wrong century, and Brother Dennis sifted through his foggy brain for the history surrounding Cossa. Had not the same fifteenth-century council, that had seen to the disposition of Clement VII, also implemented the auto-de-fait?

A hunchback chose that moment to grab a poker from the coals and shove it up a young woman's skirts. She exploded.

The monk swooned. When next he came around, the Pontiff and the misshapen monk hovered over him.

"How the hell do I know what's wrong with him?" the Pope snapped. "I'm no doctor!"

The hunchback rubbed his bum contemplatively. "Just don't make 'em like they used to. No sinew."

"Well, wake him up! I'm a busy man; I can't be standing around here forever."

There was the clank of metal and the sensation of searing heat next to his cheek.

"No, not that way! He's not one of them. He's one of us. Can't go torturing him the way you did that woman."

"Aw, hell."

"Will you quit stating the obvious and do something practical, ferchrissakes?" Clement said.

Brother Dennis gasped.

"Ah, you're awake. Come on, get up, boy, Can't loll about all day. We've got work to do."

"Work?" Dennis squawked as he struggled into a sitting

position and looked around.

He'd been wrong in his first perception of the place. There was not a single bonfire, but many fires... everywhere. Flames danced in every crevice, pooled in cracks. Molten lava ran in runnels down the clefts of rock and flowed in rivers of glowing red across the floor.

A small cry escaped Brother Dennis's lips, for the scene before his eyes was one etched indelibly in the memory of humanity. Every man, woman and child, choirboy or altar boy. In both laity and clergy. Forsooth, in every human psyche be it Catholic or Protestant, Christian or not. For even the Moslems have some version of Hell.

The cleric bent over to help Dennis to his feet.

"Are you all right, brother?" the friar said solicitously.

Brother Dennis nodded, keeping his eyes downcast so he would not see the scarred and seamed face or the distorted figure of his fellow priest.

"This is..." Dennis began to say.

"... Hell, yes." The papal lip curled into a sneer. "And I've come to welcome you."

Another friar, as twisted as the one who had helped Dennis to his feet, moved into his line of vision. The man held a pitchfork in hand and drove a living chain of human flesh into the flames.

"I don't understand," Dennis said, "we're men of the cloth..."

"Who better than us to act as custodians of the hell we created? We have centuries of experience. As shepherds of our flock, we made a profession of tormenting them for their sins in life, so it has been given unto us to continue our work in the afterlife. Who else should administer their penance in death?"

Dennis thought for a moment and couldn't think anyone better qualified.

The Pope gestured expansively. "Thus, we have been rewarded."

"Rewarded?" Brother Dennis gulped.

"We're the lucky ones." The Antipope shielded his mouth behind his hand and inclined his head toward the monk. "After all, we could've been one of them."

"But I'm confused. Aren't we — oh, I don't know — the good guys?"

95

"Good guys?" Clement VII's face began to contort, the pontifical frame to quiver, the back to heave, and the shoulders shook. A sound somewhere between a cough and a howl erupted from the papal lips.

Brother Dennis moved to give the Pontiff a thump between the shoulders, the motion arrested when he realized that Clement VII was... laughing. Not just laughing, but guffawing in a most undignified manner.

The monk was sprayed with spittle and subjected to another barrage of mirth as Clement VII doubled over and slapped a venerable knee.

"Good guys," he wheezed. "Oh," gasp, "pull the other one. I love it. I haven't laughed so much since, oh, I don't know... the demotion of the Saints."

"Saints? You don't mean..."

The Pontiff sobered slightly. "Oh, we got quite a few of them. Most of 'em switched, rather than give up swaying souls for a living," he stroked his chin, "or, more appropriately, a dying. You see, it's a hard habit to break."

Clement took Dennis's arm and started to steer him through the throng. Afflicted souls scuttled to get out of their away, or melted before them. Dennis stepped gingerly over a puddle.

When Pope Clement towed him into the central pyre, Brother Dennis balked.

"Recreant!" Pope Clement VII clutched the monk's cowl in his fast and hauled him through the fire unscathed.

They strolled — or Dennis strolled, Clement gimped — casually past a cauldron of boiling oil, the soul entrapped reached out to Clement, beseechingly.

A woman vomited. Her head twisted in a complete circle, spraying all within her trajectory with what appeared to be pea soup. Brother Dennis stared in mute terror as those struck by the substance began to dissolve.

"None of this makes sense." The monk looked askance at his host. "We don't belong here. Are we not men of God? Keepers of the only true faith? Upholders of the Holy Roman Church?" he faltered, "Aren't we among God's chosen?"

"Lad." Pope Clement shook his head. "You have a lot to learn. Don't worry. A certain amount of confusion is to be expected. That is the reason for the orientation period."

The Pontiff draped his arm over Dennis's shoulder. "Let's examine your question point by point."

A demon — or perhaps it was an imp or a fiend — gambolled close by, grabbing a hapless human who was trying to escape down a dark corridor and returning its victim to the rack.

"Yes, we were shepherds of the church, but what did you," he poked the monk's chest with a horny forefinger, "do with that trust?"

They moved past two demons who were pouring molten gold down the throat of a usurer.

"How does buggery sound? Did you sodomise a few of your flock, perchance?" He elbowed Brother Dennis and winked.

Brother Dennis stepped away from the unholy father.

"I was cloistered," Dennis mumbled.

"Oh, a novice then, or," he gazed at the monk critically, "several, was it?" The Pope stared deep into the brother's eyes, as if he could reach into the monk's soul. "And, I see, you made a habit of it."

The monk flushed right down to his cowl.

"As keepers of the flock we could either sink with the devils or soar with the angels. All we have to do is examine our consciences."

Dennis shook his head in denial.

"You preyed particularly on the young. Do I have to mention names, dates, places?"

"Ah, er, no."

"I thought not. You know, I know. We all know why we're here." He crooked a thumb at the ground beneath their feet, "rather than there." He reversed the direction of his thumb so that it pointed straight up.

"Right, now that we got that straight, what were we talking about?" The Pope mused. "Oh, yes, I remember. Of course, we are representatives of the church known as Catholic — although despite its name it is by no means universal — and that church is based in Rome. Whether it's holy is still cause for debate."

Two demons skewered a murderer on a pitchfork and cast him into a bubbling cauldron. Brother Dennis's Adam's apple bobbed up and down in his throat.

"The only true faith?" the Pope continued. "Not by a long shot. Not as the church stands, or wobbles, now on dying legs in an era as lascivious as that of classical Rome which we were trying to replace. The church didn't resemble the true faith even in my day. None of the current religions classify. In their traditions, maybe, but not in their practice."

"But —"

"All faiths are represented here. We have saints and prophets of every, er, persuasion. Even some of the majors drop down now and then from on high just to make sure we're doing our job, to see if we're, uh, keeping the faith."

Clement VII took off his mitre, breathed on it and polished it with his sleeve. Just then, a priest — by the cut of singed habit — stuck his finger in the eye of a sinner.

"Got to talk to that man," said Clement. "He's a new recruit. One of your contemporaries. What's happened to the church nowadays if that's the best punishment you can think of?"

"It seemed to work for the Three Stooges," reflected Dennis.

"What?"

"Never mind."

"Hokay." The Antipope slammed the mitre back on his head. "Let's get on with the tour."

"Tah-tour?" The monk stammered.

"Yes, all part of the service."

The papal arm took in the entire chamber with a broad sweep. "As you can see, this portion is built on a classical model. What you see before you is hell as we created it. Hell, like everything else, is what you make it, and we — you and I — end up with the hell we foisted upon others.

"Its imagery is the imagery we presented in our sermons. It's what was etched in stone or painted on the walls of our cathedrals. Here, we find the dance macabre made flesh, as it were."

Just then Death — or an image of it at least – danced obligingly past. It drove human souls toward Perdition's flames.

"You should be pleased, boy. Hell — or this portion of it at least — truly was painted in our image and likeness. Surely, you recognize the seven deadly sins," the Pope said as two inmates fell to fighting over a piece of rancid meat. "There's avarice, and sloth." He nodded at a group of malingerers who were being whipped into action by a couple of demons.

"Oh yes, and we can't forget gluttony." An imp forced a piece of meat, apparently a human thigh, down the throat of a fat Franciscan Friar.

Dennis swallowed and turned to study the vast chasm. Twisted and contorted figures cavorted to and fro. Two fiends held a bridge of spikes aloft while several more — armed with spears and tridents — coerced sinners across the jagged span.

"These are," Clement explained, "dishonest tradesman, destined to toil without the tools of their trade."

And looking closely, Dennis observed a spinner without her wheel. She sat in the midst of a tangled web, the strands of which were spewing from her navel. Elsewhere a smith laboured without his anvil.

Clement nudged the brother. "Those that gave short measure are doomed to carry their stolen goods for all eternity."

A baker struggled over the spikes, weighted down with sacks of grain. He missed his footing and slipped, impaling himself.

By this time, they reached the edge of the cavern. From this vantage point, the monk could see what had been hidden from him at its heart. The cave itself was divided into two equal parts, upper and lower which were separated by a thin line of nebula. The lower contained all the known torments and punishments of damnation, and a few Dennis had never thought of. While above it — so close that it almost seemed that you could touch it — the heavenly host flitted blissfully in a sky of brilliant blue. The three Mary's rode a snow-white stallion. They beckoned to the people below, their arms extended in open invitation.

"What about that?" Brother Dennis indicated another ladder that led up to a fairy wisp of cloud.

"Oh, that. It's fake, but we keep it to tempt and tantalize the poor miserable sinners. The fools actually believe they still might find salvation."

Pope Clement VII beamed as a faux St Michael weighed souls and, finding them wanting, gave them over to the denizens of hell. The nearest demon, Dennis noticed, kept his thumb firmly planted upon the scale.

"Having heaven, or a depiction of it, here was my idea. Adds just the right touch of desperation, don't you think?" Clement VII said.

Twin imps grabbed an unworthy soul from the ladder to false heaven and flung it into the abyss, and Dennis realized with a shock that the creatures he had mistaken for imps or fiends were, in fact, human — their forms twisted beyond belief. Their humanity made poignantly apparent by their pain racked expressions, their blistered skin which was burnt raw in places, and their guarded movements.

Clement VII followed his worried gaze. "The shapes are an outer reflection of the inner soul. You'll start to transform too, soon."

Brother Dennis crossed himself. "My God."

A thunderclap cut through the babble of a thousand agonized souls.

The Pope pressed his lips against Dennis's ear. "Ah, I wouldn't use the G—word, if were you. Also you can leave off genuflecting."

Dennis shivered as he noted the cut of their clothes. He recognized the habits, surplices and copes. They were men of the cloth, each and every one of them. In some, enough of the fabric remained that the colour could be discerned under the splattering of grime. He saw rusty-black, sullied white, and sooty grey of Benedictine, Cluniac, Franciscan, Augustine. All the orders were represented here.

"What became of the demons?"

"Moved on," Clement replied. "As we need to if you're going to get the full tour. Come on, there's a lot more to Hell than meets the eye. Not everybody adheres to the Judeo-Christian ethic. I must say they're pretty inventive. You as a twentieth-century man can probably appreciate some of it better than I."

Clement VII ushered him through a door and into a long hall. Unlike the dank cave they had just left, the corridor was antiseptically clean — a stark, harsh white. The monk's feet were swept out from under him the minute he set them on the floor. His arms pinwheeled as he fought to maintain balance. The Pope reached out a hand and steadied Dennis.

The floor was propelling them along with incredible speed. Brother Dennis stared at his feet, and yet the ground did not appear to move. It was as if they were being towed by some invisible force, or pushed along by a relentless tide.

"Demons," the pontiff explained, "are more adaptable than man so they have advanced. Gone on to bigger and better things. They're in charge of the whole thing, you see, while we — mere vicars of the church — administer to only one small portion of it. The hell we had made, F and B."

"Pardon?"

"Oh, sorry. You'll get used to the vernacular, stands for Fire and Brimstone," said Clement. "Hell like everything else is in a constant process of devolution. Human needs change, so too their punishments, along with their gods and their definition of evil. In this post-industrial age, most men don't view hell as we do. They've evolved beyond our simplistic convictions. So Satan has to be flexible."

The Antipope coughed delicately. "Let me direct your attention to the windows."

Dennis looked up, and, sure enough, heretofore unseen windows punctuated the wall.

Curious, the monk glanced through the first in another dark chamber where he saw a pile of decomposing bodies. Muscle and flesh dripped from bone. He turned to Clement.

"As you probably know, many people nowadays don't believe in life after death. The worst they can imagine is the decomposition of their mortal flesh. Ever obliging, we give it to them. You can't see them, but their souls are flitting around in there somewhere. From what I understand, they maintain full command of their faculties. They can smell, hear and see, and so can contemplate the folly of their ways — along with the dissolution of their mortal remains."

The gruesome image glided away, and they came to the next chamber where a couple stood before an altar, hand in hand. The woman was dressed in virginal white.

"Women's hell."

"Huh?" Dennis grunted.

"Surely, you don't believe in marital bliss?"

"It can't be as bad as all that."

"How would you know?"

"Although I agree with you, it is bewildering, and quite frankly I have a hard time grasping the things people call evil these days."

The floor hurried them on, and as they whizzed past several chambers the monk caught snatches of conversation.

"... Ping? What ping?"

"But I swear to you that it was pinging just a few moments

101

ago..."

"What's that?" Dennis asked as the image of a mechanic peering under the bonnet of a car receded.

"Don't ask me. I don't even know what a ping is."

"... wha'd'ya mean it's gonna cost me —" there was a mumbled number "how the hell can you charge me that if you don't even know what's wrong with the damn thing?"

The words faded and they glided up to another window that opened onto a hall very like the one they were in, only this one was crammed full to bursting. People stood — toes tapping, arms crossed, expressions sour — in a queue that stretched as far as the eye could see. Many of their faces were impassive, apathetic, but most were irritated. One man looked at his watch and swore.

"What do you think they get when they reach end? A whipping?" Clement spun to the younger man, speaking vehemently. "A beating? A scourging? Even a good haranguing? Hell no! They get a little slip of paper with glue on one side. A stamp, they tell me. A bloody stamp!"

"You don't sound like a pope."

"You hear me as you want to hear me. My thoughts are immediately perceived as words and those words translated into the nearest linguistic equivalent. So in this as in everything else in death, you get what you expect."

He directed Dennis's attention back to the queue. "Then after all that, they go back to the beginning and start all over again. Now I ask you, what's sort of retribution is that?"

"It's difficult to explain."

"And the stamp? What's the significance of the stamp?"

"None, I don't suppose. Up above, it allows you to send a letter to a friend. Assuming, of course, that the letter doesn't get lost in the post."

Clement VII heaved a great sigh. "Things were so much easier when everyone shared the same vision of hell. We could really put the fear of, ah, er, what's-his-name in them then. Here, look at this."

The belt shuddered to a halt; the monk overbalanced and fell. The Pope hauled him to his feet.

"Much of the purpose of this portion of hell eludes me and, as a representative of modern man, I'd be interested in your assessment. Does this make any sense to you?"

As previously, the chamber beyond was crowded. Too many people were compressed into a space too small to hold them. Some sat, but most clung to straps, others were only held upright by the crush of bodies around them. The walls of the hall were interrupted at regular intervals with black windows.

A voice, its humanity distorted, thundered an announcement which was discernable despite the thick glass. "... mmmr-prmph... garble... passenger action... xkkdgxerr... mmmmd the gap... crackle..."

"It's the tube."

"A tube? Of course, it's a tube," he eyed the enclosure, "or a tunnel; but what does it do?"

"Takes away your humanity," Dennis said.

"Ah." The Antipope pondered this. "Ttch, mankind is getting weak."

The people inside the car lurched and swayed.

"... mmmrprmph... garble... gerbil... chirp... shun... xkkdgxerr... sizzle, hiss... mmmmd the gappppp... crackle... SCREECH!"

A shrill electronic wail replaced the garbled message.

Dennis stumbled back. "Good Lor—"

"Sh-sh." The Antipope hissed a warning at Dennis.

"Wha—what's that?"

"That's the PA; it does that, goes on the blink some times." His eyes lost their focus. "Quite often as a matter of fact."

"PA?"

"The public address system, intercom, I think is the more common term now. You'll get used to it after a while. Follow me." Clement VII motioned ahead and limped on.

Brother Dennis put his head on one side, a term which took on an entirely different meaning in the nether regions.

The Pontiff replaced the monk's head upon his shoulders. "Pull yourself together man. We need men with their heads firmly attached to their shoulders."

The floor started up again. Clement flailed, nearly clopping Dennis with his croft, and toppled. The belt stopped.

"Give me a hand," the Antipope said. Dennis extended his arm. Clement gave the monk a considering look.

"On second thought, don't bother." The Pope fiddled with what appeared to be an elaborate digital watch on his wrist.

"I think that ought to stop it." He stood. "We can walk from here."

The opening strains of Wagner's *Der Fliegende Hollander* drifted to them from the next cubicle. Senta pledged her troth in a hauntingly powerful ballad. Inside the room, someone screamed.

The Antipope inserted his hands demurely in his sleeves. They shambled to the next window. Brother Dennis's eyes lit up when he saw an elaborate stage. Sailors coiled ropes, scrambled over riggings, and sang Ho-jo-he.

The first act had just begun.

A wail drew his attention away from the production to a young man with one of those strange, spiky hair cuts that Dennis had always found so inexplicable.

Two demons flanked the youth, restraining him and keeping him pinned to his chair. When the performance began, the kid began to scream in earnest.

Dennis pressed his nose against the glass to get a better view. These demons were the real thing. He could tell by the way their knees turned the wrong way round. Seen up close, it was easy to distinguish them from their human counterparts. These exhibited true scales. While the skin of the mortal overseers was thick and horny, it came from continuous burning, blistering and peeling.

The horns, of course, were a dead give away.

"Aaargh!"

"Beautiful," said Clement.

"Yes, I've always liked Wagner," Dennis agreed.

The papal brow crinkled in disapproval. "I was talking about the shrieking."

"Oh."

"Of course, at each level of hell —" the hall took a distinct downward turn —"there's orientation. Now here is a particularly interesting room."

They stopped again, and Dennis blinked when he saw Oscar Wilde, Marlow, Faust, Dylan Thomas, James Joyce, Pliny and a host of other authors.

"This is R and D."

"Research and development?"

"Hey, wha'd'ya know." The Pope thumped his shoulder. "You're getting the hang of it."

"But they're all writers. See there's Lewis Carroll."

"You know how he felt about children," Clement VII replied.

"Byron, Shelley and Goethe."

"Yes, we get a lot of them. Authors, that is. Actors and artists too. The sin of pride, you know. Not to mention that those professions lend themselves to a dissolute lifestyle. They're supposed to stay here until the appropriate hell has been created for them. Some of them have been here a long time."

"So this is limbo?"

"Not hardly. No this place has its own peculiar torture. Watch and listen." Clement touched a panel on the wall and the voices that had been little more than a murmur before became clear and distinct.

"Look, it is agreed that we are strange bedfellows, but this project has been given unto us, and we must complete it."

The group hung their heads, stuffed their hands in their pockets and studied their feet.

"Remember we have only one pad of paper and one quill —"

"Pen," Fitzgerald corrected the speaker.

"— between us." Shakespeare waited for argument, when none was forthcoming he went on. "Then, it is decided. I, whose name personifies great literature, will head this undertaking."

"Why you?" chimed Mary Shelley. "Historically speaking, others have been credited with your texts. There's not even a consensus that you existed. How about Francis Bacon? He'd do as well."

"Bacon? The insult!" Shakespeare huffed.

"Oh, forget about insult. Who reads you anyway? Iambic pentameter, indeed," Faulkner growled. "Besides you represent the visual medium with its eventual outgrowth, cinema and television." His mouth pulled into a tight rictus of distaste. "Your works are now done in movies and seldom seen in the legitimate theatre. No, I say we need a writer of novels like myself."

"Movies didn't do me any harm," Bloch muttered, but no one was listening to him.

"You... you," Hemingway sputtered as he stabbed an accusing finger at Faulkner. "You don't even know the basics of sentence construction. Long-winded, pompous..." Words failed him. "Old wind-bag."

"That's tautology," Yeats interjected.

Faulkner disregarded the poet, glaring at his nearest rival, Hemingway. "You should talk. I've heard about you. We all have. Your editors cut fifty percent of your text. They wouldn't have done that if it were any good."

"Those are fighting words." Hemingway tore his coat off, rolled up his shirt sleeves and presented bare fists to his critic.

"Gentlemen." Dostoevsky interposed himself between the two men. "We seem to be losing the point with all this talk of leaders. This collaboration is our greatest endeavour ever. The greatest minds have been assembled to execute it. The task was appointed to us by the Almighty — it must have been, who else would do it? — and it would appear that its purpose is to teach us co-operation. Let us not disappoint our Maker."

Plato sidestepped a roundhouse swing that Hemingway had directed at Faulkner and straightened a pleat on his robes self-consciously. "A group without rulers sounds suspiciously like anarchy to me. Surely, you must recognize that in any society, there are the rulers and the ruled."

"I take exception to that statement." Dostoevsky bristled and the two fell to arguing between themselves.

Shakespeare, his memory muddled with extreme age, awakened enough to quibble. "What's wrong with iambic pentameter? It remains the most oft-used metre to this day."

"It's a cumbersome way to communicate." said Faulkner as he dodged a blow that landed on ee cummings.

Bloch threw up his hands. "This coming from a man who had a sentence twenty seven pages long."

"You wouldn't know poetry if it bit you in the ass, Faulkner" Hemingway said.

And the scene descended into chaos yet again, as short fuses attached to inflated egos exploded. James Joyce tore off his coat and offered his fists to Pliny. Byron brandished a sword, challenging Shakespeare to a duel. While Pepys backed into a corner and fixed himself a cup of coffee, only to drop it when Cicero jostled his arm in attempting to evade a sock full of sand that was aimed at him.

In the hall, Brother Dennis ducked as a body came crashing into the window.

A voice rose above the din. "Excuse me, excuse me, has anyone seen the biro?"

Brother Dennis turned his back to the window. "That's horrible."

"It does sort of destroy a lot of your illusions, doesn't it? It gets better." The Pontiff clasped the monk's arm. "Oh, look they've brought in the heavy artillery there."

"What?" Dennis faced the glass. Two creatures, fiends or imps by the look of them were wheeling in a cart of... cream pies.

He flattened himself against the wall. "I can't watch."

A door appeared in the wall and the imps walked out.

"Feeding time at the zoo," said one.

Dennis watched the pair thoughtfully. "Where are the rest of the demons? I thought there were legions. We've only seen the four so far."

"Oh, they're around, probably watching us at this very moment." Clement glanced nervously over his shoulder. "You don't want to meet one. Trust me."

And he herded the monk down the hall.

*

Elsewhere a disgusted Astoroth glowered at the bank of television screens. "Look at them! They're supposed to be recorders of the cumulative knowledge of the ages, the bringers of wisdom to humanity, and they can't agree on a damned thing."

"Is it any wonder that mankind is such a mess?" Forcas, spoke from his man-face, one of three available to him.

Astoroth smoothed his batwings. "What I don't understand is why I got stuck with them?"

"As the patron of the liberal arts, it's only logical that you should see to their orientation to the afterlife."

"Orientation is supposed to be a short-lived affair." He jammed a finger at the screen. "Look at Aristotle, Socrates, Dante. How long have they been here?"

Forcas's cat face peered closely at the monitor. "It is getting a bit crowded."

Beside him, Bael shrugged, an interesting manoeuvre that involved the manipulations of any number of insectile appendages.

"Oh well, it could be worse." Forcas gestured at another in

107

the long row of televisions. "You think you've got it bad. How about my batch?"

The screen revealed a scene that was reminiscent of London in the worst days of fog. It cleared upon Forcas's command to exhibit a room that was almost entirely filled with a single large mechanism. The contraption was nothing more than a conglomeration of moving, clattering parts.

Men and women in standard-issue white lab coats crawled over the mechanism, twiddling this bit and that. Some of them had separated into little groups. Einstein discussed the quantum theory with Madame Curie while those nearest the engine gathered to debate what was for them the key issue.

Units of measure.

"The metric system is universal now."

"No, imperial," Rittenhouse said, "I never had any truck with this new-fangled metric."

"Well, I don't see what's wrong with the old units — like hands." Newton took a bite of a bruised apple. "They... crunch... crunch... were used for years, and everybody's got them."

"Right, that's just the problem. Whose hand do we use as standard?" asked Rittenhouse.

Alexander Graham Bell interjected: "And how do you calibrate a hand?"

"Why goof with a system that works?" said Talleyrand. "There's standard metric weights and measure locked up in Paris, London and Washington."

"Fat lot of good that does here," Newton said.

Forcas snorted and turned down the volume on the control panel. "Give me authors any day."

"Well, at least, some of them are working co-operatively," Bael said.

"Yes, but that's not the point, is it?" The broad frog mouth twitched. "They're actually enjoying themselves!"

"Yeah, well, I'm sure you'll come up with something."

"I wonder."

"Look at the bright side," Astoroth said, "if it weren't for them, we wouldn't have the infernal combustion engine."

"Still," Forcas said, "things just aren't like they used to be. Remember the good old days when people used to cringe on command..."

"... cower on cue," Astoroth said wistfully.

A third wall in the panel of screens sprung to life. Forcas leapt to his feet, as if electrified, and Astoroth sat at attention upon his dragon mount. Bael saluted with all his limbs — an operation comparable to a spider curling up and dying.

A single bloodshot eye glared down at them There was a rumble, like words all jumbled together.

Questioning my wisdom again?

"Yes, boss. I mean, no, boss. Of course, boss. Whatever you say," said Forcas as he fell into an epileptic fit.

"Oh, thank you, boss," Astoroth said before he deflated like an empty bladder and began to convulse also.

No fool, Bael maintained his shrivelled pose of death, listening to the tortured screams of his companions.

In a far hall a camera picked up Clement VII and the monk Dennis as they hurried to their next assignation. "Now for the oubliettes where people go once they've been matched to the hell of their own choosing…"

THE GATES OF HELL

Bill Gates lifted his head off the floor. He lay in a pure white room.

Featureless.

The chamber was seamless. Nothing to show where the ceiling met walls and walls met floor. He swept his hands across the smooth surface, almost glasslike, but not glass. Not metal, either. Not porcelain because even the finest porcelain had grains. Neither plastic nor PVC. He placed his palms against the wall above his head. It was slightly warm and where his hand touched, it grew hot.

Gates attempted to rise. The room spun.

He sat up and his stomach lurched to somewhere around his throat. Gates wondered if he overindulged the night before. How else would he wake up here? What hotel was this? What hotel would have rooms such as this one, without window or doors?

If this was a hallucination, then this was worse than any alcohol-induced hangover he had ever experienced.

Food poisoning? Flu?

White. A hospital made more sense than a hotel.

Gates felt for all his body parts. Two arms. Two legs. A head. Regrettably. Everything seemed to be accounted for. Gingerly, he turned his head. Walls, but no furniture. Nowhere. No bed or chair. No door or windows. What sort of hospital was this? A loony bin?

Jesus Christ, he was trapped.

Nothing but...

A computer. If there was a computer around Gates would be able to get a hold of somebody. Anybody.

Gates leapt to his feet, or tried. He flopped gracelessly back to the ground, and he couldn't decide if he should clutch his stomach or his head. Then he remembered he had two of them. Hands that is. One dutifully went to his stomach; the other to his head.

Cautiously he pushed himself off the floor, with both hands and legs, and achieved something of an upright position. He shuffled to the nearest wall and felt his way to the terminal.

He recognized the familiar logo and found some comfort there.

Gates squinted: Gates Version 2,000,000.001? What?

Was this some kind of joke?

"Damnit." He would have plopped to his chair or gone storming out the door, but there was none.

All right standing then.

He dropped the dialog box and gasped when he noted that his old globetrotter software was missing. In its stead was: MicroManage Internet Bumbler.

It's gotta be a joke.

Gates clicked on the icon. There was a whir and the following text appeared on the screen.

Program error 1,459,000.001: Sorry we cannot find that program. Please check the spelling and try again.

God, this is an antiquated mouse, and the numbers are outrageous.

Again. Drop down menu. Click on MicroManage Internet Bumbler.

Program error 2,105,773: Sorry, MicroManage no longer supports that function. Please go online to the MicroManage website to get help.

"But that's what I am trying to do, damn you," he shouted at the machine.

And again.

Program error 2,105,773: Sorry, MicroManage no longer supports that function. Please go online to MicroManage website to get help.

He lowered himself to the floor and tried to think. He knew the software backward and forward. He would run the usual tests. He should be able to get into the guts of the system and fix it, but he needed to get a line to the outside world.

Think. Think.

The corporate e-mail? The last thing he remembered he was at some kind of do, corporate celebrations, office opening or launch of the next incarnation Gates.

What city, where? And was this part of the corporation in any number of cities in one of infinitesimal bee hives that was encompassed by the MicroManage Corporation?

If this was one of the corporate offices, why hadn't they had the common courtesy to put furniture in it?

And, more importantly, why had they left him stranded? Okay, maybe he had had too much to drink, but there was no reason to dump him unattended here. "Someone's head is going to roll for this," he muttered.

He tried to think of any disgruntled employees, and if it was a hospital or the world's most bizarre hotel, then what?

Gates got up on his knees so the keyboard was at chest level. Somehow he felt like he was praying in a pew in a church.

He went to the Start Menu and viewed all programs, searching for any other internet software, like Godzilla, or any of the internal e-mail programs, and found nothing.

"Damn!"

It was time for the test. He located the proper program and clicked run.

Program error 666: "You have tried to perform an illegal function. This computer will shut down."

Gates threw his hands in the air. "No, God, no!"

He didn't know where the button was. His hands felt frantically for a power button, in the console and along the walls.

The screen went dark and with that the room went dark, as if the computer powered the lights.

He dropped down, curled in a fetal ball, head resting on the floor. "Please, God, no."

Suddenly he sensed that he was not alone. Movement. He heard the soft susurration of cloth, and the hair on the back of his neck began to curl.

"That's not who you should be talking to, Mr Gates. Not here. Not now."

"What? Who are you? Where's here? Where am I?"

"Again you ask?" There was a heavy sigh and a swish of cloth.

Gates peered in that direction and tried to follow the sound as it advanced toward him.

"Come now, Mr Gates, do we need to get the electrodes out?

"Electrodes?" He gulped.

He heard a slap or a clap, much closer than he would have liked.

The lights sprung to life and he heard the reassuring click of the computer coming to life.

The man who appeared suddenly at his side was a small non-assuming man, nondescript. Gates thought indignantly, he crushed bigger men than this.

"No, you have not, Mr Gates," the man spoke.

"What the... did I say that aloud?"

"No."

"Then how the hell did you know what I was thinking?"

"Very little remains hidden here. Unless we want it to be."

"Here? Where's here? Where the hell am I?"

"Now you're getting warmer," the man said. "You are in the same place you have been for a millennium or two.

"What?" He was only half listening. His eyes scanned the walls, the ceiling. If this guy had gotten in, then there had to be a door.

"Where is this? A hospital? A hotel? Where's all the furniture?" he said, his voice getting quarrelsome. "I'm hungry. Where's food? What sort of place is this?"

"You have everything you need. It's all on the computer. That's why we left you one," he explained with the bored tone of a man who had explained it a million times before.

"It doesn't work." Gates pouted.

"The software works as well as it's always worked. It's your baby; you created it — one of the most diabolical inventions of the 20th Century. We really must thank you for that. It drove any number of people to murder and madness. Not to mention the numbers of innocent computers killed by an angry consumer with a hammer, an ax or a gun."

The little man gestured around the room. "We don't have much use for tables and chairs and things. We're a bit crowded here, what with the population explosion and all; but they are available and can be called up." He indicated the computer. "It is what you wanted, isn't it? Everything a person could possibly want on computer. No need to shop or work, it can be ordered online. Effectively penning them inside their rooms, glued to their screens. No need to go outside. While you inflict them with more upgrades that don't function as intended."

He put a finger in his ear and dug around. "Monopoly. Control. More for you."

"It doesn't stop people from working. They can work from

home." Gates realized what he had said and frowned. "Okay, I employed thousands of people, and most of them," he said with emphasis, "didn't work from home."

The man didn't quibble. "You see, Bill — may I call you Bill? — we're all about punishment here, not tables and chairs and other frivolities. Only the punishment counts."

"Punishment? What punishment?"

The man ignored Gates's question. "You can get food, chair, tables, bed, anything you want. It's on the computer."

The little man waddled to the computer, tapped on a few keys and clicked on an item and a chair sprung up underneath Gates, lifting him into the air so fast that he was ejected from the seat.

Then the chair retracted.

"Oops! Sorry, the software still has a few bugs in it," he said. "Play around with it. I'm sure you'll get the hang of it."

"Where's the instruction manual?"

"Instruction manual? For Gates Software?" The man threw back his head and laughed, and then he vanished. Just like that. First he was there and then he wasn't. No door opened, so Gates could plot his escape. Now you see it, now you don't.

"What the hell?" Gates shouted. "You can't just leave me here like this. Get the fuck back here. I'm Bill Gates. I can buy and sell you."

The laughter echoed around the empty room, bouncing off the sterile, white walls.

The little man reappeared somewhere beyond the wall. Gone was the suit and the mild manners. He appeared as he had been described for years, with blazing red eyes, forked tongue and tail.

Another demon stood waiting. "Why do you let him get away with that, boss?"

"Because it's fun," the first said.

"But you don't have to appear like this." The second mime going through the motions of putting on a suit and tie.

"I appear like that because that's how he expects me to appear. I am nothing, a nobody, in his eyes."

The two paused. Distantly, they could hear swearing and banging.

"No. No. No. NO. NO. NO!"

Suddenly the wall next to their ears began to throb.

Bang. Bang. Bang.

"Let me out of here!"

"That's my cue."

The room went dark.

"What the fah — " said Gates.

A snap or a slap, and the lights came on again.

The little man sat on a chair next to console. "Aw, what the hell?"

He fiddled with the controls and stool came spiralling from the floor, picking Gates up and stopping just short of the ceiling.

"What's the problem?" the bland man said.

Gates scrunched up in a tight little ball, clinging to the seat just in case it continued its ascent or, worse, plummeted. His gaze swept the room. Then he saw it.

A window!

Gates pushed himself from the stool, falling to the floor. He righted himself and then stumbled to the window, seeking something, anything he could see, that would provide him with a sense of place, a sense of sanity.

The vision that confronted him caused him to reel. A man hung on a meat hook, surrounded by angry people armed with scissors, with knives, with saws and any number of garden implements. Anything, it seemed, as long as it had a point and could stab, slice or impale.

The young man's mouth was open in a silent scream.

"Would you like sound? We can give you sound if you would like?" His fingers hovered over a button that had suddenly sprouted from the wall, like a mushroom.

"Uh, no thank you."

"What's the matter, Mr Gates?" the little man whispered in his ear.

Gates flinched. "What the — ? How did you leave; I saw no door, and how did get back so fast? I didn't even hear you move."

"I can do many things, Mr Gates," he said. "Do you like the entertainment? Think of it as your own personal channel."

Gates recoiled. "If that's the case, I'm gonna change the channel."

The little man stepped back and gestured at the computer.

"You are welcome to try."

Gates shook his head. "No, uh, that's all right. I don't have to watch."

But his gaze kept returning to the window where someone hacked another piece from a pasty-faced teenager. Others darted in and out, taking him to bits, slowly, one piece at a time. Peeling off meat and flesh

His arms, or what was left of them, were bound. His hands were nonexistent.

"Stop it. Can't you stop it?"

Someone started sawing at his wrists.

"No, I don't think so." The little man pursed his lips. "I wouldn't want to."

"Why not?"

"That's his punishment."

"What he's done that is so wrong?"

"He's a hacker. What would you do with a hacker if you caught one?"

"Who are they?" He nodded at the crowd. "They look like perfectly ordinary people to me." He paused. "Or they would if they weren't slicing him to pieces."

"They are just the public."

"The public?" Gates yelped.

"I'd say they were hacked off, don't you think. I mean what would you do to hackers if you could get your hands on them? They dismantled your software."

The man studied the sculpture done on living flesh. "We do try to let the punishment fit the crime. We pride ourselves on that."

"We? We who? What is this place?"

"Hell, baby." The little man cupped his face and Bill Gates's skin began to burn.

He grasped Gates's head.

His cheeks blistered.

The tiny man exhibited Herculean strength as he twisted Gates's head on his neck. "Watch it? Can you imagine what would happen if they were to manage to get their hands on you?"

"Me? Why me? I gave to charities. I provided computers for school. Hell, I opened up the entire world to the computer."

"Keep telling yourself that," the voice said.

The hair on that side of his face burst into flames.

Gates danced around the room, beating his head with his hands.

"Whoops, someone found an axe." The man twittered.

Then he stopped. Gates approached the window just in time to see them cut the remains off the hook and chopped it up in little pieces.

At that moment, what the man had called 'the public' noticed him and recognized him. They rushed the glass. "Gates! Gates! You fucking bastard. Let's get him."

Sound flooded the room as they beat on the window.

"Think of what might happen to you who released program after program with so many errors your employees had to set up websites and a system of updates that corrected nothing? You are the man who laid their computers, their homes, their lives open to invasion, and raised obsolesce into art form where each new release is incompatible with the previous."

Gates wasn't listening as another bookish sort was skewered onto the meat hook, and the public was diverted from their attack on the window. They returned to the job at hand and began to stab, slice, parry and hack at the new version geek, starting with the fingers, one at a time.

"It's our own version of death by a thousand cuts," the man said. "Do you like it?"

"What's going to happen to them?" Gates swallowed hard. "Or what's left of them?"

"Oh, they'll be back for your viewing pleasure, tomorrow, most likely."

"You mean, this is not real?"

"It's real enough." Again the sound of the youth's shrieks flooded the room.

"Ah, don't bother."

"Oh, no bother."

Gates mused: "What a horrible way to die?"

"No one here ever really dies." The little man examined his fingernails and brushed them against his coat.

Gates backed away, but the wall came to meet him holding him pinned to the window. He looked for the little man, but he was gone.

Again.

On the other side of the wall Satan joined his second in command.

"Well, boss, has he figured it out yet? Has he figured out his fate?" The demon indicated the hacker with a jut of his chin.

"No, he never does. Not very bright, our Mr Gates. Not very bright, at all."

Horns sprouted from the scalp. The devil scratched the nubs. "Ah, that's better. What's next on the agenda?"

"We have a new customer in the waiting room."

"How long?"

"Don't know. Long enough that he is getting seriously annoyed, but we have the muzack running so that's all right.

"Who is it?"

"I believe the name is Zuckerman, sir."

Satan clapped his hands together and rubbed them.

"Oh, goody."

HELL ON WHEELS

Edward Mathers's senses were assaulted with sights and smells and sounds. Flashes of colour and light. The signal board overhead declaimed the destination, and the estimated time of arrival, with a single word: "Delayed."

A voice, its humanity distorted by static and bad wiring, blared some incomprehensible reason: "Mmrprmph... garble... passenger action... xkkdgxerr... mmmmd the gap... crackle..."

The message's pulsating cadence provided a meter to the continuous rumble of shuffling, sniffling masses. Noise swelled around him until it became a muffled roar.

His nostrils twitched at the pungent aroma of too many bodies — both washed and unwashed — confined in too small a space.

Somewhere a train clattered and growled.

Not their train, evidently, for the sign continued to blink its unrelenting message: "Delayed."

Rush hour in London.

And it seemed he could see the vague shadows of cars and hear the clatter of street traffic. But how could that be?

Mathers looked around him in confusion.

"Mmmrprmph... garble... gerbil... chirp... shun... xkkdgxerr... sizzle, hiss... mmmmd the gappppp... crackle..."

"Goddammit, we're gonna be late," the man next to Mathers cursed roundly. Behind him another harried commuter did the same.

Someone elbowed him in the ribs. "Come on, move. I'm in a hurry."

Mathers stepped aside and trod on another man's foot. "Sorry," he muttered. The crowded tunnel absorbed the sound.

"Mmmrprmph... garble... gerbil... chirp... shun... xkkdgxerr... sizzle, hiss... mmmmd the gappppp... crackle..."

"Watch it!" someone said.

"Come on, keep it moving," another interjected.

"Where are we going?" Mathers snapped. "The train's delayed." He halted in the surging crowd and was besieged on

119

all sides.

The high-pitched skriegh of feedback drowned out all other sounds.

"Oi!" Mathers jumped as someone shouted in his ear. "Get moving!"

The feedback faded, and the mutter of human voices filled in the void.

"Who's holding up the queue?"

Some exhorted Mathers to hurry. "Come on, come on. Get the lead out."

"Mmmrprmph... garble... gerbil... chirp... shun... xkkdgxerr... sizzle, hiss... mmmmd the gappppp... crackle..."

"Why? Where are we going?" Mathers said, "For that matter where are we? What line is this? What station is this?"

"Listen to him! What line is this?"

"Are you still asleep, young man?"

"The one line, the only line."

"Down here."

Each statement was issued by a successive man as they jabbed, shoved, poked, prodded, and punched their way past him. They eddied around him, pushing him along as they went.

"Mmmrprmph… garble... gerbil... chirp... shun... xkkdgxerr... sizzle, hiss... mmmmd the gappppp... crackle... SCREECH!"

Mathers dug in his heels, refusing to be budged. Rush hour. The scene was commonplace enough. One he'd faced five days a week for most of his adult life.

And that meant he was going to work.

Or coming back from.

"Mmmrprmph... garble... gerbil... chirp... shun... xkkdgxerr... sizzle, hiss… mmmmd the gappppp... crackle..."

But he couldn't recall which one. His heart jogged and the walls of the station began to press down on him. He couldn't breathe.

What time was it? Was it morning or night? Or noon, for that matter?

"We're going to be late if you don't move," someone growled and gave Mathers a karate chop in the ribs.

"Ow, that hurt."

"Move!"

Mathers shuffled forward.

A red faced man in a blue cap, huddled upon a small platform, put a cone to his mouth and shouted: "Keep to the right... Please, keep to the right."

"Mmmrprmph... garble... gerbil... chirp... shun... xkkdgxerr... sizzle, hiss... mmmmd the gappppp... crackle..."

"But where," Mathers bleated "are we going?"

"You're new here, aren't you?" A stranger spoke to Mathers out of the corner of his mouth as they surged ahead. "You can always tell."

"Tell, tell what?"

"Don't worry. You'll get used to it."

"But where's here?" Mathers tried to ask, but the man had disappeared into the throng. Mathers plunged forward in pursuit.

Just then the train rattled into the station. Agitated people rushed toward the doors. The crush was enormous, but his step was arrested as he stared agog at the train. Finally, Mathers understood.

The train was powered by a chariot with wheels of fire.

Oh, oh, this did not look promising.

"Mmmrprmph the gah... app... crackle..."

"What a plonker!" a woman grumbled as she squirmed past him. Another individual almost knee-capped Mathers with her stiletto heel as she clambered into the car.

A friendly hand clasped his, pulling him in. The doors closed behind him, and the vision of flaming wheel was lost.

A speaker overhead sprung to life. "Mmmrprmph... garble... gerbil... chirp... mmmmd the... crackle..."

*

An eternity later Edward Mathers strode purposefully through the crowd, elbows wide. He wielded his briefcase like a weapon, swinging it around him in a wide arc. He was making good progress; he turned sideways and slipped through a gap between bodies.

He was late.

Just then a man seemed to materialize right before his eyes, and the wanker was just standing there.

"Come on, move," Mathers snarled.

"Hey, wait." The other man clutched at Mathers' sleeve a panic-stricken look on his face. Mathers swore roundly as he shook off the unwelcome hand and charged through the man.

"Where am I?" he said.

Mathers shrugged. He couldn't stop now to explain. He was running late.

CINDERELLA REVISITED

The howl reverberated inside her head. Unearthly and macabre, a strident cord that plaited her dreams with the black thread of dolour and the brilliant scarlet of passion. Love lost. The clamour disrupted the flow of the woman's fair fantasy, sundering the pleasant fabric of dream with nightmare's dissonance and discord.

Boo hoo. Boo hoo, hoo, hoo. Oh, BOO HOO!

The distant weeping rent the night, reaching her even in her bed, and she awoke from her slumber, with a start.

"Damn."

Oh woe, woe, woe is me...

The woman groaned, grabbed the pillow, stuffed it on top of her head and rolled over and tried to go back to sleep again, but the wail was relentless.

Boo hoo. Boo hoo, hoo, hoo. Oh, BOO HOO!

"Oh, bother and damnation," the woman said as she jerked into a sitting position and swung her legs over the side of the bed.

... woe, woe...

The woman grunted. "All right, all right, all right already, I'm coming. Keep your shirt on." She rose, grumbling irritably. "Bloody hell, can't even get a decent night's sleep. I want. I want. Gimme, gimme. Gimme this; gimme that."

The old woman scratched her head, dislodging her cap from which a single pink roller wrapped in silver hair protruded floppily. Her knotted and gnarled hand moved to her bottom to claw at a particularly nasty itch as she yawned.

That was just the problem with being a fairy godmother. One of the disadvantages of the job. You were always getting caught up in other people's problems. Their whinges, their wishes wafted about the planet constantly, borne upon the wistful winds of human imagination.

The good fairy could ignore them, sometimes. This was easier to do in the light of day when the hustle and bustle of daily activity drove desire from the mortal mind. But in the quiet

123

of evening's gloaming when man's whims were at their strongest, they were insistent things that intruded upon her thoughts, interrupting high tea and trespassing upon her hours of sleep. And the fairy godmother knew she wouldn't get any rest until she answered the call.

The fairy godmother paced around the room. The walls flickered in the firelight, and she rebelled at another night lost. Then she cast an oblique glance at her frilly frock of gossamer pink that hung on the back of the door. Ridiculous raiment for a woman of her years. Complete with buttons and bows, and an uncomfortably cinched waist, it was the kind of dress that little girls dreamed about before time had muted their fancies, and they had developed the commodity human's called good taste. The kind of garment that no grown woman would be caught dead in. The standard issue uniform that went with the position.

The fairy godmother peered into the mirror at a lined and seamed face. The ruffled cap held recalcitrant curls hidden from view. Then with critical appraisal, she considered her dressing gown. It was also pink and had nearly as many gew-gaws and curlicues upon it as the frock. In fact, the two were identical except for the waist.

If you disregarded the rollers and the fuzzy pink slippers, you could almost forget that she hadn't changed. With a shrug, the fairy godmother opted for comfort. At this time of night, who would know or care if she hadn't dressed for the occasion?

"Right," she said, hiking up her skirts to glare at the slippers. "Hell with it."

With a sigh and sharp whistle to fetch her magic wand, the fairy godmother dissipated in a dazzling cloud of gold dust. The sparkle flitted indecisively around the room a couple of times and then streaked away, zooming across the night-dark patch work of woods, field and stream to trouble's source.

The castle looked vaguely familiar, but dark, or darker than the last time she'd seen it. The shimmering mist hovered before a parapet, trying to remember when she'd been here and couldn't.

Boo hoo. Boo hoo, hoo, hoo. Oh, BOO HOO HOO!

The billowing vapour zipped through the narrow of slit of a tower window. As the fairy godmother spiralled into a human shape, words of indignation were vented from the approximate location where her lips should be. She stepped fully formed from the glittering corolla.

"You!" exclaimed the fairy godmother, and she pointed an accusing finger at the human source of the heart-rending sobs.

"You!" retorted the weeping woman, in a voice even more petulant, if possible, than the other's.

"I've already done you," the fairy godmother said.

"I'll say you've done me, all right," the woman conceded.

The fairy godmother drew herself up to full height, all four feet of it. "Sorry only one wish per customer. I'm afraid I can't help you again."

"Help me?" the woman parroted as she lifted a haggard face to gaze upon her nemesis. "You call this help?"

The fairy godmother grimaced. The woman did look terrible. The once blooming cheeks were the white of new fallen snow – and hollow. Purple circles of exhaustion ringed eyes gone dull and dim with despair.

Mortals were always making such a mess of their lives. If they didn't, she'd be out of a job.

"Of course I helped you," the fairy godmother explained as though talking to a thick-witted child. "I gave you your heart's desire."

"My heart's desire? You call this my heart's desire? I asked for someone to love me. Someone gentle, caring and kind. Someone who would treat me like a queen."

"And I did you one better than that," the fairy godmother said. "You are a queen."

"Of what?"

The fairy godmother paused to gaze around the tower, with its dirty rushes and greasy tallows.

"I wanted devotion. I wanted tenderness."

"No, I'm sorry but those concepts never entered into the equation," the fairy godmother informed her charge. "If I may quote you: You asked for a handsome prince, someone wealthy who could afford to take you away from the cinders and the ashes you had known to a palace rich beyond your wildest imaginings."

Cinderella stopped sobbing and looked around her. "Well, I certainly never imagined this." She gestured vaguely around the grim castle.

"Well, it does look like the place has got a little run down

125

through the years; but as lady of the manor, you are responsible for its upkeep."

"And what about my husband? Am I the only one to be held accountable? The only responsible party in the realm? I've got fifteen children to take care of. I've lost my shape."

The fairy godmother examined the once trim frame and nodded in agreement.

"And the hired help you get nowadays." Cinderella threw up her hands in disgust.

"The quality of the local labour is not my concern," the fairy godmother huffed. "I did, at least, give you the finest man in the kingdom. What you do with it..."

The light of rage gleamed in Cinderella's eyes. "My husband is a liar, a cheat. A dissembler of the first order. Duplicitous. I can't believe a word he says."

"All perfectly predictable, even laudable traits for a royal who must enter into delicate negotiations in which honesty may be a distinct disadvantage," the fairy godmother remonstrated the distraught wife gently.

"All right, I concede that some deception may be required for a ruler, but what about as my husband?"

"Well, you married him, despite all the difficulties you put me though. What with losing the glass slippers, and all," the fairy godmother harrumphed fluffily and patted a flounce back into place. "Those things don't grow on trees, you know."

"If I'd've known, I'd have broken the damn thing." Cinderella hobbled about the room, baby clasped to her deflated breast.

"Well, I never," the fairy godmother sputtered.

Cinderella ignored her, continuing with her complaint. "He's a philanderer. You'd think that fifteen children would be enough..."

"A goodly number, I confess."

"... but he's got to spread his seed among every lady-in-waiting, serving maid or kitchen wench in the kingdom."

"That is the royal prerogative. One of the perks of the job, along with," she coughed genteelly into her hand as she studied Cinderella's stained gown, "er, fine clothes; sycophantic courtiers, this draughty, old castle and all the peasants you could rape and pillage in a lifetime. Believe me, I know, I've seen the job description."

"Why didn't you warn me?" she asked.

"It's not my place to explain the consequences of mortal wishes to a human."

"Oh," Cinderella wailed, a sound that sent chills rocketing up and down the fairy godmother's spine. And the fairy godmother decided she'd do anything to shut the queen up, even if it meant breaking a few rules.

Cinderella flopped down into a chair. The glowing brazier threw her face into stark relief, each wrinkled highlighted, each line underscored. "I wish I'd never listened to you."

The fairy godmother canted her head to one side to contemplate the woman, and she wondered if she dared stretch a point and grant the wish. With a shake of lace cap, the fairy godmother decided the whole proposition of turning back time was much too risky.

"I think I would rather be back with my stepsisters, than here." Cinderella gestured around the dingy tower.

"Oh well," the fairy godmother said, "now that's something I can help you with."

With that, the fairy godmother rapped the ageing queen soundly on the top of the head. The woman began to waver, her image thinned as the molecules disbursed. Another howl echoed about the room.

The fairy godmother stared into the coals of the fire where she could view Cinderella as she rematerialized in a dank dungeon. The woman made a fist and shook it at the empty air. Then she deflated next the cold grate of an empty hearth.

"Sorry, kid, it's the best I can do," the fairy godmother said.

The mouth opened in a silent scream as rats clambered up the long skirts and onto Cinderella's lap. The head bent to rest upon bony arms and the thin shoulders shook.

Weeping again. There was just no pleasing some people.

Good deed done, at least now the fairy godmother wouldn't have to listen to it.

Peace at last, she thought as she too wavered and vanished.

When the fairy godmother next appeared beside the bed, the normally sweet, old-lady face had turned sour. Her lips twisted into a feral sneer.

No one ever really appreciated what she did, or just how hard she worked, chasing after mortal fancies.

The fairy kicked off the great pink slippers to examine the cloven hooves which were her feet. Then she yanked the cap from her head — pulling the candy floss of white curl wrapped in rollers with it — to reveal a knobbed skull and bald pate from which two curving horns jutted proudly. And she wondered what she had done in life to deserve this.

LAST LAUGH

Rick Simpson came to with a groan. For a moment he lay, trying to remember where he was and how he got there. The last thing he recalled was putting down the gas can and... and...

His mind went blank.

He moved experimentally. His head swam. Every muscle in his body ached, and it was hellaciously cold. The unnatural chill penetrated. Icicles stabbed deep into his spine and sent shrieking messages shivering throughout his frame and into his viscera.

Still unwilling to open his eyes, Simpson noted the hard, unyielding surface which felt somehow familiar, like... the harsh, uncharitable table upon which he had been strapped in preparation for electroshock therapy.

No!

Simpson jerked upright, heart pounding. His foot hit something metallic and sent it spinning with a loud clatter. The scruffy young man inhaled sharply. Only then did he notice the overwhelming odour of gasoline.

His eyes popped open, and he blinked at his surroundings. Old newspapers were stacked against the walls. Piles and piles of them — some bound, some loose. They spilled in a glorious cascade to the concrete floor. Abandoned paint cans were scattered here and there. Many of them open and, if his nose could be trusted, still fresh. Turpentine soaked rags were draped over the open cans, invitingly, ready to ignite like a candle wick. He let out his breath in a long ecstatic sigh.

He must'a died and gone to heaven.

Sniffing, Simpson detected the faint aroma of toluene, dipentene. His mind rattled off a list of chemical names unknown to the uninitiated, but that ran throughout in his brain like the hymnal lyrics. Sweet-smelling benzene, sickly, head-spinning glycol. Here close to the floor, there was the dull thick odour of paraffin. Pungent.

The young man picked himself up off the floor, brushed clenched fists against his pants and inhaled again. Higher up, he perceived cloying acetone, acrid acetylene and tangy butane, along with the octane-rich aroma of methanol and the ever-present gasoline. Simpson did a quick mental shuffle.

He'd been about to start a fire. There was the empty can and the puddle of pink-tinged liquid at his feet. But he didn't remember this particular warehouse. Neither could he remember blacking out.

He must have been overpowered by the fumes.

Again, Simpson sucked air in through his nostril, relishing the heaven-sent smells of flammable fluids. His head spun deliciously and the heaped piles of debris grew fuzzy. He stumbled, tripping over the red and yellow can. It rattled away from him. He chuckled. Looking at his surroundings such formalities as gasoline seemed a little redundant.

A smile oozed across his face. His eyes glinted with the faintly iridescent glow of burgeoning madness. With shaking hands, he began to pat his pockets looking for... matches.

*

The phone rang, tearing into a dream where Detective Immanuel Rodriguez fought back a blazing fire. The tingling bell set a vibrant counterpoint to the alarm screaming inside his brain.

He struggled out from under the tangled covers and groped for the phone. Even now Rodriguez could hear sirens shredding the velveteen night. A voice buzzed on the other end of the line, and his features changed from disturbed fuzziness to animate wakefulness.

"You're kidding. You really think this is our man?" he paused, listening for a second and then said, "I'm on my way."

A muffled voice issued from the tousled blankets, moaning. "Not again."

Consuelo sat up, her face twisted into a disapproving scowl. He reached for his clothes, hastily discarded after yet another late night over the back of the overstuffed chair

"We got him," Rodriguez said, excited.

"Got who?" she mumbled, peering at him with one eye still closed and a voice thick with slumber.

Rodriguez gave her a disbelieving look that was lost on her, still befuddled by sleep as she was. How could she forget his personal nemesis, glibly dubbed by the media, alternately, the

Shy-town Torch or the Chicago Scorcher.

"Never mind. Get some sleep."

"Too late for that now." She leaned across him to grab the clock and glare at the time.

"The Scorcher, love. Someone answering his description was sighted at a warehouse near Wabash."

Rubbing the sleep from her eyes, she was instantly alert. "What do you mean? No fire?"

"Not yet. He gave her the thumbs-up sign and, almost as an afterthought, his lips touched her dishevelled hair in a hurried kiss before Detective Immanuel Rodriguez bounded from the room.

"Be careful," she called after him. The apartment door closed with a bang. Sighing Consuelo settled back disconsolately.

Why couldn't she have married a lawyer, a plumber, a used-car salesman, a stock broker? Anything, anything but a cop.

*

Simpson's right hand went to his breast pocket, a gesture made familiar by rote, automatic by time and repetition. His deformed left, crossed into his view, and he hid it instinctively. A spiderlike webwork covered both front and back. Poorly executed skin grafts, improperly healed, had resulted in scar tissue that twisted it into a mocking parody of a human appendage.

Simpson hid it from prying eyes and remembered jeers which still echoed in his ears.

"Claw!" they hissed.

The warped fingers twitched as an older voice screamed recrimination, and a stronger, larger hand held the child's quivering digits over the open flame of a stove.

The tremulous right hand went from pocket to brow, wiping away sweat and memory with a single motion.

A one-time psychiatric aide had contemptuously claimed Rick Simpson was a few sticks shy of a bundle. Shy indeed! Hah! Yes, he would heat things up a bit.

He would show them. He'd set a blaze that would set Chicago on its ear. Simpson looked around him, awed by as much by the cathedral-type silence as the delicious assortment of flammable, both solid and liquid.

A holy conflagration. Apocryphal, divine retribution against a cold and indifferent world.

With everything he saw here, he was gonna start the fire of century. Mrs O'Leary's cow had nothing on Mrs Simpson's baby boy, Richard. The Chicago Scorcher.

Simpson felt for the small, hard rectangle of his lighter. His fingers delved into the dirt-stiffened cambric cloth of his shirt pocket, idly pondering the manufacturer's lifetime guarantee.

*

Rodriguez yanked the light from the glove box, slammed it onto the roof of the car with a metallic twang, and turned on the car radio with a savage wrest of the knob. It squawked its protest, crackling to life, and Rodriguez winced at the sound so akin to flames.

This time, this time, they would get him.

*

The good fingers on his right hand spun the striker. Nothing. No response. Not even a spark. He shook the lighter and then beat it against the dead meat of his twisted left hand.

Again. And again.

It felt light.

Muttering to himself constantly, Simpson tore it apart, clasping the outer casing with contorted fingers and wrenching the body from the shell. The cotton was devoid of fluid. Dry. Dead.

Agitated, he patted first one pocket and then another, searching for the less desirable, but always handy, Bic. Nothing.

Matches, then. He always kept some on him. They were easy to come by. He'd grab a handful everywhere he went. The seven-eleven, Pizza hut, wherever. After all, a fellow never knew when he'd need a match.

The flat books were more difficult to find. He probed and poked, digging into his shirt pocket, then his pant pockets. Right front and then left. Hip pockets.

Nothing.

Unbelieving, Simpson repeated the ritual a second, third and then a fourth time; meanwhile his eyes made a nervous circuit of the room, taking in this time what he had failed to notice before.

Discarded canisters, dented and disreputable-looking. Butane. Rejected medical supplies, their labels torn and chipped, containers of nitrous oxide, oxygen and ether. Further back, half-buried by old papers and other refuse, were several propane tanks.

The demonic fire in his eye flared as his gaze lighted upon each new treasure. A pyromaniac's paradise.

Leaves crackled underfoot as he paced back and forth, both hands flailing after his unproductive search.

Right hip pocket... slap... left hip pocket... whack... right front, left front... thwack! thwack! Breast pocket... RRRIP!

The information finally filtered into his reluctant brain that he, Rick Simpson, alias The Torch, was without a match. It couldn't be!

He bellowed his rage. The eldritch sound got lost among the stacks of debris, muffled by the heaped paper and rags.

His eyes scanned the room. Surely, somewhere in this Mecca of human detritus there must be something. A not-quite-spent Bic with one forlorn light left. A forgotten matchbook, a single phosphorous-laden stick.

With that thought, Simpson dove into the nearest mound.

*

The car radio cackled with a reproving catcall as he replaced the handset with a now tremulous hand. They had just contacted the owner of the two major warehouses in the area to see what, if anything, was stored in them. The news was not good. If either of the two went up, the results would be in an inferno straight from hell.

Thank God, the station commander was on the ball. The fire department had been notified and was on its way.

Chewing on his lip, Rodriguez squelch the urge to speed up and reviewed what little information they had on the case for the umpteenth crime. A few meagre descriptions of a man seen loitering close by on numerous occasions.

It was vague and shadowy at best. Average height, average weight. Hair described variously as sand-coloured or mud-coloured. Eye colour: none. Scars: none. In other words, nondescript except for one rather peculiar trait. He kept his hands in his pockets. He and half the city. No law against that.

The truth was the man could be any John Doe, and they weren't even sure if the man lurking in the area was the same man or one of a group of miscellaneous misbegotten slobs that just happened to enjoy a good fire.

Even his clothing was no help. Dirty blue jeans, a work shirt or a tee-shirt, which was something of a uniform for most working class citizens, not to mention any derelict who made their home in the industrial wasteland that surrounded the Loop.

Tonight's caller had not identified himself. It was just as likely that the tip was part of a vendetta, a strategy to rid the area of a newcomer who had horned in on someone else's territory or took over a particularly choice sleeping place, a good piece of real estate or profitable rubbish skip. Assuming, of course, that their so-called Samaritan, a wino most likely, had a quarter to waste. Rodriguez wouldn't be at all surprised if in the end he found himself waking up some drunk from a liquor-induced dream.

The hell of it was that they weren't even sure if they were working with one arsonist or many. There was no distinctive MO, besides perhaps a delight in seeing things burn.

This had to be him.

Rodriguez's job wasn't worth a tinker's damn if it wasn't. The media was having a field day with this one and soon enough heads would roll.

He clasped the steering wheel in a vice-like grip as he raced along Lake Shore Drive. With a sinking heart, he searched the horizon to the west for the fatal glow that would tell him that once again he was too late.

*

Somewhere.

Anywhere.

There had to be a match.

Simpson leapt from one pile into another. Here his spatulate claw was a more effective tool than the dexterous right, acting like a shovel. He pushed sweet-smelling rags and dry debris aside, driving deeper and deeper into the refuse.

No luck.

Like a mole Simpson surfaced, blinking. By this time, he had made his way from one end of the warehouse to its opposite when his eyes lit upon several metal magazines, and he was arrested by the bright red and white DANGER logo. His gaze darted to the orange DOT sticker with the fracturing ball decoration.

EXPLOSIVES A

And he began to tremble.

EXPLOSIVES B

And C... A chill ran a plummeting course from his scalp to his toes, travelling at breakneck speeds. For the first time in his life, Rick Simpson, whose life and breath was fire, found himself looking for a door.

This job was too big even for him.

Anxious eyes scoured the pockmarked brick and saw nothing except more brick. No window. No door.

No outlet at all.

His bladder let go and warm urine spread across the crotch of his jeans as childish laughter reverberated inside his head, and a single image rippled across his consciousness as though planted by some evil demon...

The burning bright eye of a gas range and a small child's hand forced into the flames.

Simpson took a deep breath and steadied himself.

A cardboard flap flitted at the periphery of his vision as though brushed by an unknown breeze. The sandy-brown head swivelled on its neck, drawn by the flash of red and a single word...

La Salle

He scrambled up the nearest pile, the loose papers slipping and sliding beneath his feet. His arms pinwheeled, and he was caught in a morass of litter only a few short steps from his goal.

Frantic now, Simpson clambered on toward the top of the mound, scrabbling through the debris — oblivious to the presence of explosives, forgetting his momentary fear and the lack of egress. Only one thought on his mind. He must get a hold of that matchbook.

Success!

The fingers of Simpson's good right hand wrapped possessively around the matches.

*

Kaboom!

The speed of the screeching unmarked car lagged as Rodriguez's foot recoiled from the gas and hovered over the brake.

KABOOM!

It sounded like the earth had been split down the middle and the legions of hell loosed upon the world. The street buckled and bucked, and the strength of the convulsion was such that the car did a skittering sideways dance. The buildings, their dingy brown brick brilliantly adorned with day-glo gang names, around him shook violently. The windows rattled and many of them already broken by a rock thrown by a delinquent hand rained glass on to the road.

The detective cursed soundly as a series of small explosions followed the first ear-splitting blast. And then the sky was alight with perdition's flame.

"Holy Mary mother of God," Rodriguez crossed himself,

Too late, too late.

His helter-skelter pace slowed as he turned west toward Wabash. Nothing he could do now except hang around and watch the fire department pick up the pieces.

*

The matchbook turned in the young man's grasp, seeming to mock and defy him, and fluttered down to get lost among the rest of the litter.

Simpson threw back his head and gave an unearthly howl, a mixture of frustration and despair as his prize again evaded him to sink deeper among the rags.

Only then did he notice the presence of another man standing at the foot of the mound staring up at him amazed. The stranger's skin was the ashen grey of a Rush Street bum; his haggard eyes sunk deep into a skeletal face.

Simpson froze.

136

The man peered up at the youth puzzled. He scratched a grizzled scalp and then rubbed a stubbled chin.

"Hey, do you know where we are?"

Simpson's head wagged from side to side, and for an instant his eyes lost some of their maniacal gleam.

"Strange this," the other man mused, "The last thing I remember I was in Intensive Care. All these people running around like chickens with their heads cut off. They said I was going to die. Lung cancer, you know. Told me to quit smoking."

He snorted. "Guess I beat it again."

The man fished in his pocket, digging out a cigarette. "I don't suppose you have a match."

Simpson's gaze flicked down to the elusive matchbook caught amongst the heaped rubbish.

*

Rodriguez heaved himself from the car. No point in hustling now. Flames leapt higher and higher in a frenzied caper, and the sapphire night, brittle with stars, was softened to a burnished rose.

Moving leadenly, he went to join his partner who looked as sleepy and bemused as Rodriguez felt.

Somewhere, someone shouted. Both men looked up just as firemen hauled a charred body from the burning building. The two policemen broke into a shuffling run. Firemen wound between them, yelling at each other between rasping breaths.

One of them bumped into Rodriguez and he was bounced aside like a pinball. His partner slowed to a trot, shouting: "Is that..."

The fireman shrugged, indicating another man behind him with a jut of a chin. His partnered hurried on while Rodriguez lingered to examine the corpse.

The skin had pealed away to reveal muscles the colour of well-cooked beef, and the fingers were fused together, creating a spatula. The words "crispy critter" flash momentarily in Rodriguez's beleaguered brain.

The mouth-watering aroma of broiled steak meat wafted around him as the fireman dropped the body unceremoniously to the ground.

Rodriguez swallowed hard, and his mind blathered hysterically: "A Big Mac with a side of thighs, please."

Another yellow-garbed man slogged through the writhing hoses toward them, a warped gas can held gingerly in his gloved fist. Its once-yellow-and-red paint was bubbled and blackened.

"We found this beside the body. I think we got The Scorcher at last." The fireman grinned broadly, his teeth a white half moon in a charcoal grey background.

Rodriguez only half listened, his eyes glued to the charbroiled corpse. Nobody deserved to die like that, and he whispered a short prayer to a forgiving God as the other men talked.

*

The young man awoke with a groan. For a moment he lay, trying to remember where he was. The last thing he recalled he was putting down the gas can, and... and...

His mind went blank.

It was hellaciously cold. Every muscle ached; his head swam. The unholy chill penetrated, and icicles stabbed his spine to send shrieking messages coursing through his body and into his viscera...

SISTERS

Evangeline Adams shifted into fifth gear. It had been a horrible day — the little bar stewards had outdone themselves — and she had been delayed. She wanted to get home to her small cottage on a quiet estate in Shrewsbury where she lived with her sister.

School was pure, unmitigated hell.

Eve knew, even when she started that she was ill-suited to be a teacher. It was a job where other people's little darlings became her holy terrors. But back in the olden days, she gave a dry laugh, when she was young, it had been the only acceptable profession for a woman.

She needed employment because she had followed in her sister's footsteps, leaving her husband and, in Eve's case, she gave up the children. It hadn't been a match made in heaven, the man was an oaf. She kept the name, and now she was stuck raising someone else's kids.

Most parents didn't know the first thing about discipline. The unsuspecting students soon learned they had to mind their teacher. Eve knew all about punishment. For her there had been hell enough to pay.

Do one lousy thing wrong, and you're taking care of snotty midgets for the rest of your life. Jeez.

Eve's heavy hand in the classroom had earned her the nickname, Attila, and she relished her name, as much as she relished her spinster status. She had no man to interfere with her, no man to demand what he felt was his due. No sweaty hands to grope and fondle. Eve shuddered. Filthy beasts.

The wipers strove valiantly to keep up with the rain. Between each monotonous stroke, the landscape before her dissolved into a grey-green blur. The portion of the A49 just past the 'Hound In The Lane' was a twisty, turny affair. Her eyes flicked to the mirror, temporarily blinded by the glaring lights on the articulated lorry behind her. The driver seemed to be hell bent on getting somewhere fast and oblivious to the conditions of the road.

Eve pulled over to let him pass. Her gaze slipped from the

rear view mirror to the washed-out world of sodden grey and green. "Don't worry about the other guy," she intoned, in memory of driving lessons past. "You can drive only one car at a time."

Her vehicle was doused as the lorry thundered around it.

She started swearing. Her invective became more creative when she realized that she was supposed to go to store before going home. She had been so anxious to get home she had quite forgotten. Eve made a u-turn – not a three-point turn or a four-point, more like a five- or six-point turn — and headed back to Shrewsbury. Eve rounded the bend near the gypsy camp. The Rover hit a hole and floundered where water had collected in a small pool.

Instinctively, Eve slammed on the brakes. The car skated sideways. "Damn, damn, damn, damn."

Eve checked her watch and then glared up at the sky painted the hues of winter drear. Night came so early these days. Here, it was around four o'clock and it was already dark.

She arrived at the Tescos car park and cruised up and down the aisles. She and everybody else in the town was here to shop. She parked at the far end.

Eve raced for the entrance, but she was still soaked when she stepped under the overhang. The supermarket doors whispered open. She had to get something to go with that evening's tea, and she was already late. A quick dash to grab some vegetables and some sausages and that would be it.

Eve squared her shoulders and strode rigidly into the store. Her pace faltered and she sputtered her dismay. There were little old ladies everywhere — trundling in front of trolleys and tottering behind carts, and she wondered what had brought them out this late. Usually, the pensioners had come and gone by this time, riding in on the 'free bus'.

She picked up a metal basket and dove into the madness. She didn't need this. Her legs ached and her feet hurt. She didn't want to run the gauntlet through humanity. She'd had enough of them for the day.

Eve lowered her head. Arms akimbo with elbows placed defensively out, she barged through the group of seniors, only to be confronted by some businesswoman who read every label, looking for an E or some other polysyllabic word used to disguise preservatives.

Or, maybe, she was looking for the country of origin to see if it was proscribed. Once it had been South Africa, later Guatemala, then this country and that country. Who knew what was popular now. Such people were always easily recognizable; their faces bore a scowl; their lips moved as they read, and their carts were filled with items marked 'green'.

To the woman's right, a bachelor was picking up that night's lager and some mince. Eve hurried on past husbands, clutching little slips of paper in their hands and wearing the same bemused expression. Periodically, they squinted at the illegible list and then the signs above their heads.

"... ground Chuck is on special this week... go the flashing red light in aisle..." BEEEEEEEEEEEEEEEEP, and the rest of the announcement was lost as it disintegrated into static and feedback.

People stampeded away. Eve shuffled sidewise to make sure she wasn't trampled. She just moved to the next aisle to find entire families — husband, wife and ranks of screaming children. Her eyes narrowed. In twenty years of teaching, she had learned to hate children. Not that she was particularly fond of adults, who usually exhibited the same emotional maturity of their offspring.

The child's voice rose to a falsetto and went all wobbly and thin that grated on the nerves. Further down another toddler clinging to another mother threw a full-body tantrum.

Why were they always crying? You never saw a happy baby in a supermarket

She grunted.

Some mothers were too solicitous, far too indulgent, and others compounded the problem by whacking the child and making it cry all the louder.

The fathers were no help. Eventually, they would scurry off, supposedly to search for some hard-to-find item at the other end of the store where it was quiet. They would spend the rest of their time in the supermarket, putting as much distance between themselves and their caterwauling mob as possible.

It was a recipe for insanity. It didn't used to be this way, this crowded, back when she was young. People spent far too much time procreating. "Haven't you ever heard of birth control?" she said under her breath.

Just then a man skulked past her, glancing furtively over his shoulder, an unmistakable sign, and somewhere to her left a child screeched loudly. A young man wearing a pad or a pod, or some such nonsense, was texting and carrying a bottle of cheap wine. He was more reminiscent of the normal evening crowd. He nearly bowled over an old woman. She threatened him with her cane. Eve thought of Monty Python with their gangs of marauding grandmothers. Grandmothers from hell. Killer grand- mothers from space.

Eve chuckled quietly to herself. She needed to get off her feet, and she needed to get home to her sister where she had dinner cooking.

Basket held before her like a shield, Eve veered around the crowd. She spied the tinned beans and homed in on them, congratulating herself on her progress so far, and as if on cue, a woman with blue-tinted hair, hauling a shrieking child, stepped in front of her to peer myopically at the labels. Eve stopped and rocked back on her heels to avoid collision.

Her temper started to flare.

This was hell.

She felt her body temperature rise. The blue-tinted head ducked and reared like a ferret doing the death dance, until finally the woman decided which was the best buy and raised a palsied hand with arthritic fingers.

What seemed an eternity later the can bounced to the bottom of the cart, and the two debated where to go next. Eve clamped her jaw to cut off the angry expletive she felt forming on her lips when someone concentrating more on the contents of his trolley than the world around him ran into her.

"Uh, sorry," the man said.

She bit back a retort and scooped a can of green beans from the shelf.

Sorry! She fumed. Everybody's sorry. The principal is sorry when he keeps me fifteen minutes late. The children are sorry when they misbehave. Eve made sure of it. An eye for an eye, a tooth for a tooth was her creed.

Their parents, though, weren't sorry until the teacher stared them down and let them know just what she thought of their darlings. Then they were insulted, and most were sorry they came to the school to complain.

The grandmother bent over the urchin, spit on her hand and smudged dirt across the boy's face. He wriggled.

"Candy, little boy," Eve muttered. Children. They were so cute, she could just eat them up. Eve liked hers fried.

Eve pushed aggressively into the crowd, repressing the desire to run over someone's nan or, preferably, a child.

Her legs felt like lead. Something warm trickled down her calf and into her shoes. Blood. Eve dipped her finger in the blood and then put it in her mouth. The cut must be deep. She cursed him roundly. Someday, she would have her revenge. Maybe she would teach his progeny.

A kid ran tearing up the aisle, shrieking. A harried mother shouted after him. Eve murmured, "Women should be sterilized at the age of thirteen."

Eve entered the next aisle and there she was, the cliché, the fat woman with the bum of a water buffalo. The silly cow waddled along while her brood fanned blocking the entire aisle. The woman paused every few feet, fat jiggling on buttocks and thighs.

It was time to leave before she decided to kill somebody. People had no sense of humour when it came to throttling the aged, the obese, the young.

The husband, a scrawny little fellow with rheumy eyes, mumbled something to her. "I'll go get the..." and the words were lost in the wail of a child. The husband fled and the fat woman squatted next to one of four children. Its nose ran with thick catarrh, and the woman resurrected a greyed hankie from somewhere and reached down to wipe the child's face, smearing green from cheek to cheek.

Eve felt nauseated. She decided that there was nothing else she needed and made good her escape. She shook herself like a dog before getting into the vehicle. The drumming of the rain on the windscreen was soothing after the chaos of the supermarket.

She put her car into gear and headed for home.

Eve's stomach growled. "Quiet," she said. "You'll get fed soon enough."

She pulled close to the kerb after she entered the cul de sac. Not ready to brave the horizontal rain, she studied the residence with its abundant statuary of fairies, elves and garden gnomes. A neighbour commented once that it looked like a gingerbread house.

 If she only knew...

In the past, a few misguided neighbourhood children had entered their garden to play. The little buggers always received a warm welcome from the sisters, and those who did never came back again.

Eve scooped the soggy newspaper from the stoop. Once inside the door, she unrolled it, glanced at the headline and left it in the reception to dry.

"Lilith? Lilith, I'm home."

Somewhere a child squealed. Eve rolled her eyes. Thin walls.

"How was the supermarket?" her sister shouted.

"Hell."

"You should expect that. We age and see how the world is going to hell in a hand basket."

"Easy for you to say, you stay home," Eve groused. "What's for dinner?"

"The usual," Lilith replied.

"Paper says another child is missing," Eve said as she entered the kitchen.

"Oh, imagine that," said Lilith. "That's a shame. Let's hope they fatten up nicely."

The sisters twittered as Lilith clattered across the floor and yanked the toddler from the cage that hung in the back of the room. She twisted the tiny neck and shoved the body into the roasting pan.

Eve opened the oven door for Lilith. Her sister placed the roaster inside and slammed it shut.

"There, that's dinner taken care of," she said as she began to empty the grocery bags.

"How's Mr Scott?"

"Oh, him? Mr Scott is well contented. He thinks he's landed in hog heaven..."

The sisters cackled.

"He's got someone to clean up after him, and all the sausages he can eat. I'd say he should be ready next week." Lilith washed her hands.

"So, how was your day?"

A COLD DAY IN HELL

So this was it, John Ryan thought. One minute you're trying to chat up some bint or bonking some bimbo, and the next you're mincemeat, taken to bits.

The man eyed the corpse and winced at the blood pouring from between its legs and the detached scrotal sack. He drifted away from body and bed, getting snagged in the curtains.

"Bloody hell," Ryan murmured, but no one was listening. The woman was screaming as she clambered out from underneath the corpse, and the husband... well... the husband was circling the bed, waiting for Ryan to flick a finger or an arm in self-defence.

"You're gonna wait a long time," he muttered, "'til hell freezes over."

No one laughed at his wit. They were caught in their own little psycho drama and paid little heed as Ryan attempted to untangle himself from the curtains with their cloying floral print. He could see each thread of warp and woof. Never had his senses been so acute, and he risked getting lost in the weave.

Katie Ryan's boy, John, probably should have expected this. It had to happen eventually. Another man's woman had always been fair game, but he was always cautious, studying the situation for weeks, noting the husband's schedule and the woman's availability before approaching any woman.

John Ryan was also a pragmatist. He didn't waste his time on lost causes. If John did stray into another man's territory, you could bet he'd been encouraged. He didn't go where he wasn't invited. Hell, he didn't have to.

Oh, there'd been fights in the past. Usually in pubs, never in a woman's home. Not that the arguments lasted long, because John always backed down, with a mumbled apology, an avowal of the woman's innocence and a compliment to the man on his good taste.

As for the disputed woman?

Well, there was always tomorrow, or next week, or next month if need be. If the invitation was valid, it would remain until he chose to accept it. In fact, it would be enhanced by a certain debt of gratitude for his gallantry.

All part of his philosophy of being a practical man. John reasoned, rightly enough, that you couldn't enjoy much of anything if you were dead. You certainly couldn't enjoy sex if some bastard had cut your goolies off. He stared in dismay at his testes, a forlorn testament to his failed philosophy and then at his deflated willy where they lay next to him on the bed.

The concept had stood him in good stead for years. It had got him in and out of any number of women's beds. That and availability. His chosen profession of window washer had helped. He was around when women's husbands were not, and it was amazing how many got frisky during the day. Even more amazing what the average suburban housewife was willing to do to satisfy this itch during the day when they were left to their own devises. John was always around, ready to provide service with a smile.

John sort of figured that he'd get caught climbing out of the wrong bed at the wrong time. It was inevitable. What he hadn't reckoned on was that his reflexes would be so slow, so sluggish, caught as he had been mid-orgasm. Or that his wits would be so dull.

This had been a horrible miscalculation on his part. A fatal miscalculation. John frowned at the twelve-inch kitchen knife protruding from his back.

A battle raged around him. As husband and wife shouted at each other, not about who had done what to whom — it seemed the time for accusations and recriminations was past — but what to do with the corpse.

And John realized as he looked at the triumphant gleam in the woman's eye that she had known this would happen. The husband's arrival had been no accident. She had set him up. Both of them, John corrected himself.

"Bitch," he sneered.

The woman, whose name he could no longer recall, had her husband by the short and curlies, for sure. John grimaced at the choice of expression — seeing how his dangly bits, and a few pubic hairs, were now permanently severed from his person. She was clearly in charge — telling her spouse to take the body to the bath and then to bring an axe and a saw from the garage.

146

"No!" John roared soundlessly.

The woman glanced frantically about her, flinching away from the cooling corpse and belatedly slipping into a dressing gown.

Meanwhile John took a stab at removing the blade from his back. Ephemeral hands passed through the handle, and the action caused him to float away from the bed, pass through the closet door and into a row of neatly hung suits. The scent of aftershave tickled at his nose, and he sneezed. The force of it propelled him through the wall and into the back garden.

This was ridiculous. He swam back toward the house, but bits of himself were getting tossed about by a fragile breeze.

Think solid, and his body — or some semblance of it — reformed.

Hovering above the rose bushes, John contemplated his quandary and wished himself back into the house. The bed was empty. The wife was stripping off the bloody sheets.

Now where was he, John wondered, and his mind followed his wish into the bath where the husband was busily applying cleaver and saw to the already ravaged flesh.

It was the final insult, John decided. Bury him in the back garden, fine — he'd never been much for funerals or cemeteries — but don't cut him up and distribute the pieces all over the bleeding country. There was something unholy about that.

John paused to consider the body that he appeared to possess at this moment. The one that could zip, zoom or swoop from here to there with a whispered wish or a whim. It looked familiar enough, floating somewhere underneath his head. He patted the chest, the torso. It seemed solid enough.

"PSSSST"

John spun, which means he revolved in mid-air, too fast to control the movement or stop it when his 'body' was pointing in the right direction. When at last he'd pivoted to a woozy halt, he faced an open door. Not a door that had existed before. John could still see the closet, the bedroom and the distant hall clearly enough. The aperture did not appear to be a part of the room or the house, opening instead onto a stair that couldn't possibly exist in the bungalow.

A glow that should have been blinding, or would have been had he been quite himself, emanated from beyond the door.

147

Instinctively, John put his hand up to block the glare and was not pleased to note that the light shone through his palm and fingers as if they were nothing more than thin tissue paper.

"Psssst."

"Yes?"

"There's not much more you can do around here. You are dead, you know, and you can't influence events any more."

"You don't have to remind me," John snapped.

"No point in getting crossed. I didn't get you into this mess." The voice was one of mild reproach.

John squinted, trying to discern the speaker's face in the light.

"I can haunt them," he retorted.

"I suppose you can, but do you really want to spend your afterlife stuck here in this house? Or see what lies beyond?"

Suddenly, John could distinguish a hand in the doorway — its forefinger extended — and beyond that he saw a staircase made of silver and gold. And crystal, or perhaps it was diamonds. The steps sparkled invitingly and John wondered if this could be the source of the strange light. He sailed forward, tantalized by this glimpse of brilliance, and he realized that the stairs were moving.

Straight up.

Heaven? John thought and he heard a dim chuckle.

The invitation was too tempting to resist. He had to know what lay beyond the door and where the stairs led. His feet paddled forward even while his brain signalled alarm.

Something was wrong with all this. He didn't belong in heaven; he belonged... well... elsewhere.

The next thing John knew he was on the steps, and he was being towed up. Up. Ever up.

This could not be right. He had sinned.

John shrugged. He had given pleasure to women, as many women as would take pleasure in his company, but never without their consent. He enjoyed a good pint or two. Okay — so maybe it was more than that — but, any road, were his sins so very great?

The proof was in the pudding, so to speak. Here he was, John Ryan, riding on these stairs through blue skies and fluffy white clouds. He leaned over the golden rail. The ground was not visible. He had not expected it to be. Neither did he see sign of hell's fire.

Up. Up. UP.

Until it got boring. Ryan was growing weary of eternally blue sky and candy-floss clouds. There was nothing to do, but think of his ultimate demise and what he might have done to get revenge if he'd chosen to tarry a little longer in the world below.

No matter how many different means Ryan devised or implements he used to castrate the husband, the entertainment value paled after the first few hours or so.

And John yearned to arrive at their final destination. He began to walk up the stairs, perhaps to speed the process just a bit.

Up. Up. Ever UP!

If this was heaven, John thought, then it was damned dull.

As if some omniscient power divined that Ryan's not considerable patience was at its limit, the escalator ride ended abruptly — spewing him on to flat ground, or cloud. He sprawled face down. As he extracted pieces of fluff from his eyes, nose and mouth, John noticed not one but several similar stairways, likewise unloading their confused burdens. Some fell; others — those wearing pious expressions — did not.

"Mind the gap. Mind the gap," a melodious voice intoned.

"Bloody hell," John said and a wizened little man frowned at him.

"Please take a number..." the same disembodied voice continued.

"From where?" John huffed.

A scroll materialized before the perplexed Ryan and, when he unrolled it, he was confronted with a number so long that he could have easily wrapped himself, mummy-style, in the paper upon which it was written and still have some to spare.

"... and join the queue."

He cocked an ear, listening to the celestial voices that chimed mundane messages with heavenly harmonics.

"No pushing, shoving or queue jumping will be tolerated. All will be served in their time."

The messages were repeated for each new arrival. "Mind the gap... take a number..."

The mellifluous voices began to grate upon his nerves, and John was fuming by the time he reached the head of the queue.

"... all will be served in their time."

"Like hell, they will," he grumbled. "My time is bloody up already. I'm dead. I had to put up with enough of this in life, I shouldn't be stuck in some fucking queue."

The man behind the counter looked him up and down, then typed something into a computer.

"Hey, don't you need this?" John brandished the scroll at him.

"That's for you not for me," the man said.

"Pardon?"

"To verify the records."

"Some heaven," John sputtered. "Fancy gates, maybe," he pointed at the gilt and mother-of-pearl inlay, "but so far it's not a whole helluva lot better than the London Underground, or signing up for the dole."

"You would be John Ryan?"

"Yeah, how did you know?"

The man swung his terminal around so Ryan could read the screen. The number flashed on the top of the screen. In fact, it filled it.

"Check the number, please?"

"What? You've got to be kidding?"

"Do I look like I'm kidding?"

John grimaced. "You don't look like you've heard a decent joke for years."

Ryan checked the number, getting lost after the first ten or twenty digits.

The man pressed a key. The number vanished, and there it was. John Ryan's life in a nutshell. His age at time of death — correct, no doubt, down to the second. A piss-poor photo — and wouldn't you know it, it was the last picture he'd had taken for his travel card.

RYAN, JOHN. NATIONALITY. BRITISH BY BIRTH; IRISH BY EXTRACTION. RELIGION: LAPSED CATHOLIC.

And... what could best be described as a character assessment, a none too flattering character assessment: WOMANIZER, PHILANDERER. Then came a list of days, dates and names. Evidently of women he had had in the past, more even than John could remember. He blushed.

GAMBLER... John couldn't argue with that.

ALCOHOLIC...

"Now wait a second, I may like a tipple or two, but I'm no fucking alcoholic."

The man blinked. "Did you ever have a single sober day in your entire adult life?"

"Well, I don't know. There must have been one..."

The screen had changed, listing — for lack of a better term — vital statistics. Much of which John didn't understand. Names, dates, places continued to scroll across the VDU until it terminated in: FINAL DESTINATION AFTER CUSTOMS AND EXCISE PROCESSING AT UNLOADING STATION NUMBER...

John Ryan's eyes widened. His pupils dilated, and his skin went a funny shade of green.

"What the hell is this? Come on, I wasn't that bad. I never even knew half those women."

"That's just the problem, Mr Ryan. You did know all of them, in the most Biblical, intimate and carnal sense of the term."

"Well, I never hurt nobody. I mean those women enjoyed themselves." John preened. "Never had a dissatisfied customer. Besides, they all knew what they were doing."

"Yes, and they are answerable for their sins as you are for yours." The man scowled. "However, your actions precipitated at least two divorces and God only knows how many beatings..."

There was a rumble overhead; a series of clackings somewhere within the computer, and a number popped onto the screen.

"Why I never hit a woman in my life!" John shouted indignantly.

"No, you didn't, but any number — what does it say there? — of irate husbands have."

"Look, Saint Peter," John said.

"Cyril."

"Saint Cyril," John amended.

"Just plain Cyril." The man sighed. "We aren't saints any more. Forgotten by the church and demoted by God for being too lax. Now everything's been standardized and centralized."

"The point is," John interrupted, "are you gonna believe some fucking machine? Or me?"

"The machine, of course."

"What's this," John slapped the terminal, "computer doing here anyway? I would think God would be above this sort of thing."

"We must keep up with the times. Do you realize how many people we service here? We are just fallible mortals, after all." The man behind the pearly counter looked wistful.

"Gone is the day when saints manned the desks. Too many people are born. Too many people die. Famine is not enough. You must have global war. Do you realize how many places are at war even as we speak? You have Aids. We get people from Rwanda, Ethiopia, Somalia, the former Yugoslavia, Cambodia. Have the lot of you gone nuts?"

The man gesticulated widely. "And we service everyone. People from all religions, races and creeds. Whether your final destination is Nirvana or Valhalla, we do not discriminate. In your own faith alone, you have four possible alternatives — purgatory, limbo, heaven, hell — and within those an infinite number of gradations." The man behind the counter examined the glowing screen myopically.

"Seventh level," he mused. "Could be worse. Satan starts to get a little creative on that level. Something beyond the same old fire and brimstone. He likes people like you; people whose crimes have radiated outward in ever enlarging circles. You should count your blessings that you are a lowly womaniser and not a politician."

John glowered at the machine, willing the red, yellow and orange flickering letters of his ultimate destination to vanish.

"The computer assures absolute justice without personal bias. Straight from the big man above. And it speeds you on the way. You were getting a little impatient, weren't you?"

John gulped. "I'm not in that big of a hurry."

"Well, I am. The next person is waiting. It is his time, if I'm not mistaken, the doctor is filling out the death certificate even as we speak. Hang on to your number. You will need it down stairs."

The one called Cyril motioned vaguely to the left. "Just follow the orange, yellow and red..." As he mentioned them, lines flared brightly among the cottony tufts of white. "... flashing arrows to the lift. Don't worry about the floor. The lift has been pre-programmed to the correct level. Just step inside and

152

wait. Someone will greet you."

"And if I refuse?"

"I'm afraid that's not really an option," Cyril said. His lips kept moving, but John didn't hear the words because the ground had been whipped out from under his feet. Or more appropriately, it dragged him along — his feet seemed to be glued to the conveyer belt. John didn't even fall, as it lurched to a start. Only bounced a bit. His nose hit cottony soft cloud. He righted himself — or rebounded — and sneezed.

The first arrow whizzed past, and the desk, the pearly gates, escalators vomiting innumerable dead, and the long winding lines of queue receded.

Then he was thrust into a small cubical so hard that he hit the opposite wall of burnished copper with a clatter and a bang. The doors, also copper, brass or some warm, red metal, closed without forming so much as a seal. And John was surrounded by burnished flame.

John bellowed — "Oi!" — and threw himself against what he thought must be the door. The metal was cool, the flames were etched or sculpted into the surface. Yet, as he watched they seemed to coil and uncoil, writhe and leap.

He backed away from the door, dusted himself off, and straightened his shirt self-consciously.

Maybe this wouldn't be so bad.

Something bonged stridently and an arrow appeared pointing down, but John sensed no movement.

He whistled, also self-consciously. He began to search for imaginary lint among the folds of his shirt. He considered his clothes, wondering where they had come from. He'd hardly been attired when he died.

Some kind of uniform?

The door opened, not with the same swoosh and whisper with which it had shut, but with a rasp, like the rattling of chains or a banshee's wail. John's hair stood on end and he was welcomed by the same wrinkled and wizened man he had seen upstairs.

"No, no uniform. We're not formal here in Hades, John?" the old man said. "Quite casual, really. Hi, I'm Nick."

"Right, don't tell me let me guess, Old Nick."

With as much bravado as he could muster, John strolled from

the lift, thumbs looped in his belt. "You really should get that door greased."

"What? You don't like the unholy cacophony?"

The door swept shut with the sound of tormented souls screaming.

"That's the supreme being," the man put his thumb to the side of his nose and made a rude noise, "for you. He insisted on it. Something to set the stage, the mood, if you will."

The man tapped the doors. "The lift was whipped up by the special effects department. God's big on that sort of thing. Special effects. Parting the Red Sea and such like. All theatrics and thunder. No real substance."

John opened his mouth to argue that the parting of the Red Sea was a bona fide miracle and decided against it. Nick halted just outside a second door.

"This space has been specially reserved for you. I don't think you'll be disappointed. It's not at all what you are expecting." He gestured for Ryan to precede him. "After you."

John hung back, reluctant to step inside despite the devil's assurances. Satan, himself, looked innocuous enough, but his words sounded more than ominous. John searched inside his head for a reasonable excuse to prevent taking the final irrevocable step which lead to his own personal hell.

Then John paused to scan the area around him and realized there was no place left to go. The lift, or whatever it was, was gone, and the room — a wall of solid flames — was contracting around them.

And, unlike those burnished in the metal, these flames were real. They were hot. Extremely hot. His skin began to shrivel and his hair to sizzle.

"Uh, thank you?" More a question than a statement, and John scuttled sideways through the door, trying to avoid the devil as he followed the trembling Ryan.

The minute Satan set foot inside the threshold he began to moult and change. His near-human skin split, to reveal glistening scarlet flesh underneath. It sloughed away in great clumps, and his face began to melt. The chin to stretch, the lips to twist up into a leer. While horns sprouted from his scalp.

But John had didn't waste time on the transformation. He'd half-expected it anyway. Instead his eye was trained on the other

154

occupants in the room he had just entered.

Women. All women. Tall ones, short ones. Fat ones, skinny ones. All sizes and shapes — from the willowy waif to luscious plump peaches. Black, white. Blond, brunette. Women to suit every taste, to satiate every wanton lust or desire. Women to fulfil any appetite.

Flabbergasted, John returned his attention to his diabolic escort and recoiled.

The creature was hideous!

"I am only a reflection of what is on your mind right now," Satan said.

Ryan's gaze dropped, and John admired the huge erect penis that throbbed between goat-like legs and cloven hooves. A young girl drifted by, delicate, nubile, her breasts blossoming with the first faint touch of adolescence.

"Oh God." His Adam's apple bounced up and down in his throat. His voice shook, and he cupped his groin protectively.

"I thought you'd like this. Wait a second, there's more."

The boudoir dissolved around them and the next thing he knew they were in a storeroom filled with rows upon rows of bottles. Like its predecessor there was enough variety here to fulfill any fancy or satisfy any palate, and enough booze to keep him and a whole fucking army legless for an eternity.

He moved between the lines and lines of shelves, reading labels. The expensive Moët... The mundane Thunderbird. Scotches, bourbons, real Irish whisky. Ale, bitter, stout and some of that wet urine Americans call beer.

You name it and it was here, somewhere, he was sure.

"Jack Daniels... Chevas Regal..."

"Blimey," he said.

Satan beamed benevolently. "We aim to please," he said.

"I don't get it," John said.

"Get what?" Satan began to shrink and fade.

"This is supposed to be hell. You know, punishment? But I spent a lifetime, chasing woman..."

"And a fine service you did there too, John," Satan said — a cloud of so many shimmering dots.

"I always thought so." John puffed with pride. "But this is hell. It's supposed to be something I hate, isn't it?"

"Is it?"

"I don't know." John scratched his head. "I don't get it."

The dots coalesced into a boiling ball of flame. "You will."

The ball exploded, and John wiped his brow. It was getting pretty hot in here and he was getting thirsty. He licked his lips and rubbed them with the back of his hand. John surveyed the bottles and wondered how he was supposed to get back into the first room.

A door appeared among the shelves.

"Ah," he said. Now that he'd found the entrance, he decided that there was no rush to get to the women. He had all eternity, didn't he? Perhaps he'd sample some of the wares in this room first. The surrounding heat was building a powerful thirst within him.

This wasn't bad. This wasn't bad, at all. He must have done something right. Katie Ryan's boy, John, must be pretty high in the Big Man's favour to deserve this.

John wandered among the shelves, unable to choose what to try first. How about some of the good stuff? He'd never been able to afford anything other than cheap plonk during his lifetime.

He sauntered over to a bottle marked Moët and grinned. He reached out, but before his fingers had grazed the glass, John hesitated.

This had to be some kind of a trick.

His eyes darted back and forth, searching for imps or fiends to brush his hand away or take the bottle from his grasp. Nothing, just rows upon rows of lovely bottles.

No corkscrew. That was it. There was no corkscrew.

A corkscrew appeared.

"Well, I'll be damned," he said.

Someone somewhere laughed. He pulled his hand away. The thirst hit him hard. It felt like someone had stuffed his mouth with cotton.

"The hell with it," John said, and the twitter deepened.

John picked the bottle up.

There was a soft ping, like the shattering of glass, and all the champagne ran in a bubbly, pink stream out of the bottom of bottle. He lifted it to his lips, trying to catch the last drops before they escaped. Too late.

"Son of a bitch."

A guffaw.

"Son of a bitch!" He seized the next bottle, with similar results. A taunting ping and all the precious fluid drained away too quickly for him to partake.

Again!

And again!

He tried one bottle after another. They all had holes in the bottom of them. Or if they didn't have holes before he touched them, they burst as soon as his fingers stroked the glass.

Frantic now, John switched to another set of shelves. The whiskies...

He grabbed some Jack Daniels and the bottom shattered.

"No!" He let the bottle drop. It was replaced upon the shelf with another full one. He clutched at that.

Nothing. Not a sound. He lifted it.

Ping. Tinkle.

And the precious amber fluid cascaded down to the ground. John dropped to his knees, trying to lap up the liquid, but it was immediately absorbed by the spongy floor.

John scrambled to his feet, clenched his fists and lifted them into the air. "NO!"

He raced from one line of shelves to another, indiscriminately lifting bottles. Not a single one survived his touch.

In a fit of pique, he swept a row of bottles from their perches and they rematerialized. He halted, gasping for breath, and stood, arms akimbo, forcing himself to be calm.

"Okay, so no booze, what about the women?"

The door gaped invitingly; he regarded it suspiciously. Then his gaze returned to the bottles. They shimmered, full of false promise and unattainable fluid. Every single one had a hole in the bottom.

"Sweet Jesus, holy Mary mother of God, no!"

The laughing ceased, and John bolted through the door.

Grabbing first one woman and then another, he noticed what his initial swift perusal had missed. They had no mouths. Not a single one. Oh, the woman had lips, but they were drawn on, just for show. There were no holes. John pried at the woman's mouth, trying to expose gap, teeth or tongue. She stared back at him in mute horror.

Ryan hurled her away and plucked a voluptuous red-head from the crowd. His hand dipped to cover the hard mound of pubic hair. His fingers probed between the woman's legs to find more of the same.

More hair, more flesh, more bone, and no hole... anywhere.

CHEAP SHOTS

"And here's a picture of Allan standing on the edge of Grand Canyon... oops... no, I'm sorry, that's my thumb. The next one's... uh... Yes, yes, that's right. There's Allan again. That's... out of focus."

She fiddled with the projector. "That's the donkey I rode all the way down to the bottom. Blasted beast, my bum hurts just thinking about it.

"Oh, yes, here's my cousin Edna next to a fruit stand, and look at that view..." The woman dug an elbow into his rib.

Andy Earl winced. He saw nothing but sky.

"And this one is... upside down. Sorry."

He never should have accepted the offer to do that series on nature photography. He had no business being in Africa. It sounded all very romantic, but when you're running for your life from 300 pounds of overgrown cat, it lost a lot of its appeal.

Killed by a pride of lions. Andy understood the term now. The animals had looked inordinately pleased with themselves as they munched his goolies for an entrée and his arse for a main course.

The crew had been no help. They had filmed his demise for posterity. He knew he had posterity and he could watch the video anytime he wanted. Andy preferred the slide show.

"Okay, that's fixed. This next one is... upside down also. 'Scuse me," she trilled. "Won't take a moment."

Earl shifted away from her and prayed for this torture to stop. The metal chair beneath him began to heat up. He smelt sulphur, and burning cloth. He stopped praying. It did no good. He tried to leap up from his seat. It stuck to him.

"There, that's got it. Well, let's see what's next? Better be good after all that, eh?"

He shot her a withering look; she was oblivious.

"Heh, heh. My thumb again, I need one of those big long lenses like you have, Andy. Of course, I'm not the photographer you are. I try. I watched all your shows, though. Never could get the hang of it, but," she brightened, "slides are just for fun. They don't have to be good. I take `em all the time.

"Here's another one. Now what's that shot doing here? It's from the cruise. QEII. See that dot there." The shadow of a finger stabbed at a smudge, dead centre, in a sea of blue. "That's a seal."

Another image flashed on the screen. "Now what have we got here? Let's see," his hostess mused, fingers in her mouth. "This is, this is, I don't know what this is. No matter, I may have bungled a few, but don't you worry, I've got thousands of them."

She twittered. "Millions of them I shot some twenty-seven rolls of film on this trip alone. Wait'll you see all the pictures I got on the QEII..."

WHAT THE DICKENS

Charles John Huffam Dickens stopped in front of the mirror and examined his neckcloth minutely, looking for flaws in the compact artistry of its many folds. He fiddled with it, rearranging the pleats yet again. Then Dickens gave the points of his waistcoat a tug to ensure they jutted out from under the broadcloth cutaway at the proper angle. He performed a similar ritual with the creases of his trousers, giving them a twitch to make sure they were straight. He completed the effect by grasping his lapel and striking a scholarly pose which allowed him to look down his nose at his editor.

Then he clasped his hands behind his back and paced some more. His editor was late. Late beyond all sense of decency and propriety even for those for whom lateness was the fashion, and his editor was not such a man. Dickens appraised his reflection in the mirror.

The man was late even for somebody who may be in the midst of contract negotiation. Then tardiness was a weapon, meant to put one's opponent on the defensive, intended to intimidate as well as inconvenience. The author was not amused.

At least Dickens thought he'd been called into discuss fees, money or some such thing, but he wasn't completely sure. Come to think of it, he wasn't completely sure he had an appointment with his editor.

Dickens pulled his watch from his pocket and frowned. His gaze flicked nervously to the clock face and he pondered the bizarre arrangement of twelves that went around the circumference of the clock. The timepiece itself peeked from the belly of a sculpture depicting overripe womanhood, a naked crone. The body was bent, the legs bowed, the belly and breasts drooped. The latter swung pendulously. The hag's face twisted in terror. Her skin was creased, and its folds had all the complexity of his neckerchief, with none of its artistry. She was bronze, but she was engulfed in gilt flames. The timepiece was grotesque. Dickens shivered. He didn't particularly relish the idea of a clock that always read midnight.

Or noon, he reminded himself. His eyes slid up from the clock face to the sagging breasts.

Midnight, definitely, midnight.

This was not his editor's office. It could not be. He would remember that clock. His publisher's offices — the one Dickens remembered, or thought he remembered — had housed a single large room filled to overflowing and made dark and dusty thereby. It had been almost completely furnished with books. They lined each wall, and they formed a wall between editor and assistant. They were piled in precarious stacks here and there on the floor and stacked in front of the desk. Magazines covered every available work surface, spilling from the table tops.

The clang and clatter of London traffic echoed faintly throughout the office — muffled, but not muted, by the insulation of books and outside wall. The street beyond resounded with the cries of vendors, the clop of hooves, the jangle of harness and the rattle of wagons and carriages. In other words, all the typical sounds one normally found in the teeming city.

But this office was quiet. Dead quiet. He could hear the swish of his trousers and dull thud of his feet despite the thick carpeting. He could hear the beating of his heart as his disquiet rose.

And the office itself was no office Dickens had ever seen before. Nor imagined in his wildest dreams. There wasn't a single memento or knack knacks one would expect to find. The stand of pipes with its array of ashes and tobacco. No indicator of the character of its possessor. No silver framed pictures, with the family sitting stiff and rigid in front of a camera. The sole ornament was the clock, with its belly of glass and twelve radiant twelves.

It went beyond Spartan; it was sterile. Barren, without life or personality. The lines too straight, too harsh. Without adornment or embellishment.

Although it was elegantly appointed, after a fashion. A strange sort of opulence oozed from every fixture. The carpet was plush, thicker than the most luxurious Oriental rug. Yet it was devoid of pattern, flowers or any of the flowing fantastical curlicues that one commonly found on the carpets from the East. The rug was red, a conventional enough colour, but this was a strident scarlet. The hue harsh, glaring. Not the normal deep maroon that cooled the eye and soothed the spirit, but something left one feeling agitated and aggrieved.

The furniture was obviously expensive. The chairs made of some fine-grain, if unrecognisable, wood. Like the room, they were Spartan. The backs went straight up and down, with none of the lovely rococo carving so much the rage nowadays. They looked uncomfortable.

The room itself was dominated by the desk. It was immense, huge. Impractically so. In fact, as a functional piece of furniture, the desk was most unsuitable. Sitting at one end, it was unlikely that any but a chimpanzee could reach an item at the other, and it was made of glass, smoky glass.

Dickens would have been afraid to work at such a desk or to put anything on it, and it would appear that its owner felt the same. Not a single slip of paper, book or note marred its pristine surface. None of the usual accumulated clutter Dickens normally associated with his editor or with his desk. No pens or pencils, only a single box made of some bizarre substance Dickens didn't recognise.

Neither wood nor metal, the box was warm to the touch like wood, but had neither grain nor none of wood's suppleness and pliancy. Rather it was brittle, like metal, but with none of its frost. When Dickens pressed a thumbnail into the box as hard as he could, it took neither imprint nor scratch. And it hummed.

Someone had taken the trouble to hang pictures. The artwork, if one could call it that, was representative of nothing. Simply broad swathes of colour and splashes of pigment, as though someone had taken paint and thrown it at a canvas. Dickens could do better than this, and he was no painter. The pictures did not even depict recognisable geometric shapes. They had no pattern, no rhyme nor reason. The paintings did not enhance the room, only emphasised the abominable taste of the unseen owner. Here as elsewhere, the colours seemed to be chosen in such a way so that moving about the office, they clashed with each other, and with the room itself. The only painting that came close to being illustrative of something hung above the empty desk and even that was peculiar.

Dickens wandered around the desk. The canvas was split into two squares, one white, one black. That was it. A single rectangle, half black, half white. It had neither flower nor stray feathering of line or brush. Nothing. Not even a signature. And Dickens wondered who would be so foolish to waste his time painting this.

Neither were there any visible lamps. No hiss of gas, no flicker of flame. Dickens contemplated the ceiling which provided the only source of ghostly illumination. It glowed with a pale blue-white light that bleached his reflection of all colour.

What sort of heathen place was this?

Dickens was sure he had an appointment. He was sure it was here — wherever here was — or he thought he was sure. At this point things got really fuddled because Dickens wasn't sure of anything any more. He couldn't recollect an address. Neither could he resurrect one — from any one of his pockets no matter how many times he searched them — to confirm his recall or, more appropriately, its lack.

Worse, Dickens could not even check the number on the entrance to see if it might jig some memory, for when he tried to walk through the door, he'd discovered that it was locked.

The author began to fuss at this clothes again, unwilling to look at the holes in his recall, like wool attacked by summer's moths. His agitation was understandable, for nothing in this situation could bear too close scrutiny. Could Dickens be blamed if he chose not to examine the fragile fabric of his memory?

"Ah, Chuck." A voice rang out behind him, brash, brassy, and clangourous. "Sit, Chuck, old boy, sit."

The accent was decidedly American, which explained the voice. In no particular hurry after having been kept waiting for so long, Charles John Huffam Dickens pivoted stiffly on his heel and stopped.

Dickens' eyes grew round and large, his mouth gaped. The unknown editor was, if possible, even more garish than his office. His suit was made of some kind of shiny material. Pink, so bright that even the most hardened harlot in Piccadilly would be ashamed to wear it. Broad stripes of a radiant green, orange and yellow ran down the sleeve and rumpled trouser leg. The collar was non-existent. The gathered cuffs around wrist and ankle were black.

The man's face was flushed, almost as pink as his garb. His black hair was slicked back with too much wax and his goatee sharpened almost to a point.

"Sorry I'm late, Chuck. I've been running. Must keep fit, you know."

The strange man patted a flat torso, and Dickens pondered the action. If the gentleman referred to his attire, then he was sadly mistaken. The suit fitted him like a sack.

The editor flopped into his chair and kicked his feet on his desk.

"Well, Chuck, I bet you're wondering why I called you here."

"Charles. My name is Charles, not..." he gave his most disdainful sniff, "Chuck."

"Huh? Oh yes, right," the editor said. "Let's get down to business, why don't we, Chuck. Have a seat."

Dickens opened his mouth to correct the editor again, as the man motioned the author toward a chair.

With a huff, Dickens swept his tails to either side and sat as instructed, totally nonplussed. The chair was as uncomfortable as it looked, despite the fat cushions. Horsehair protruded through the cloth as stiff and unyielding as the upright back. More like prickers or cockleburs, they penetrated the trousers leg, making him itch.

"Look, Chuck, we're gonna have to do a little work on this." The editor opened a drawer that couldn't possibly exist in the smokily transparent desk, extracted a dog-eared manuscript and threw it down. It skidded across the broad expanse of the desk and shivered to a halt before the author.

Dickens glanced at the first page.

A Christmas Carol

"I'm sorry, Chuck, I know you're a big name and all, but I'm afraid it's a bit trite. Out of date. Behind the times." The editor flipped through the pages and shook his head.

"And how many time do I have to tell you, Chuck? We want 'em typed. Double spaced. One inch margins. SAE. That sort of thing. You're lucky you are a name, or you'd never get away with it. Look at the condition of this manuscript. Cross outs, things written in the margin. The typesetters are gonna go nuts trying to interpret this."

Dickens managed to look affronted.

The editor didn't notice. Instead, he leaned forward eagerly. "Mind you, Chuck, I'm not saying it's gonna need a lot of work.

Just a tweak here and there to make it more marketable. You know what I mean."

"No, I can't say that I do," Dickens said.

"It's got no sizzle, no pizazz."

"Pah what?"

"Pizazz."

Dickens gave him a blank stare.

"Pizazz, you know. Dazzle, flash. Style," he snapped his fingers impatiently at the author. "Come on, get with it."

"My good man, I can't understand a word you're saying much less get with it."

The editor removed his feet from the desktop and leaned forward. "You want to go through it point by point?"

"Actually," Dickens said archly, "I've got another appointment."

The slick smile dropped from the editor's face.

"No, you don't," he growled, "there are no other appointments here." He pointed at the clock. The sneer slid across his features again. "Besides, I told I'd meet you at twelve, and twelve it is."

Dickens winced as the editor settled back in his chair.

"First, let's discuss the overall aspects. It's dull, boring. I'm afraid we've gotta spice it up a bit. I'm talking sex, violence, blood, guts, gore. Do you realise that there isn't a single erotic scene in this entire book? We need a little of the ol' bump and grind. How about making Scrooge a paedophiliac, maybe a couple of lurid scenes with him molesting what-his-name? You know the cripple." He opened the book and poured over the text. "Tiny Tim. Yeah, that's it. Let's have Scrooge bugger the kid. Great pathos and child abuse is all very topical now."

"You mean sodomy?" Dickens blushed crimson. "This is an outrage!"

"Now how do you expect to sell without sex? Okay, so no buggery. How about something a little more mundane? Something..." he paused for effect, "autobiographical, for instance? Like having Crotchet send his wife away so he can carry on an affair with some heartless hussy."

"Sir!"

"Don't like that idea, huh? Well, it makes good reading and don't forget it got you where you are today. Let's face it all your books are autobiographical in some way, ask any lit professor."

The author crossed his arms.

"Okay, forget the autobiographical crap. Just heat it up. I want lust; I want passion; I want sweat and semen oozing out of every page. Of you don't want Crotchet..."

"Cratchet."

"... to have an affair, then how about having his nephew visiting a few whores on the way home? It's Christmas; people get a little enthused with Christmas spirits, and then they can't be held accountable for their action."

"If I refuse?"

"You ought to know by now, you can't refuse. Even Stephen King, one of my best authors, has to be negotiable sometimes."

"Stephen who?"

The editor peered at the discomfited author over steepled fingers. "The language is tedious. Pedantic. Look at the length of this sentence. Don't forget the stats..."

"Stats?"

"Statistics, marketing statistics. Your average reader is fifteen years old, and in a day and age when over twenty percent of all students leave school functionally illiterate... Well, I don't have to tell what sort of vocabulary they have. Think stupid. That's the ticket. Stupid."

"Which words did you find too difficult?" the author said disparagingly, but the editor continued.

"Yes, and blood. Lots of blood. You've got a couple of good arguments in here, with Scrooge telling the do-gooders just what they can do with their charitable institutions, and I love allegorical images of Ignorance and Want. Is it Ignorance and Want?" The editor began shuffling through the pages again. "Whatever, it doesn't matter. The point is those are really nice touches. I love the ghost of Christmas Future. We need more of that And violence. A gun fight, a fist fight, a chase scene. Something."

The editor tapped the manuscript with a gnarled forefinger. "There's no action! Don't just have Scrooge quibble with the men and shout Humbug. What the hell is humbug anyway. Let's have the old man trounce the philanthropists out of the office. Have Scrooge beat 'em up. Do a real kung-fu number on them. Or karate would be good."

"Do you actually mean that you want my Scrooge to participate in pugilism? I'm sorry that wouldn't fit the character. He may be a miser but he's too much of a gentleman, too dignified, for that."

"Ah, yes, Chuck, and that was something else I wanted to discuss with you. Why does Scrooge have to be so old? We've gotta be thinking movie rights here.

"I see Sylvester Stallone playing the part. Instant box office hit, Stallone. Or maybe Clint Eastwood. I can just see him standing there in the gloomy office, lots of smoke, with a submachine gun in his hands telling those fucking, bleeding-heart liberals: 'Christmas? Make my day.'"

"Pardon?"

"Of course, that will never work if Scrooge is some doddering little old man. So you'll have to fix it."

"Excuse me the whole theme of the book is about a man — grown old, but not wise — given his last chance at redemption."

"Redemption? Well, we'll talk about that later," the editor said as he stared myopically at the notes that had miraculously appeared before him. He scowled. "That's number thirteen on the list."

"Thirteen?" Dickens squawked.

"And cut the Father Christmas crap. Nobody believes in Santa Claus any more. This whole spirit-of-Christmas thing is schmaltz. It's gotta go."

"What?"

"We just can't sell it any more. No holiday is more cursed than Christmas. It's just a royal pain in the old' wahzoo for most people."

"I don't know what a wahzoo is, sir, but if you are saying that people don't treat Christmas with the same tradition and respect..." Dickens faltered. "Well, that is the entire point of the book, isn't it?"

"Too bad, it's gotta go."

Dickens rose abruptly from his seat. "I will not sit here and listen to this. You are not the only publisher in the world. I'm sure I can find someone else that's interested."

"SIT DOWN!" The eyes behind the spectacles flashed at Dickens; the order was barked so loud that his ears rung, and forgetting his indignation, Dickens dropped back into the chair.

"Come on, this is the twentieth century," the editor crooned, "nobody believes in that sort of hocus pocus any more. Good fairies, and that kind of shit. Spirit of Christmas, my ass. Showing people the error of their ways. Be real. Your audience is much more, uh, sophisticated than that."

"Twentieth century?" The words were murmured, and Dickens's eyes glazed as he finally recollected where he was, where he had been for more than a century, and where he would be for the rest of his days, if the term applied. Eternity stretched dark and bleak before him as the voice droned on and on and on.

"Now, Chuck, about this concept of redemption..."

*

Dickens's head still rang with the clamour of his criticism.

"Now, Chuck, I'll leave you here to rewrite on it." He moved over to the box, touched it and it began to hum and glow. "Type it up while you're at it. You can use the computer."

Dickens gaped at the device. Then the editor flicked another switch.

Dickens stopped him. "Was it so bad?"

"What do you mean? How can you ask when you've condemned humanity to this?"

One of the blank walls burst into a montage of colour. The wall itself was divided into several different squares. Each contained a miraculous image that danced and moved, like a tintypes brought to life.

"And now, lest we forget our goal, for the ghost of Christmases yet to come."

Large print scrolled into the centre of each square.

"Scrooge," one said, "based on a story by Charles Dickens."

"Christmas Carol," said another while yet another identified itself as being: "A Muppets' Christmas Carol."

"What in heaven's name was a Muppet?" said Dickens, but his editor was gone.

WHEN HELL FREEZES OVER

John Ryan leaned back and surveyed his domain. For that's what it was, his own private domain. All his. Uniquely his. Oh, the bottles in storage may just be for show, but John could imagine still. He could remember what alcohol tasted like, what it was like to have his thirst slaked, and that was almost as good. At least, you didn't get a hangover that way.

And the women?

With a grunt, he pushed the full-figured brunette off his lap, where she was attempting to enervate his inert plonker with lively hands and an eager expression.

It didn't move. It wasn't fooled by this fake feminine form.

Saint Cyrus, or whatever the fuck his name was, had been right. Satan could get quite inventive. Ryan snorted.

But it could have been worse. The bloke upstairs, at what John Ryan not-so-affectionately called immolation, had been right about that too. Things could have been a lot worse.

All things considered, things had worked out pretty damned well. The women were his. All his. He shared them with no man. They came at his beck and call. They may be... well... flawed — and John tried not to stare at the mouthless lips of the brunette who was grovelling at his feet, her hands extended imploringly. Even this apparent disadvantage had less obvious advantages. They never nagged.

And they looked good.

What Cyrus hadn't mentioned, perhaps hadn't even considered, was that Satan couldn't be at all places at all times. He set you up in your own little corner of Hell and let you get on with the business of suffering whatever your fate decreed.

The bottles may have holes in them and the woman may not, but if a man had imagination, if a man was inventive...

John chuckled, snapped his fingers at a lovely dark-skinned beauty and folded his arms across his chest. The raven haired matron crept away on all fours as the nubile youth picked up where her predecessor left off.

There were other things than vaginas. Other things besides

mouths and tongues. Although those would have been nice. Still, there were other clefts. Between breasts, buttocks and thighs. There were hands. Warm folds between arm and flank.

Satan had really slipped up this time. John was actually enjoying himself, and he sunk lower in his chair as the girl thrust his throbbing penis between melon breasts and squeezed tightly.

Ryan had done pretty well for himself. He'd managed to pull a fast one on Old Nick, and he wondered if any other man in Hell would be able to make the same claim.

When hell freezes over, John thought, and the dark chill of premonition rippled up and down his spine as he ejaculated.

BAD MEDICINE

The incessant beep of the IVAC, the bubble of oxygen, and the thud-whoosh-whisper of a respirator penetrated the fog of consciousness. The subtle murmur of the staff was broken by the intermittent bray of laughter. In other words, he was surrounded by the all too familiar sounds of the hospital.

And something that was not so familiar in this environment, the physician was flat on his back. Not that doctors never layed down — despite the common belief that they reposed dangling by their feet from the rafters — but no physician in his right mind ever lay down in a hospital bed. Not unless they had no other alternative.

I won't open my eyes, he thought, maybe if I don't open my eyes and pretend I'm somewhere else, it'll go away.

It didn't. He could hear the rustle of stiff cloth against rubberised sheets and the liquid dribble of someone relieving himself into a urinal. That called to attention the fact that his bladder was filled near to bursting and his nose itched.

"Dr Trotman? Dr. Trotman?"

The doctor recognised the less than dulcet tones of the duty nurse. Oh, God, now I've had it.

"Dr. Trotman? Wakies, wakies, Dr. Trotman?"

How come they always sound so bloody cheerful all the time? So sweet. When you knew, you knew, the sister probably had all the personality of a pit viper and looked like something that had just crawled from the Black Lagoon.

"Wake up, Dr. Trotman, it's breakfast time."

Oh, please God, not another low-sodium, low cholesterol, pseudo-egg and soy-bacon fry-up.

"I'm must say the kitchen has outdone itself to day."

He whimpered. He was in trouble.

"Come now, Dr. Trotman, I know you're awake. Rise and shine. We haven't got all day."

You got some place else to go? he thought. And like any five-year-old child, he kept his eyes tightly shut, his jaw clenched. He wouldn't speak. He wouldn't stir. Maybe she'd just go away.

"Now, doctor, you know if you don't co-operate, I'll have to force feed you."

Two rough hands grabbed him and wrenched him into a sitting position. He gave up and opened his eyes.

"Ah, so you are awake. I thought so. How are we doing today?" she said with a too jovial voice.

"Got a frog in your pocket?" Trotman snapped.

"Still haven't lost that lovely sense of humour, have we? Give it time, we'll get rid of it. Perhaps we can have it surgically removed." The voice was still pleasant, but the bright yellow eyes sparkled a brilliant orange and the cat-like pupils constricted into slits.

The world swam into focus, and he wished fervently that it hadn't. The sister placed the tray on the over-bed table. He glanced down.

Liquidised! Good grief. His breakfast consisted of green slimy stuff, brown slimy stuff and something that looked suspiciously like the recycled remains of someone's emesis basin. Only the complex jumble of tubes — IV, piggy back and monitor cables — that kept him strapped to his bed prevented him from throwing it back in her face.

The nurse shambled around the room, prattling about inconsequentials, picking up this bit and that bit, rearranging everything for no particular purpose.

"My, isn't it a nice day... lovely weather we're having..."

It was a lie. All of it. It wasn't a nice day. There wasn't anything nice about it. And there wasn't any bleeding weather, not down here.

Neither was Trotman fooled by the jollity. It was all a trick — the running monologue just the kind of thing health professionals did to put you off your guard.

The doctor closed his eyes to shut out the image of this morning's fodder and let the chatter roll over him.

"Dr Trotman! You haven't touched your food."

He opened a single eye to peer at her and asked, "Would you?"

"Doctor, you of all people should know the importance of nutrition..."

A bald-faced lie. He'd been a bloody MD and not some goddamn nutritionalist. Besides, he didn't see what this swill had to do with nourishment.

"Come on, this is chuck roast. Chuck died."

"What!"

"Just a little kitchen humour."

She glared at him and continued to glower until he took a bite of the glop. It actually tasted worse than it looked, if that was possible. He waited until the nurse's back was turned and scraped the meal into the bedpan.

He eyed it speculatively. It looked just about the same. He was just sparing the middle man, that's all.

"... paging Dr Who..."

Doctor who?

"... Dr Who, please report to the operating theatre..."

WHINE! The hall echoed with the sharp shriek of electronic feedback.

The rattle of curtain rings alerted Trotman to another presence within the small cubicle.

The consultant, thank God! An intelligent life-form. Maybe now he could get someone to listen to him. Dr Ian Trotman pushed the over-bed table away, eyes alight and full of hope until they settled upon the doctor.

No, not a chance; Trotman had forgotten where he was.

The consultant wore the blood red coat that seemed to be standard issue around here. A lot more practical really than white, it didn't show the stains.

"Watch the tail," the consultant murmured as the overeager nurse nearly trod on it. Turning to Trotman, he said — as if he cared: "So how are we today?"

Trotman knew what he was supposed to say, but his mouth formed the words of his protest before his teeth could clamp down on his disobedient tongue. "I tell you, there's nothing wrong with me. You can release me."

The consultant chortled. "Unlikely."

"Why won't you listen to me?

"Not my job. You know that."

"But –" Trotman couldn't argue the point. After a while, a doctor learned to turn a deaf ear to people's gripes and a blind eye to their pain. All patients started to look and sound the same. The young and the old became one amorphous, androgynous face with an expression which is either surly or suffering —

depending on how long they've been kept in the waiting room. And all voices became a single strident voice — individual complaints just so much background noise. While human flesh became meat to be poked and prodded.

You started out in a caring profession because you cared, and you ended up so you couldn't care less.

The consultant pulled the nurse aside for a conference. Their heads tilted conspiratorially toward each other, and they whispered. Trotman began to quake in his sheets, wondering what sort of deviltry they would come up with today.

"Very good, sir," she said.

With a swish of snaking tail, the consultant clattered back into the ward.

The nurse smacked her lips. "Well, Dr Trotman, it would appear we have a busy day ahead of us today. The consultant has ordered some tests."

"Wonderful!"

"And a gastric lavage." She held up a tube the size of a fire hose.

"What? I just ate. You just forced that, that –" words failed him "– stuff down my throat."

"Oh, but this will be much more fun."

Trotman struggled to get out of bed, but she pinned him against the mattress. "What clinical purpose can that possibly serve?"

The reptilian face scowled. "He's also ordered a high-colonic." She snapped her fingers — at least Trotman thought it was a she; it was a little hard to tell down here — and an enema bucket materialised in her outstretched hand.

"And after that," she checked the notes, "a bleed." She tapped the jar of leeches in her pocket.

"I tell you I'm okay. I'm healthy."

"Who are you to judge?" she said.

"I'm a goddamn doctor is what I am."

"Not in here, you're not. You're just a patient."

They said that doctors make the worst patients, and Trotman had to admit that that was true. Doctors had no illusions about their profession. They knew what was going on, and they knew the staff were only human — Trotman cast a sidelong glance at the nurse — or almost. All he saw was her rump.

175

A doctor knew, when looking into the bleary eyes of the resident physician, that they were watering, not because of care and concern, but because, he'd had too little sleep the night before. Or worse, too much to drink. Because sleep like everything else requires time and doctors got little enough of that. So on those rare nights off a doctor felt almost obliged to make up for lost time — drinking himself, or herself as the case may be — into an oblivion of forgetfulness.

"Look, I want to talk to someone in charge here."

She wagged her great horned head. "No, you don't. Trust me."

Trotman considered her for a moment and decided she was probably right he didn't want to talk to someone from the top.

"We want you all cleaned out for surgery," she explained. She grinned. "Right on down the line, if you get my meaning."

"Couldn't I just fast for a few days?" he squawked.

"What and miss lunch?" She picked up the bedpan. "Well, well. This looks familiar." She stared at the doctor. "Tomorrow's breakfast, perhaps."

He couldn't meet her gaze. "What sort of surgery?"

"An amputation." She took a swipe at the stub of his arm.

He groaned, although he shouldn't have been surprised. He'd been an orthopaedic surgeon and what could possibly be a greater loss?

The limb always grew back until they decided to hack it off again.

"Ah-hem, Dr. Trotman, it's time for your bed bath."

NO! It was too much.

He squeezed his eyes shut tight, and counted to ten. How many times had he witnessed a patient's discomfiture at this procedure and simply ignored it? After all, the nurse did the dirty deed while the physician buggered off somewhere to some budgetary meeting or some-such.

"Fill this up with ice water for the good doctor here."

Trotman heard the scuff of paper slippers and hazarded a peek at... human feet! He looked up in time to see a woman with stiff blond hair turn her back to him. She wore a typical hospital gown with the split up the middle.

Even from behind, he could see her glance between the bath basin in one hand and the enema bucket in the other, as if in a quandary over which appliance the nurse had meant her to fill.

"The bucket, you cretin," the sister said, "you can re-use the water for the bath."

"Sweet Jesus." Trotman felt faint.

The nurse turned on him.

"What did you say? Haven't I told you you're not supposed to use foul language in here?"

But his eye was trained upon the woman, obviously a fellow patient, as she bent over the taps. Her bottom was laid bare for all to see, but she seemed too old or too tired to care. Her buttocks were wrinkled with age. He swallowed feeling slightly ill.

Then it happened. The Velcro tabs that held the gown together at the back of the neck and the base of the spine vanished. They must've, for the gown fell from her shoulders, revealing a one-quarter view of sagging stomach and breasts.

The doctor felt his own gown. The tabs were missing from there too.

"Hurry up!" the nurse snapped. "Give him the back rub first, the enema next. What the hell, you know the routine by now."

And before Trotman knew what was happening, the sister had picked him up, flipping him over as if he had no more weight than a pancake, and slammed him back down on the bed.

"Then we have some bedpans for you to clean," the sister informed the woman. "After that, we'll see what else we can dredge up for you to do."

The nurse stomped from the cubicle. Someone, the woman he presumed, slapped him on the rump. Hard!

"Ow!"

"Shut up." Her hands were cold as ice and her touch was anything but gentle.

"What're you doing here?"

"You have to ask?"

He cocked his head, the voice sounded vaguely familiar.

"Lie still," said she, shoving him hard against the pillows.

"I mean what are you in for? What's your diagnosis?"

"Terminal apathy, or so they tell me." The woman squirted her hands with lotion that was, he discovered when it touched his back, even colder than ice.

"Sounds like the type of thing they'd come up with here.

177

You're lucky; you've at least got one. I've been here for years..."

"What did you expect considering the nature of the place?"

Trotman ruminated on this and could find no suitable response. He changed the topic.

"It's not fair," he groused. "If I had only known this was going to happen, I might have chosen a different occupation. Never in my wildest dreams did I think my reward would be this, an eternity of cold baths, low-sodium diets and superfluous surgical procedures. I wasn't a bad doctor. Not top notch maybe, but not bad. All in all, I'd say I was better than most. I never passed out pills indiscriminately. I never did an unnecessary surgery, like they do in the States. Cadillac payment due — whoops! 'Excuse me, Mrs Smith, I think we ought to take out that nasty old gall bladder. You don't need it anyway.' I never did that."

"Looks like you missed a financial opportunity."

"Huh?" Then, sure he had misunderstood, he persisted. "Mind you, there was that hip replacement, something of a bodge-job, but I did the second operation for free, even paying for the operating theatre and the anaesthesiologist's fees out of my own pocket. It didn't cost the patient or the NHS a thing."

"What do you expect, applause?" She punched his shoulder.

He began flopping around the bed trying to get a look at her. "Who the hell are you? You make the sister seem like the angel of goodness and light."

"Nix to the former." She dug a bony knee into his spine. "But you got the latter about right."

Angry now, Trotman gave a mighty heave, throwing her off. She sprawled on the floor just under his face, and he stared at a well-known visage.

"But you're — "

The grand dame got up and dusted herself off.

" — Margaret Thatcher."

"So? What of it?" She fondled the tube in her hand almost lovingly. "You know, I get really sick of you doctors, always whinging and moaning and carrying on. First there, now here. As if you had something to complain about." She rammed the tube home. "Welcome to the new NHS."

WRONG NUMBER

"... drugs..."

Miles Arden sat up at the word. This was quickly succeeded by the static and clicks of a satellite relay as the computer locked onto a key word and began to play the conversation back to him.

There was an answering mumble of acknowledgement, and then the woman's reply: "Yes, mom, can you believe it? The doctor changed my prescription again... no, no diagnosis yet."

Miles Arden kicked his feet up on his desk, folded his arms across his chest and sputtered. He couldn't believe it would come to this. He was eavesdropping on some middle-aged housewife talking to her mother.

Protecting Queen and country from subversive nans. Bloody ridiculous.

Normally, it was a thought that would have amused him, but not today, not when he was so bored. Arden glowered at the equipment. It must be malfunctioning. It wasn't supposed to patch through calls like this. He pressed the button to silence the call and the callers, but the machine persisted stubbornly in recording the conversation. After all, the woman had used one of the 'magic words', drugs.

The voice droned on. "Little Jimmy's fine."

"Wonderful," he mouthed the word.

Somehow when he'd joined the security section of the Home Office, he'd expected something more glamorous than this. Not that he cherished any delusions that operatives lived like James Bond. With more people riding desks than in the field, you could forget fancy cars — spitting oil and armed with laser beams. If you were lucky you ended up with some dumpy little Montego, specifically designed to go from A to Z unnoticed. No flash gadgets or gizmos. Hell, they'd just mastered the art of putting plugs on appliances.

Neither were there bevies of beautiful women at his beck and call. No steamy blonds, only muggy hotel rooms. In fact, women seemed to be in short supply, and the few he ran into were of the type you wouldn't pause to give a second glance, but then it was a job where the greatest asset was remaining nondescript.

His training had been about what you'd expect. He'd received instruction in the martial arts (damned little of it); small weapons (preferably those that made little or no sound, the garrotte or the knife); and firearms (all kinds) — along with the correct handling of explosives, particularly syntax. Enough to convince a person of the potentially lethal nature of the job.

Then there was cryptology, along with the more mundane internal rules and procedures. Lessons on the proper papers and protocols for everything from filing a field report to obtaining a motor pool chit. At the end of it all, you were a finely greased machine who snapped to attention on cue and always spoke in code.

Disillusionment came at the end of the orientation when you found yourself working as a glorified clerk in some anonymous office at the MOD. After all, someone had to do it, why not the new recruit? Generally speaking you spent more time shuffling through T 04s than anything else. Eventually you realised that advancement depended more on wearing the right tie than on skill. If you knew the right people, you might make it out of the stifling confines of the office. You might, you just might, get to fill in your first 4L 00 field report.

If Agent Arden's own experiences were to be the judge, the halls of the Ministry were strewn with the corpses of shattered careers, splintered dreams and men broken by the sheer weight of the paperwork.

Unless you were a total git, though, you ultimately made it into the field where the rest of your illusions were crushed and ambitions thwarted. Where you discovered you were as often as not acting as decoy — carrying an empty brief to your next assignation with the ducks of Hyde Park rather than the vital documents you thought you possessed. Subterfuge layered upon subterfuge upon subterfuge. But that was the name of the game, wasn't it?

Until you got shot protecting useless documents or still worse blank pages, like the pages of your life. Because once you signed on, you ceased to exist for all practical purposes. You never really knew if you had the real thing or you were just one of many blinds.

Then the Cold War warmed, or perhaps melted would be a

better term. In other words, it fizzled out. The Berlin Wall fell while the Krauts got soused, and ancient animosities were drowned under a deluge of placatory words and media coverage. The traditional adversary dissipated like the London fog. Even the less traditional ones became undecided, as Jordan signed peace treaties with Israel and Israel with Palestine. Now the IRA were taking a sabbatical. People were declaring peace all over the place. It was disgusting, really.

After decades in his post, job security became a thing of the past and you were given a choice: Go to the GCHQ monitoring centre or find yourself another position.

Didn't find many ex-agents queuing up for the unemployment benefit.

He could see the interview now. Previous employment? Decoy... "I'm afraid we don't have many openings here right now. Have you tried Libya?"

All he got for years of service was his scar — he fingered the hard knob on his temple where a bullet had grazed his brain — and this.

"Well, mom, I guess that's about it for now. My love to Auntie Edith."

Not many openings for a spy when you come and think about it. Disappointing to think that monitoring overseas calls at GCHQ was the best he could do after all his years of loyal service. Miles sighed as the recording automatically cut off at the sound of disconnect.

Enough. It was time to eat. He plugged into an outside line and dialled a number.

"Tombstone Pizza,"

In olden days when telephones had had proper receivers, he would have pulled the handset away from his ear and looked at it, unsure of what he'd heard. Instead, he chewed on his lip and wondered when they'd franchised.

"I'd like to order a pizza. Something, ah," he thought for a bit, "hot and spicy."

There was a click.

"Hello, welcome to Tombstone Pizza's telephone system. I'm afraid we are not able to take your call right now. All our lines are busy at the moment, but you have been put in a queue. Do not hang up or you will lose your place. Rest assured, though, if you just stay on the line one of our sanitised nurse-operators will be with you momentarily."

And the bland tones of canned Muzak burst into his earphone playing an insipid, instrumentalised version of 'Devil with the Blue Dress'.

Again Miles regretted the days of old fashioned telephones, instead of having this thing attached to his scalp. It would have afforded him the pleasure of slamming the phone down into the cradle. He settled for swearing vehemently.

"Hello," a voice crackled.

"Yes, great," he rubbed his hands together. "I'd like to order..."

The voice continued as if he hadn't spoken. "Welcome to Tombstone's new computerised ordering system."

Oh no, since when had pizza gone computer?

"If you would like to order something, press 'star'. If you would like to register a complaint, depress the disconnect and try again."

Miles pressed star.

"Our special this week Doner Kebab. The doner of the week is Bob, unless you prefer the ever popular ground Chuck."

"What!"

"Or you could try our rump roast. If you'd like one of our specials, press the hash sign. If you want to go directly to menu, press 0."

Arden pressed 0.

"Each pizza is listed by name followed by a short description and an alpha-numeric identification code. Press the appropriate alpha or numeric designation when you get to the pizza of your choice. If you would like to create your own press one to get out of this menu."

Thereafter he listened to an inventory of garbled names and even more garbled numerical designations. The selections came at him so fast and furious that he had not assimilated the information about each pizza, much less heard the number, before they moved on to the next option.

This went on for several minutes when the computer informed him, "You have not pressed a number. If you would like to hear the menu over again, press two. If you would like to create your own pizza press one."

Miles dawdled. Did he really want to hear the list again? It was unlikely that it would be any more comprehensible this time. He dithered too long.

"I'm sorry, you have made too many errors entering this system. Please try again some other time."

A few jejune chords of Devil with the Blue Dress drifted over the line before his was disconnected.

He dialled again and took his place in the queue. The musical selection had changed to Sympathy for the Devil played by — he looked perplexed — of all things, The Vienna Boy's Choir. He found himself humming along with the tune, even singing part of the chorus... "won't you guess my name."

The line went dead.

Angry, Arden dialled the number over again even though he wasn't sure he wanted a pizza anymore. He wasn't going to let a bloody machine get the better of him.

Fingers drumming against his desk Miles sat impatiently through the Mormon Tabernacle Choir sings Black Sabbath's Greatest Hits.

Eventually he got the same set of instructions, and when it got to the menu, he stabbed at number, any number, no longer caring which pizza he ordered.

"We are all out of that selection. If you would like to hear the menu again..."

He jabbed at another number.

"Very good, sir. You've ordered our Doner kebab. The doner this week is... "

"No," he roared and he started hitting one number after another.

The next time he could hear something over the combined sounds of his shouting and the numerical tones, the voice was saying: "Would you like small, medium or large? Large, press three; medium, press two; small, press one."

He must have done something right, because it would appear he was getting a pizza.

"Jesus Christ," he muttered as he picked three. After all this trouble, it better be big enough to be worth something.

"If you want anchovies, press star. If you want extra cheese, press two. If you want thin crust, press..."

He was disconnected.

"Hello, Mom?"

He buried his face in his hands.

"No more, no more," Arden mumbled. "I can't stand any more."

*

Lucifer sat upon a blazing throne in Hell's central headquarters. From here, he could view all that happened in his domain. Four major screens dominated the room, providing a direct link to the other control centres in the vast labyrinth of the abyss, where he could watch his demons, imps and fiends as they did his ruling and orchestrated infinite punishments of Hell.

The smaller screens were set to continuous scan that allowed him to observe the many chambers and caverns of Hell. Flames flickered here and there. Occasionally, the camera would stop on a particular scene. Here, a hospital room where a woman with a pinched expression was getting ready to shove a tube up a man's arse. There, a supermarket and a tube station somewhere else again. In one room a wormlike creature thrashed in agony as an imp poured salt on its quivering flesh.

All the individual hells man had created.

Not just man, although he was the most creative, for other species were represented. They were all here. All the life forms God had made after man — on some whim or fancy, from all the possible planets or worlds, all the possible galaxies and universes — for God had experimented with an infinite variety of sizes and shapes. Some of them more hideous to the human eye than the demons that had stewardship over them. Walking fungus, giant slugs, animate slime. Indicative, Satan thought, of the divine disillusionment with the original design.

Yet, each species shared one common trait; each contained the kernel, the seed or rudiments, of intelligence. True to form, Lucifer had given them the same gift he had given to man: knowledge. Why should man be the only one so honoured?

"It's a dirty job," he mumbled, "but somebody's got to do it."

"What? What was that?"

Satan frowned at Buer, who hopped to attention and saluted, clopping himself soundly with a hoof.

"Ah, er, what, Sir!" he added, circumspectly.

"Oh, nothing." Lucifer zoomed in on the orientation centre. The smaller screens continued their search.

"... infernal combustion engine..."

Satan looked closer. Forcas and Astoroth were discussing the inductees, some new, some not so new.

"Still," Forcas said, "things just aren't like they used to be. Remember the good old days when people used to cringe on command..."

"... cower on cue," Astoroth said wistfully.

Suddenly they noticed that Satan's baleful eye was trained on them. Forcas leapt to his feet, as if electrified, and Astoroth sat up on his dragon mount.

Lucifer growled a thought at them and the two were quick to respond.

"Yes, boss. Of course, boss... whatever you say... oh, thank you, boss..."

The demons began to jerk spasmodically and the screen faded to black.

"Fools!"

Gathering courage, Buer turned from one wall screen to another. "They're right though. Things aren't like they used to be."

Lucifer turned back to the screen and sneered as a mechanised voice spoke. "If you want anchovies, press star," it said. "If you want extra cheese, press two. If you want..."

Satan regarded Arden hunched miserably over a telephone terminal. The man dug ineffectually at the surgical implants — which bore a banal, if somewhat predictable, resemblance to horns and transmitted the audio directly into his cerebral cortex.

"Hello Mom?"

"No more, no more," he moaned. "I can't stand any more."

Lucifer glanced from Buer to the man, and back again. "Oh, I don't know. I think they're better."

A SNOWBALL'S CHANCE

John Ryan followed his erect penis around the room. It twanged and thwanged with a mind of its own, pulling him along like some useless appendage.

"Damn... damn... damn... damn... damn," he chanted with each pulsing beat of his prick.

He'd been caught out during the devil's most recent clean-up campaign, and boy, had Satan been furious about something; Ryan didn't know what.

His willy throbbed redly, twitched, and his entire body was jerked forward another step.

"Damn."

The normal sounds of the cave-type dwelling which was his own private hell — the swish of veil and skirt — were silenced. For the women no longer moved. They were frozen — quite literally — statues, maintained in the postures they had held when Satan had so precipitously arrived on the scene. How long ago? He couldn't recall; it seemed an eternity.

No amount of stroking could relieve this erection, and John wouldn't have rubbed his prick against the woman even if he had been so inclined. Ryan had tried it once and they were cold. So cold, that the skin of his dick had stayed stuck to the frozen female form.

Katie Ryan's son, John had performed his own circumcision right then and there. He'd had to. The wound still hadn't healed properly because his continual hard-on didn't permit the skin to close completely. The sore still oozed.

Old Satan had been pretty wily, after all, as he materialised into Ryan's personal cell twittering about some movie. John had been wrong when he thought the devil was lacking in imagination; he'd proven himself to be pretty goddamn inventive.

The women were still beautiful. Gorgeous. But cold, hard as ice. The only thing that told John that they were still alive were their eyes which followed him around the room. Taunting, pleading.

The thirst he had felt before, the lust, remained.

With Satan's infinite blessing, the holes in the bottles were now plugged. You would think that was a comfort since John could drink to his heart's content. He could drink himself into stupor. But Ryan couldn't piss if his life depended on it, and a full bladder ensured he didn't sleep, no matter how drunk he got.

All because this God... damned... e... rec... tion. John Ryan thwacked his penis against the wall to punctuate each syllable.

Neither did masturbation permit orgasm nor release from the perpetual state of arousal.

Somewhere a fly buzzed. The sound was driving him around the twist, and Ryan wondered as he followed his penis around the room in search of the fly: "Who the devil Miss Jones was, anyway?"

DEVIL WOMAN

"I say, Holmes, what are we doing here?" Watson grumbled, as he solicitously assisted Miss Mary Morstan through a particularly soggy patch of ground. "I thought you said we were going to the country."

"But this is the country." Holmes gestured around them at the melancholy flats of the tidal plain. "It's the Plumstead Marshes."

Watson sniffed. "Hardly the place to bring a young lady." By this time, the group had drawn up close to the Thames. From here, they could see Barking Level, where a few scant days before Jonathan Small had been apprehended in the mystery which would later be called, 'A Sign of Four.'

It had been one of their first cases together, and the prim and proper Watson had yet to adjust to dealing with what he called the criminal element. This normally critical attitude was reinforced by the presence of Mary Morstan, whom Watson would've preferred to protect.

Holmes rolled his eyes towards the heavens. The man was positively infatuated.

"Really, Holmes, this is most inappropriate." Watson stroked his moustache to muffle his voice. "Don't you think coming out here is in poor taste. I mean, Mary is a real trooper, but don't you think it's a little hard on her?"

"Watson!" Holmes snapped, and then modulating the harshness of his tone he went on, "the good lady wasn't present when Small was arrested, so how, do you suppose, will she be able to recognise the place? I don't plan to tell her. I would advise you not to mention it either."

"Good God, man, she can read. She knows where we are." Holmes dismissed the topic and squatted down to study the ground. Brought up short, Watson asked. "Why are we here?"

"Our friend, Tonga," said Holmes.

"That black devil! Why, he's drowned."

"I'm not so sure."

"Not sure, why not? Small said he'd weighted the poor

blighter down with the treasure."

"Ah, yes, and he also said it would do no good to drag the Thames. That he thought it would be better to have the jewels scattered across the length and breadth of the river than falling into other's hands. If that's true, then the gems must have been loose. Now I ask you: if he had no container, how could Small attach the treasure to the creature?"

"Pockets?"

"Doubtful." Holmes scanned the broad expanse of the river. "Don't forget, our friend Tonga came from the Andaman Islands, and most islanders are good swimmers. We have no reason to believe that Tonga is different."

"You mean that black devil might still be alive somewhere in the city?" Watson clasped his hands behind his back and whistled.

"Watch where you step, Watson."

"Huh?"

"Why don't you go entertain your little guest?" suggested Holmes as he whipped his glass out of his pocket.

Before Watson had the chance to retort Holmes was off, body folded almost double, his face thrust between the long leafy fronds of marsh grass. His long artistic fingers swept the blades away to reveal the soft earth underneath.

Watson sauntered back Miss Morstan who had wandered further up the river and away from the scene under investigation.

Holmes stopped him. "Can you move away from the bank, I haven't been able to pick up the path yet?"

Immediately fascinated, Watson swung around to face Holmes. "Path? What path? What have you found there, Holmes?"

"His footprint."

"By Jove, are you sure?"

"Of course, I'm sure. It could be none other. The size of the print, the spread of the toes — which indicate a foot unaccustomed to shoes — all confirm that this is our friend, Tonga."

With a worried glance at Miss Morstan, Watson reversed his direction and began wading through the tall grass toward Holmes.

"Please be careful, Watson. This wet river mud is the perfect medium for taking an imprint. I want to pick up the trail. Therefore, I would prefer if you and Miss Morstan please stay where you are."

Watson's back went stiff and rigid as a poker. "If you insist," he groused.

Intent upon his quest, Holmes didn't notice his partner's reaction. His long, thin nose twitched like a bloodhound on the scent. His deep-set eyes gleamed as he muttered to himself and finally gave a crow of delight.

"Aha, here we have it, Watson. The game is afoot."

And, still squatting like a duck, Holmes ploughed through the waist-high grass. Companion forgotten, Watson raced to the bank and glanced at the telltale spoor.

"Ah Holmes, it looks like a hoof print to me."

Watson lumbered after his friend, who despite his peculiar posture — legs bent, bottom high and nose pressed close to the ground — had still managed to attain a certain speed. Watson was quite out of breath by the time he caught up with his friend.

"Holmes..."

The great detective straightened. "Stay back."

"What's the matter? Why have you stopped?"

"The trail ends."

"Just like that?" Watson asked incredulously.

They had come abreast of the first scraggly growth of trees.

"Probably not just like that. He must have gone somewhere. But, see here, how we've run into something that more closely approximates his native habitat." He pointed at the brush. "Remember, Andaman Islanders are fierce warriors, fully capable of escaping the attentions of their enemies. I'd say from here he probably took to the trees."

Holmes examined the branches. "Ha! See here, some of the twigs are broken."

"Couldn't we pick up the trail on the other side of the copse?"

"We probably could, but I think what happened to him when he first came ashore is more important than finding out where he went." Watson shot the detective a dubious look. Holmes elucidated. "He seems to have lost weight somewhere back there."

"Lost weight!"

"You see how the prints here aren't as deep."

Watson considered the imprint. "No, not really."

Holmes clapped his friend on the shoulder. "Trust me, Watson."

Watson shook off his hand. "Couldn't the change be accounted for by the fact that the soil here isn't as damp?"

"Not entirely." Holmes stooped and stuck his finger into impression to measure its depth.

"Besides, as you pointed out earlier, this is no place to keep a lady waiting."

"Mary!" Watson exclaimed. "My word, I quite forgot."

"Such a memory lapse is not very commendable for a man who's supposed to be in love," commented Holmes, but Watson was already gone.

By the time the detective had returned to the river, Miss Morstan and Watson had wandered well away from the grizzly trail. Holmes ignored the couple, heading back to the place where the track began.

"I say, what's this?" Holmes cried as he shoved aside a tuft of grass and spied a second print. "This looks like a lady's foot print."

He glared at Mary Morstan.

"Uh, sorry," said Miss Morstan, "it's probably mine. I thought you were all through here so I went over to see what all the excitement was about."

Holmes frowned, giving her a sidelong glance, but she only had eyes for Watson. The young woman leaned forward eagerly to listen to his animated explanation of events. Holmes brushed his hands on his trousers and stood up.

There was nothing more to be found here.

*

It was a cold, grey December day — appropriate weather to mark the anniversary of the Prince Consort's death. Winter had long since stripped the leaves from the trees in Regent's Park, and fog settled upon London like a shroud.

Holmes and Watson sat in companionable silence, Watson with his nose tucked in the pages of *The Times* while Holmes hunched over the detritus of an experiment. The room was littered with tubes and beakers and the air reeked of foul-smelling chemicals. Intermittently, the detective would stop what he was doing to jot down notes for his next monograph.

Watson grunted. *The Times* shook in his hands.

Holmes looked up from his test. "I say, Watson, anything wrong at home?"

"No, of course not. Why? Should there be?"

"You've been coming to Baker Street a lot lately. I would have imagined that you would spend more time at home now that you are a married man," Holmes said.

"Humph, hmmpph," Watson puffed energetically.

"How is your lady wife?"

"Mary? Oh, she keeps busy — charitable concerns, what not."

"Is she involved in any particular organisations."

"I don't know. Naturalists or spiritualists or some such nonsense.

"Naturalists or spiritualists," Holmes chuckled. "There is a big difference between the two. The naturalists believe in the study of nature, excluding the supernatural, while the spiritualists are banned still under the old witchcraft laws."

"Witchcraft? My Mary? Good heavens, no, nothing of the sort. Taking care of sick sparrows, comforting the elderly. You know, womanly things."

"You seem agitated." He indicated the trembling hands. "What caused you to exclaim? Bad news?"

"It's this situation in Schleswig-Holstein. It's getting out of hand. If we don't watch our step, there will be war right on our doorstep."

"Yes, it is ticklish a situation," Holmes agreed. "It is claimed that only three men in England understand the issue; The Prince Consort, who is unfortunately no longer with us. Some wretched clerk in the Foreign Office who has gone irrevocably and irretrievably mad. And Palmerston who, by his own estimation, forgot."

Holmes rose from his seat, went to the fireplace to pick up his pipe from the mantel. "It's quite interesting that you should mention that particular article."

"No, it's not. The paper was opened to this page."

Holmes disregarded Watson's observation.

"Because we are expecting a very important visitor about this

192

very issue." There was a knock on the door followed by footsteps on the stairs. "Speak of the devil, I believe that's him now."

"Him? Who?"

"Lord Palmerston."

"What? You mean Lord Palmerston is here now?"

Holmes didn't have time to answer. The study door opened to reveal Palmerston himself. A man of singular appearance, he was easily identified by his mode of dress, the well-known shock of red hair and florid complexion.

"Good Lord, Holmes, how did you know?"

"Nothing particularly perplexing, Watson," Holmes said as he made his way across the room to receive the visitor. "We had an appointment."

To Palmerston he said, "Welcome, sir. Please, make yourself comfortable."

The gentleman sat on the edge of his chair. The gaze he settled upon Watson from under big, bushy eyebrows was intent.

Nonplussed, Watson stammered a greeting.

Palmerston scowled. "Mr Holmes, I didn't expect you to have company."

"This is Watson. Surely, you have read some of his case studies, amusing little tales, if woefully inaccurate."

"Inaccurate!" Watson huffed.

"This is no time to delve into the area of literary criticism, Watson."

"I should say not," said Palmerston. "This is a matter of the utmost importance. We want no stories about it."

"I can vouch for Watson. His services have been invaluable to me in the past."

Watson's chest swelled. "Why thank you, Holmes?"

Holmes turned to the doctor. "You can keep a confidence, can't you?"

"Of course, you know I can."

Palmerston gave Watson a searching appraisal, sniffed and relaxed. "As my communiqué explained this is a matter of national security. The future of the crown may be at stake."

"How awful!" Watson ejaculated.

"Good God, man, can't you control yourself. It's worse than you could possibly imagine," Palmerston said gloomily.

"Yes," said Holmes, "but your communiqué didn't give a

clue as to what was so urgent."

"Of course, I couldn't risk putting the details on a paper that might possibly be intercepted. This concerns the safety of the queen."

"So I'd gathered." Holmes took a seat directly across from Palmerston. "May I ask, why you?" He coughed into his hand. "I mean you and Her Majesty are not known to be on the best of terms."

"What do you mean? I like the old girl."

Watson gasped at the temerity. Holmes simply smiled at the parliamentarian over steepled fingers.

"Her Majesty is fully cognizant of the missive I'm about to disclose to you. She is aware of these threats and forbids her staff from acting upon the information that has come to light. Against all logic and reason, she forbids even the mere mention of it."

The man leaned back. "Quite honestly, I'm afraid that her mind has become unhinged since the death of the Prince Consort. Look at the way she's handling the Schleswig-Holstein succession. From some misguided sense of loyalty to Albert, she continues to support the Germans despite public sympathies for the Dutch. I never thought I would say this, but I miss the Prince. He would have been more flexible, thinking first of the public good instead of old family alliances." Palmerston paused. "He would, at least, have listened."

"Ah, so that is what all this is about, the Schleswig-Holstein issue."

"No, no, although it may be related. In terms of national security, it's worse."

"Worse!" cried Watson.

The lord's shaggy head wagged from side to side. "I just want you to understand," his eyes sparked with almost demonic light, "why I dare go against Her Majesty's wishes."

He thumped his chest. "I'm out of favour with the Queen, no doubt, but that doesn't mean I don't know where my allegiance lies."

Holmes nodded in a conciliatory manner. "I'm sure you have Her Majesty's best wishes at heart. However, it would help if you could explain the matter you came here to discuss?"

"Let me start at the beginning. A couple of months ago, it came to the attention of Hardy, Duke of Buckingham, that a plot was afoot to abduct the Queen from Osborne."

"And how did he find out about this?"

"The Duke of Cambridge received an anonymous letter."

"Do you put much credence in these letters?"

"Not normally, but a warning such as this cannot be ignored. Besides, this is not an isolated incident. There have been other, ah, threats from America where abolitionists would like to see us become involved in their little war."

"Do you have a copy of this letter?" queried Holmes.

"Why yes, I do,' Palmerston said.

"May I see it?"

"Of course, that's why I brought it along." Palmerston handed it to Holmes.

He scrutinised the envelope. "Good quality paper. I'd say six penny a packet. Expensive." He paused in his examination to open it, extracted the letter from inside and unfolded it. "Cotton bond." Holmes turned the paper over in his hands. There was only half a sheaf of paper there, the page having been torn along a central line. "Obviously, a man of means. Funny that he should tear it this way, as though it were part of a larger letter that the sender didn't want seen. Did the paper arrive in this condition, or was it torn after its receipt?"

"It came that way."

The detective's lips moved ever so slightly as he read the text.

"Hmmm. There's a flourish to the long letters. A man of strong character." He passed the letter to Watson. "But this was written in September, why are you coming to see us now?"

"A number of reasons. There was that dreadful accident at Altnagiuthasach. That happened within days of the receipt of this letter, and since then there's been other rumours and threats."

"Any reason to give them more credence than is usual?"

"Ah, yes, there's been addition at court. A mysterious woman in black.

"A woman in black at court!" Watson snorted. "Good God, man, the Queen is in mourning. All the women at court wear black. How can you tell one from another?"

Palmerston glowered at the interruption. "That's just the problem we can't, but I can tell you it's an addition."

"Can you describe her?"

"Well, she wears widow's weeds and a thick black veil."

"Of course, that much was implied." Holmes prompted Palmerston to continue.

"The point is she uses this to cover her face and hide her identity. There's no way to distinguish her features. We only know that she's not part of the normal staff. Someone always meets her at the gate and escorts her directly to the Queen, so we cannot stop and question her without provoking the queen."

"Have you tried asking Her Majesty?"

"Yes, and she won't talk about it. She's being down right secretive.

"When General Grey notified her of this letter — " he tapped the missive with a thick forefinger — "her reaction was not favourable. She says she's a virtual state prisoner at Osborne. When pressed, she said she must not have this again mentioned. That was in response to a tangible threat. What would happen if we were to question her about her personal visitors?"

"What can you tell me about this woman in black?"

"Only that she seemed to arrive on the scene not long after the Altnagiuthasach affair. Something I personally find suspicious. However, I believe they met before that at the unveiling in Aberdeen."

Eyes closed, fingers pressed to his lips, Holmes mused aloud. "Yes, I seem to remember that, as Her Majesty's first official function, got a lot of publicity."

"Well, with the incidents happening so quickly after the receipt of the letter, it seems more than coincidence. The accident occurred the seventh of October. The unveiling was on the thirteen, and since then this mysterious stranger has become a fixture around the palace."

*

"What do you make of that, Watson?" said Holmes as the door closed behind their visitor.

"Well, I can't say I see the peril. Not with this mysterious woman in black. She's obviously bereaved, a widow, like the queen herself. It's not unusual for a woman, even a queen, to find comfort in someone who has been through similar experiences."

"A grieving widow, Watson? How do you know that?"

"The mode of dress."

"Anyone can dress in black and affect veils, particularly if they want to remain unnoticed at court."

"You have a point there, Holmes. Even my Mary wears black more often than she used to in deference to the Queen."

"You see, you prove my point? What better means to avoid detection than to adapt to your environment?"

"Like a chameleon!"

"Precisely."

"Well, what do you propose to do?"

"I'll start with the most concrete clue we've got –" he rubbed the letter between his fingers. "– this paper." Holmes moved over to the tables that held his chemicals.

Thirty minutes later he surfaced from his analysis and fingered the paper. "There's something very familiar about this. It's twenty-five percent cotton bond. The pulp is mashed fine and... As a matter of fact," he got up and went over to his desk. "The same paper as we have here."

"What? You're not saying that the letter came from here."

"No, not at all, Watson. Expensive as it may be, I don't have paper specially made. I have to order it, granted it's not common stock at the local stationers, but not made. What a bit of luck!"

"Luck? I don't understand."

"Yes, I know what you mean. I don't believe in luck. However, it gives us a starting point for our search. I think a visit the stationers would be in order."

"You don't think that this mysterious woman in black frequents the same stationer."

"Now that would be a bit of luck, but no, I don't. Still, he can give us the name of the manufacturer who must keep a list of retail and personal orders."

Grabbing his hat and coat, the detective stalked from the flat with Watson on his heels. A few minutes later they entered a shop on the corner of Melbourne and Baker Street. The shopkeeper greeted the detective like an old friend.

"What can I do for you, sir?"

"What can you tell me about this?"

"It's paper, Mr Holmes."

"I know it's paper. Can you tell me anything else about it?"

"Well, it's got writing on it. Good lord!"

197

"Don't read it," Holmes said snatching the torn sheet away from the stationer.

"Uh, sorry, sir," the stationer mumbled.

"What I mean is can you tell me if there's anything special about it?"

"It's the same paper you use, but then you probably already know that."

"Yes, I do. Can you tell me if it was purchased here?"

"No, sir, you're my only customer on this particular stock."

"Isn't that strange?"

"No, not really. Not many 'as can afford it in this neighbourhood. It is very costly, you know, sir," the shopkeeper said.

"I don't mean isn't it strange that the paper didn't come from here."

The stationer gave him a blank stare.

"It's just the coincidence that it happens to be the very same paper that I use, as if..." He tapped his chin with his index finger. "Where else can you find this paper?"

"Oh my, sir, at any of the finer shops, although it may have to be ordered."

"Does it always have to be ordered?" queried Holmes.

"No, I doubt it. Certainly, you'd be able to find it easily enough in Mayfair."

"What about the manufacturer?"

"The manufacturer? Oh yes, I can give you the name and address of the manufacturer."

"Very good." They waited while he wrote the information down and passed it to Holmes.

"Thank you." The detective waved the slip at the stationers. "Come along, Watson, I must send a telegram and then I believe we have a job for the Baker Street Irregulars."

"Holmes, you don't expect that any self-respecting shopkeeper in Mayfair would be willing to let those street urchins in the door much less give information to them?"

"No, I'd recommend that you and I take Mayfair, leaving our young chums the rest of the city."

"What about the manufacturer?"

"That will take some time and we can be do some preliminary investigation while we are waiting for a reply."

"Sounds like an awful lot of leg work if you ask me."

Two hours had passed before they heard the slap of unshod feet upon the stair. There was the chirp of many high voices, and the boys, Holmes had so glibly dubbed the Baker Street Irregulars, tumbled into the room, a single ragged creature of many legs.

Holmes surfaced somewhere within the group. "Wiggins?"

One of the older boys detached himself from the rest and wiped his nose upon a filthy sleeve. "All here, sir, except for Kenny. He's sick..."

"Yes, yes, well. How would you like to earn a few bob?"

"Please, sir," the scallywags chorused in unison. Their bodies inclined slightly toward Holmes at the mention of money.

"What I need you to do is check every shop for paper like this." And he thrust pieces of his stationery into each grubby hand. "I want to know who stocks it and who does not. More importantly I'd be interested in a woman, a widow possibly, who came in to purchase it or order it sometime in September."

The leader Wiggins exhaled explosively. "That's a long shot."

"The stationery, if not the woman, is distinctive,"

"But that was months ago, do you think they'll remember?"

"Well, this woman would have been wearing a thick veil to obscure her features. That should help."

The boys sniggered.

"Not 'arf," said Wiggins.

"A shilling for each of you now and a guinea to the boy who brings back news of our mysterious woman in black."

Grumbling, the filthy Arabs exploded from the room, colliding with Mrs Hudson on their way down the stairs.

There was a shout and a mumbled apology.

"Now, Watson, if I could trust you to do the Mayfair end of the investigation..."

"What me? Why me?"

"I've got another matter to which I must attend."

*

A weary and frustrated Watson climbed up to the Baker Street apartment that night. As he had expected, his efforts had been next to useless. As predicted, the paper was easy enough to find in the finer shops, but the woman was another matter. Until he started his enquiries, Watson had never been completely cognizant of the number of women who wore black in the city of London.

"Futile. Bloody foolish," he muttered as he walked into the room. He checked his complaint when he noted the presence of a rough looking blackguard leaning over Holmes's desk and rifling through his papers.

"By Jove, what are you doing there?"

The man leapt guiltily to his feet, knocking a stack of correspondence onto the floor.

Watson, who was particularly sensitive about the issue, what with all the commotion a single sheaf had engendered in the last twenty-four hours, advanced upon the stranger brandishing his umbrella like a sword. "Get away from that desk."

"Watson, please!"

"Holmes is that you?"

He laughed. "I would have thought you'd be used to my little disguises by now." He looked ruefully at the tangled disarray on the floor. "You surprised me. Look at this mess. Now, we'll have to get Mrs Hudson in to clean it up."

"Why are you dressed like that, and where have you been?"

"You evidently didn't notice the day."

"The day? It's Thursday. What of it? Thursday usually falls between Wednesday and Friday.

"Remember when our esteemed visitor said that the woman in black usually came to the palace once a month. Today is the day for one of her regularly scheduled visits. So, I went to see if I could catch sight of our mysterious lady and, if I did, to follow her."

"And?"

"Well, Palmerston was right. There's not much to distinguish her from a thousand other ladies in the streets. With the volume of her cloak and gown it was difficult even to gauge her size."

"Did you manage to follow her?"

"I tried. I trailed her to Chelsea and lost her in the crowd."

"Oh." Watson's face fell.

"One thing is I know for sure, this woman is no innocent."

"What do you mean?"

"She knows the rules of the chase,"

"Pardon?"

"She knew she was being pursued and she went about losing me in a very professional manner. Which makes me wonder if she hadn't let me follow her that far."

Seeing Watson's perplexity, Holmes explained. "An honest women who noticed some scruffy individual," he gestured at his attire, "following her, she would have notified a policeman immediately. She wouldn't take it upon herself to lose him.

"No, this woman had reason to suspect that she was being followed, which can only mean she has something to hide. Not all is lost, though. It gives us an area in which to concentrate our search."

"Assuming she wasn't leading you on a wild goose chase."

"Assuming that, of course," Holmes said. "Also, Watson, I did get close to her. She wears quite an unusual scent. Floral, but not the usual lavender. I think I would recognise the scent again."

Watson pursed his lips and Holmes could tell he was biting back some sneering commentary. The detective hurried on. "I sense another hand behind all this."

"You don't mean..."

Holmes nodded. "Moriarty."

*

Holmes stuck his long beak-like nose in yet another bottle of perfume and inhaled deeply.

"Rose water," sniff "extract of lily," sniff, sniff, "and carnation." He turned to Watson and smiled, fully expecting the typical ejaculations of praise such ready deductions usually elicited from his friend. But if he'd wanted this, Holmes was woefully disappointed.

Instead Watson clutched at his head and moaned, "How many more to go?"

Holmes counted the row of bottles. "You don't want to know."

"How you keep them all straight? How you can tell the difference between one perfume and another after so many? They all smell the same to me."

"Nonsense, Watson," said Holmes. "As senses go, the olfactories are the most neglected by man, even though they are just as important as any other. Surely as a physician you are aware of the significance of smells as a diagnostic tool. Well, the same is true in the science of criminology. Accurate investigation utilises all five senses, and not just the often overworked visual perceptions."

The detective upended the cut crystal vial, sprinkled a single drop of the amber fluid onto his little finger and tasted it.

"Sperm whale oil is used as a fixative, I believe," he said. Holmes repeated the action. "Yes, definitely sperm whale oil."

"My word, I never thought perfumes were so complex. I just thought they extracted the fragrance from a particular flower and distilled it."

"Essentially, that is true, but what is distillation but a complex chemical process?"

Watson rubbed at his eyes. "I can't say I ever paid much attention in the past."

"Quite an interesting topic, really," said Holmes, "once you subtract the romantic foolishness normally attached to perfumes. Their manufacture requires a lot more than just the essential oils that impart the scent, it requires fixatives to ensure the odour lingers and other ingredients that fuse the amalgamation of fragrances."

He opened another bottle. "And scents don't act singly. Certain fragrances can be used to enhance others. One can be added to another, augmenting the smell of the original without masking it."

"I think," said Watson, "I know more about perfumes than I ever wanted to know. Have you found what you were looking for?"

Holmes grimaced. "Well, ah, no. Not so far. The problem is that a fragrance is altered by an individual's body chemistry. Thus, perfume in the bottle will smell different from the same scent once it is put on. Of course, the perfume may have been specially made."

"Do you mean we have gone through all this for nothing!" Watson yelped. "Oh, my aching head."

"No, not for nothing, my good man. I believe I've been able to isolate some of the probable ingredients. Now I can analyse the paper for traces. If present that would permit further analysis and breakdown of the chemical composition. Not to mention provide a direct link between the letter and our mysterious woman in black."

"And how would that help us, since we suspect as much already?"

"I would have thought that would be apparent," Holmes mused. "It would tell whether we have two separate plots here, or just one."

"Oh, I see what you mean." Watson dug around in his side whiskers, "Quite right." More emphatically. "*Quite right!*"

The detective daintily washed his hands before reaching for the next bottle. Watson stopped him.

"Ah, Holmes, I don't know if I should mention it, but if there's a connection between the woman and the kidnapping plot, wouldn't it be rather silly of her to warn the Duke of Cambridge about it?"

Holmes scowled at the implied criticism. Marriage had done very little to improve Watson's temper.

*

They stood on Knightsbridge. Watson breathed deeply of air untainted by the smell of flowers.

"You don't look well," said Holmes

The doctor peered at the detective with eyes shot through with red. "I am feeling a bit gamey."

"Too bad, I was going to ask you to come along. I have an appointment with the Good Brown."

"You mean John Brown, the Prince Consort's gillie?" Watson cried. "Good Lord, how'd you arrange that?"

"I didn't. He contacted me. It would appear that Palmerston isn't the only one who is concerned about the Queen. Brown too is worried about the influence the woman in black is having. He's come into town today specifically to meet me."

"It sounds all very interesting, but I'm afraid I can't join you. Sorry, Holmes. The wife gets back today from Edinburgh."

"I didn't realise she had been away," Holmes said. "No wonder you've been hanging about Baker Street so much."

"Yes, well, an aunt of hers was taken ill in October."

"Hmmm," said a preoccupied Holmes. "Sounds serious."

A funny expression passed fleetingly across Watson's face.

His jaws clenched and the tip of his tongue protruded from his mouth as he bit back some comment.

"Are you all right, old man?"

"Ah, er."

Holmes didn't wait for a reply. "I must be off now. I wouldn't want to be late for such an important interview. This the first time of member of Her Majesty's personal staff has been willing to confide to me; I would not want to strain that confidence."

*

"Praise the Lord with heart and voice..."

The final chords of Prince Albert's chorale had faded. Cleansed of original sin by the rite of baptism, the proud parents, the Prince and Princess of Wales presented their heir to the congregation. Cheers rocked the cathedral as they welcomed the new addition to the royal household, but it was a much subdued crowd that gathered outside to await transportation to the official reception.

Holmes shifted nervously, weaving his way through the throng. He had little use for pomp and ceremony, and less for the concept of original sin. But this was work. He craned his neck to get a better glimpse of their sovereign and was surprised to note Dr Watson and his wife amongst the assembly.

The detective started to elbow his way through the crowd to reach Watson, as much as propriety and circumstances would allow. As he drew close, Holmes could hear Mrs Watson chastising her spouse.

"Stop fidgeting, John," she said. Watson tugged at his collar.

"Not used to the old regimental uniform, Mary."

For a brief moment, the eyes of the detective and the wife locked over Watson's epaulette, then she turned to examine her husband disparagingly. "Well, you have gained a few pounds, dear." She leaned close and whispered something in Watson's ear before moving away.

"Watson!"

"Holmes!"

"I'm surprised to see you here."

"Are you? I thought you'd arranged this," Watson said.

"I? No, it was difficult enough to get myself included on the

204

guest list, much less you and —" he indicated Mrs Watson where she stood a few yards away.

"It must have been my cousin, then."

"Ah, yes, the good doctor, Thomas Watson. I forget sometimes that you are related."

"We've never been particularly close."

"I had rather hoped that the baptism would bring out our mysterious woman in black."

Watson nodded at the group of black-clad ladies-in-waiting that surrounded the Queen. "How could you tell? Women dressed in black are twelve a ha'penny?"

"Well, yes, there is that."

"What did you learn from John Brown? Anything useful?"

"Well, the Good Brown was able to shed some light on the enigmatic woman in black."

"Oh really? I thought only her ladies-in-waiting were privy to their activities."

"True, but evidently Her Majesty is relaxed enough around the Good Brown to let some information slip."

"Yes, and what are they doing that's so mysterious?"

"Séances."

"Séances? You mean, with rattling tables and demonic voices, that sort of thing?"

"Not demonic; I believe the process is much more earthly than that," said Holmes. "Yes, it would appear that Her Majesty is trying to contact the Prince Consort, and our woman in black is the medium."

"Incredible," Watson said.

"I don't know, Watson. What could be more natural? A grieving widow, a husband dearly missed." Holmes added, "I had anticipated just such a development early on. Why else would the Queen be so secretive? What activity would be so censured that the Monarch would have to hide it even from her own ministers? She is the Queen, after all. Who has the right to interfere with the sovereign of the realm? Her advisors may suggest that she curtail her outings in Osborne and Balmoral; they can caution her; they can even cajole her to resume her duties. But they cannot force her to do anything against the royal will. But spiritualism, as you said before, smacks of witchcraft."

"And the Queen is the head of the Church of England."

"Yes, I know, Watson. That's probably why she has been so cryptic. Her Majesty cannot afford even the slightest whisper of heresy. If word got out, she could feasibly lose all." Holmes expounded, "She's already being criticised by the press for excessive grief. Some have even questioned her reason. What would happen if this became common knowledge?"

"I shudder to think."

Holmes stroked his chin. "Did you know that spiritualism is a capital offence. Illegal under statutes that date back to medieval times, and punishable by a most gruesome death."

"Well, if this as you say the most natural thing in the world, then we can assume that there's nothing sinister about the woman in black."

"I didn't say that," Holmes countered. "What about the letter?"

Watson sputtered and then said: "I don't know. Coincidence?"

"You know I don't believe in coincidence. No, I've been trying to trace our woman in black through the spiritualists." Holmes pursed his lips. "One would think that like any other underworld community, theirs must have some sort of network for communication."

"And?"

Holmes lifted his shoulders in a shrug. "Nothing. Spiritualists are even more close-mouthed than their criminal counterparts. If nothing else our woman in black is discreet. The Queen's patronage is not common knowledge, which I'm afraid doesn't bode well for the monarchy."

"Why do you say that?"

"If this woman were simply a medium, then you would think she would have talked about it, at least among her peers."

"You said they were a tight-lipped group. Maybe they didn't want to talk to you, an outsider."

"Watson, you should know me better? I passed myself off as one of them. Since when have I gone blundering about unprepared?"

The doctor snorted. "There have been a few incidents. Remember –"

Holmes forged ahead before his friend could relay some of their more notorious experiences. "Just because they keep their own council doesn't mean I wasn't able to find out anything about the group," said the detective. "It is quite a large group that embraces all levels of society — meeting anywhere from the backrooms of shops down in Hackney to the old priest holes of the aristocracy — and they do have quite an underground network. Yet, there's not been a single word of the woman in black anywhere. Don't you think that the advocacy of the Queen would be quite a coup de grace for spiritualists everywhere?"

"You don't know. The woman in black may not belong to any particular group."

"I wonder."

"If she were truly innocent, then discretion and prudence, respect for her queen may still her tongue."

"What are you two talking about?" Mary Watson inquired as she rejoined her husband. "Some dreadful murder or other, no doubt."

Watson plucked her hand from his sleeve and tucked it under his arm.

Someone jostled Holmes, forcing him closer to Watson and his wife. His usually mobile features froze. He studied the couple.

Then, bowing slightly to Mary, Holmes said, "Excuse me, Mrs Watson, I believe I see my brother Mycroft. I must go speak with him. Then it's back to work. I'm afraid for me this is not a social function."

"What an extraordinary man," she said.

"Extraordinary," Watson agreed.

*

"Hello, Watson," Holmes said without looking up from his violin.

Watson shook his head. "I wish I knew how you do that."

"Do what, my good man?"

"Know it's me even before I walk in the room."

"You don't think that after all this time I can't tell your footsteps from another's?"

Watson extracted his pipe from his pocket. "I'm surprised you could even hear me." He indicated the violin on Holmes's lap. "A most disconcerting habit." Watson settled in the chair.

"Particularly since I try to vary my gait just to see if I can fool you."

"A dead give away. Who else that I know would bother? Besides you can't change weight and foot pressure by a simple variation in the rhythm of the tread." He set the violin aside. "As usual, you're timing is impeccable, Watson. The Baker Street irregulars should be here any minute now." Holmes looked pleased with himself.

"Oh, yes? What's bringing them here today?"

"The woman in black."

"Heaven's, Holmes, I would have thought you would have solved that one by now."

"It turned out trickier than I imagined."

Watson examined his friend's face. "You know who's behind all this, don't you?"

"Yes, I do." Holmes's noble countenance darkened slightly. "I believe I mentioned that I sensed another hand behind this, another intelligence other than the woman's."

"Yes, I remember you did say that."

"Well, I know for a fact it's our old adversary Moriarty, because he paid me a visit."

"By Jove! That he would dare..."

"He dares," said Holmes, and proceeded to relate a most remarkable tale...

"... and when I tore the veil off, who do you think I should see but Moriarty?"

"No!"

"Yes."

"You mean to tell me that he came here dressed as a woman?"

"Remember that our woman in black has always been garbed in such a way to conceal her features with the thick veil and heavy cloak."

"Then how did you figure out who it was?"

"Size for one thing. Our visitor was just a little too broad through the shoulders, and a little too tall. And don't forget the all important scent."

"Ah." Watson thought about this for a minute. "But why wear a dress?"

"Because he didn't want to be recognised, not immediately at least."

"Then why come here at all?"

"There, Watson, we must delve into the criminal mind, which is narcissistic at the best of times. Your average villain is conceited."

Watson gave Holmes a strange look. The detective didn't notice. "I've made a study of it, and I don't know if you're aware of the fact that the first thing a criminal does upon his arrest is ask for a newspaper, assuming, of course, that he can read. It's always the same. They want to see their name in print. The more heinous the crime the greater this desire. In fact, I have a philosophy that the severity of the crime often reflects the individual's need for notoriety." He paused. "What must it be like for Moriarty to be behind the scenes orchestrating most of the major crimes within this city, yet receiving no credit? I can imagine it would frustrating."

"Yes, but –"

"All criminals, even a master criminal like Moriarty, covets renown, and the only place he is likely to get that acknowledge-ment, that acclaim, is from me." Holmes stopped to light his pipe. "Moriarty knew I was on to him. He knew that I knew the woman in black was a convenient tool, and he couldn't resist the challenge of confronting me in person."

"Then all this time, it was Moriarty visiting the queen?" Watson shivered.

Holmes let out a sharp bray of laughter. "Hardly. I don't think Her Majesty could be so easily duped by a wolf in sheep's clothing. No."

"Then the woman in black really exists?"

"Of course, she's an accomplice, but for the time being she's unimportant to our quest. It's Moriarty we're after."

"Why would he do such a thing?"

"I'm surprised that you would have to ask. Imagine the power Moriarty would have if he had the Queen under his influence?"

"So now what?"

"Now, I've let the sturdy legs and stout hearts of the Baker Street irregulars take over. We have several leads. Moriarty, the woman, the neighbourhood. I've tracked her twice to the same area of Chelsea. They should be able to find her eventually."

They didn't have to wait for long before there was a great pounding upon the door, the soft murmur of Mrs Hudson followed by the ebullient warble of youth. A breathless Wiggins burst into the room trailed by another of the dirty little beggars.

"We found her!" said Wiggins.

"We found him!" shouted the other boy.

"Moriarty?" cried Holmes. Wiggins nodded.

"The woman in black?" said Watson. "Good Lord, Holmes, which one do we follow? Perhaps, it would be better if we split up."

"No, Watson, we go after Moriarty. The woman is of little consequence. Wiggins, fetch a cab." He riffled through a drawer. His face clouded. "You are not, I don't suppose, carrying a weapon."

"No."

"Here take this?" He handed Watson a gun. "I would not have either one of us face Moriarty unarmed."

The door behind them banged open.

"What's that? Oh yes, Wiggins. Have you got a carriage? Good. Come along, Watson, our conveyance has arrived."

*

The cab rattled at breakneck pace down Gloucester Place and caromed onto Oxford Street. People scattered to get out of the way of the maddened horse. Watson was thrown against Wiggins as the carriage jounced along Park Lane. Holmes kept his eyes firmly fixed on the green fields of Hyde Park until they skidded around the corner onto Knightsbridge.

"See, Watson, I told you," Holmes said.

Wiggins elbowed the doctor in the ribs.

"Told me what?" he growled, glaring at the lad.

"Chelsea."

"Oh, yes, Chelsea."

Occasionally, Watson recognised one of the Baker Street irregulars standing along the road, waving the carriage on.

"How much farther, Wiggins?"

"Dunno, I was following the woman."

"Not far," replied the other lad.

They stopped near Cheyne Walk where it veered away from

the fashionable houses close to the embankment, into an area that was a mixture of dismal warehouses and workmen's terraced cottages.

"Hey!" In his excitement the older boy Wiggins began to pound on Holmes's knee. The detective stared at the youth down an imperious nose. The scallywag looked down at the offending hand and blushed. "This is where we followed the lady. See Kenny there, that's where I told him to wait right outside the door."

"There's Eddie too."

The men turned to regard the boys playing nonchalantly with a broken wheel near the end of the terrace.

"Good heavens, what does that mean?" said Watson.

"Elementary. They're both here."

"By Jove, that's a bit of luck."

Holmes hedged. "I'm not so sure."

"Perhaps, we should send for police. Moriarty is a pretty dangerous fellow. We shouldn't face him alone."

Holmes laid a restraining hand upon his friend's shoulder. "No, Watson, I think in this instance discretion is needed."

"What? Oh yes, right. Whatever you say. Don't want Lestrade to grab all the glory, do you? Should we wait," Watson eyed the busy street, "until after dark?"

"I said discretion, not foolhardiness. We have the element of surprise. If we just loiter about, don't you think Moriarty will get suspicious?" Holmes examined the house and then asked Wiggins, "Is there a back entrance to the place?"

Meanwhile Watson, pursuing his own investigation, meandered around the end of the building. "I say, Holmes, there's an open..."

He clapped his hands over his mouth as the brickwork of the nearby warehouse caught the sound of his voice and amplified it, sending it back to him. He paled and then strolled casually back to the street to look for Holmes. He was gone.

"Holmes?" Watson said in a forced stage whisper guaranteed to be heard in the back of any large auditorium. "I say, huh –"

He glanced at the house and thought better of it.

"That's right," he muttered, "Leave me behind, why don't you? Most impertinent."

He returned to the window. "I don't need you," Watson

211

puffed. "I'll apprehend the villain myself."

Light shone in the doctor's eyes at the thought of, just once, being the hero of his own story. He thrust his stick through the crack between window and sill and jimmied it open.

Holding his breath, Watson plastered himself against the wall of the building and listened for sounds of movement within. When he was sure that he hadn't been overheard, Watson climbed through the window, immediately getting tangled with the curtains. He went sprawling.

Another breathless minute passed before Watson picked himself up off the floor. With the curtains drawn, the room was black as pitch. Unwinding the cloth from his legs, the doctor waited for his eyes to adjust to the gloom.

His heart thundered in his chest. Thud, thud, thud.

Shadows took on form and shape in the darkness.

Thud, thud, thud. Bang! Crash!

It was only then that the doctor realised that the knocking that he heard was not the sound of his own heartbeat. It did not come from within, but from without.

Then he heard a groan. It increased in crescendo until it had become a banshee wail. His blood ran to ice in his veins.

The blackguard was beating her!

All the instincts of repressed chivalry stirred within the military breast.

Their mysterious lady in black may be a criminal, but she was still weak, still vulnerable. Still a woman!

"Ah... ah... ah... ah!"

His blood, so cold before, began to boil.

Bump, thud. His ears pricked as he tried to locate the source of the noise. He inched along the wall to the stairs.

Bang, crash! Watson's gaze fixed upon a door at the top of the staircase. He crept cautiously up to the first floor.

Thump, thump... CREAK!

His foot faltered on the last step.

"Aaargh!"

"That's it!" Lowering his shoulder, the doctor sprinted down the short hall and crashed against the door.

Partially open, it gave without resistance, and, caught short, Watson overbalanced and went staggering into the room.

A woman's face, flushed and slicked with sweat, lifted to

greet him, and it felt like he'd been punched in the stomach with a fist.

The woman in black wore her veil no more. Her blond hair was tousled and her contorted features were as exposed as her long delicate legs which were wrapped around Moriarty's waist.

"Mary!"

The large blue eyes widened; her mouth rounded to an O.

"John?"

"How could you!"

Mrs Watson began to struggle, pushing her lover away.

"I... he..."

The man whipped around and started to laugh. Watson fumbled with the gun in his pocket and dropped it.

Tucking bits of himself back into place, Moriarty fled, but Watson's eyes were trained upon his wife as she straightened her skirts.

"So now you know." Seeing they were alone, she glanced anxiously around the room. "Where's your friend?"

"Holmes?"

"Who else?" The look Mary Watson turned upon him was hateful. "You didn't think for one instance that I was ever interested in you, did you? You ridiculous little man. It was Moriarty's idea, to plant me close to the great detective. You were just a... necessary evil." She sneered the final word.

Watson groped blindly for the gun. Emotions warred with reason, throwing his face into spasms. Somewhere beyond the door came the din of tumult, but Watson paid it little heed, for the pulse that bounded through his body drowned out all other sounds.

Mary chuckled, and it was as if someone had thrown cold water upon his face.

"Bitch."

"John, you've never used such language before."

Watson heard footsteps on the stair. Holmes!

And he knew if he was going to act, he must act... swiftly.

The subsequent events became blurred. The next thing Watson knew, his finger flexed. There was the loud report and the faint tang of gunpowder. The force of the gunshot hurled her back against the wall. Red blossomed out behind her. She hung for a moment, big blue eyes locked in his, and then she folded.

A tendril of smoke drifted across his line of vision, obscuring his view of his wife.

Watson waved it away so he could see her face.

The surprise he had witnessed there when he'd walked in the room was nothing in comparison to the incredulous expression that flitted across her features now.

"Watson!"

The doctor froze. Holmes charged into the room, releasing Watson from his paralysis.

He thrust the gun from him. "Mary! My God, what have I done?"

Watson rushed to her side and knelt beside her. Gingerly, he lifted her to his lap and made some small attempt at staunching the flow of blood from the wound.

"How could you go blundering in here like that. Thanks to you Moriarty got away!

Watson raised Mary to his breast, cradling her.

"But my wife."

"Oh, yes, her."

Watson rocked Mary slowly back and forth and crooned.

"Pull yourself together, man!"

Watson stared at Holmes. "But Mary –"

"The woman in black," Holmes said.

"You knew!" The accusation flung between them like a gauntlet.

Holmes grimaced. His gaze flicked momentarily to the door and he deflated. "Yes, I knew. I've known since the baptism of young Albert Victor."

"But how? Why?"

"The scent. You know, the perfume," and Holmes took a pontificating stance, "although the paper was a clue. Probably the end portion of a note I'd sent to you. My own stock," he growled indignantly, "Moriarty knew that would drive me crazy."

"John?"

Watson dropped his wife.

"Ooph."

"You're alive."

"Help me please," she said, "It hurts."

A choking sound came from deep within his throat.

Holmes turned to her and scowled. Then he scrutinised Watson's face. As though reaching some decision, he strode across the room and helped Watson to his feet.

"Let me, uh, take care of this."

"John!" Dainty hands thrashed wildly in the air.

"We must do something for her," Watson said as Wiggins led him away. "We must... help her!"

With a look of disgust, Holmes reached into his pocket and removed the neat Moroccan case, extracting the hypodermic syringe from within.

"Ahhh." Watson breathed a sigh of relief.

Holmes fished around in his pockets for a bottle.

"Morphia?"

Holmes said nothing, carefully inserting the needle into the bottle and retracting the plunger to extract the mind-numbing fluid.

"Good God, Holmes, that's too m–" And Watson watched in horrified fascination as the needle slid into the vein.

"What became of the treasure?" inquired Holmes.

"Treasure? What treasure?" Her voice was weak.

"You know what treasure." He made a movement as if to withdraw the hypodermic needle from her arm. "You took it, didn't you? You stole it that night Watson accompanied you to that fabled aunt of yours."

Mary Watson nodded, with a single duck of her head. Even that small gesture caused pain. She stifled a cry.

"Holmes stop!"

"Yes, I always thought it was you. I would've warned Watson, but by the time I was sure, it was too late, the dolt had already married you." Like a miser, Holmes apportioned another small measure of relief.

"Do you want surcease from pain? Tell me what happened to it?" He wiggled the needle around in the vein. Her eyes widened. "Answer me now!"

"Moriarty. It went to Moriarty."

He depressed the plunger ever so slightly. "What about Tonga?"

"He got his reward."

"I'll bet he did, poor devil." And with that, he applied steady pressure to the plunger.

"Holmes, that's enough. You must stop!"

The detective swung on his friend. "Do you want to hang, Watson? Look at the wound, man. She'll never survive."

Her body went limp in his arms.

"No!" cried Watson.

The detective stood briskly and clasped Watson's shoulder. "I'm so sorry, old man. If I had known she was going to be here..." He didn't finish the thought. "Will you take him home, Wiggins? I'd better stay behind and, uh, clean up."

*

"Are you sure you want to publish this particular case, Watson?" Holmes returned the manuscript marked Sign of Four to his friend. "You didn't tell the entire story, I see."

"What do you mean I didn't tell the entire story!" Watson got up and began to march angrily around the room.

"I also noticed you changed the names and dates. A wise precaution."

Watson halted next to the chair and frowned down at Holmes. "I don't understand what you're going on about."

Noting his friend's growing agitation Holmes decided to let the topic go. He gripped Watson's arm and squeezed. "That's all right, old chum, I understand why your memory is a bit... selective."

"I don't like your condescending tone. Humph!" He yanked his arm from Holmes's grasp. "Don't forget for one moment that I wrote you! You're not real; you're just a character in a book." He strode over to the mantel, mumbling to himself. "... Pompous, pedantic, pontificating, arrogant, self-important... "

He whirled, addressing himself directly to Holmes. "It was as if someone had plucked the image of you from my brain."

Holmes gave his friend a side-long glance and had to stop himself from shaking his head in dismay.

Ever since that fateful day when he'd lost his first wife, Watson had all gone queer — his behaviour more and more eccentric — and he was getting worse as time progressed. Since then Watson had developed some sort of delusion where he was not, in fact, Watson — physician and sometime writer — but some chap named Doyle. Who, the detective noted wryly, was also a physician and a writer. And this fellow Doyle — like Watson — wrote about Sherlock Holmes.

In this fantasy world, Holmes was not real but a writer's invention. A figment of Watson's, or in this case Doyle's, imagination. Not only Holmes was fictitious, but Watson too was a fiction. Thus, Watson tried to expunge his conscience by fictionalising his life.

Nothing could shake Holmes's old friend from this belief, and the detective supposed it was a mechanism Watson used to distance himself from the event. Far easier to pretend that it had happened to someone else. Just a good yarn. Although Holmes found it interesting that Watson managed to retain those elements of himself that were integral to his functioning. Like his profession and his avocation.

Watson picked up the bottle of morphine. Holmes patted his pocket, checking to make sure the syringe was still there.

Four wives, now. All dead. Would the man ever give up his hatred of women?

Would Holmes ever stop covering for him?

Probably not. Too late now, for Holmes's reputation as well as his friend's liberty rested upon maintaining the myth. If Holmes was going to do something about it, he should have done it then. The first death even the dolt Lestrade would have understood, and the courts would have been lenient.

Watson rolled the bottle around in his hands. Watching the movement, Holmes wondered for the umpteenth time, if, perchance, he had drugged the wrong person.

As if reading the detective's thoughts, Watson said, "I should have killed you when I had the chance."

Taken aback, Holmes blinked.

"I tried," Watson mumbled. "Lord knows I've tried but my publisher, my public..."

Trying to make light of an increasingly untenable situation, Holmes interjected with mock enthusiasm: "Yes, Watson, I've been meaning to talk to you about that. Couldn't you have waited before publishing those case studies? You'll loose your credibility if you keep announcing my death prematurely. Although I suppose I should thank you for the legend that seems to be growing up around me."

Watson continued as if Holmes hadn't spoken. "I've written

plenty of books, hundreds of stories. I don't want to die with people remembering me only for you!" Watson cum Doyle complained. "Why couldn't you stay dead?"

"As you can see," Holmes extended his arms and bowed dramatically, "the reports of our demise, to paraphrase a contemporary of yours, was an exaggeration."

"CUT!"

"What?" Holmes jumped and swung to gape at empty air.

"What the hell are you doing, quoting Twain? Can't you read, you idiot?"

Holmes looked down. The chiselled jaw flopped uselessly as the detective struggled for breath.

"Read the script, damn you!" A small black man, a midget actually, shook a sheaf of papers at him. "This isn't Twain's story; it's —" he wagged a hideously misshapen head at the author "— his. What'd'ya think we pay writers for."

"Tonga! Watson, that's Tonga." Holmes stabbed his finger at the creature.

Watson sighed. "You twit, Holmes. How many times do I have to tell you that I'm not Watson; I'm Doyle, and that's not Tonga."

"What do you mean? Look at him."

"There is a striking resemblance, I agree, but that's —"

The thick lips twisted into a leer, exposing strong yellow teeth, and the creature completed the sentence for Doyle. "— a black devil."

"Huh?" said Holmes.

Watson continued. "And this isn't 22 B Baker Street. That address doesn't exist. This is —"

"Belay that. We've got work to do." The midget turned his back on Holmes and Watson and waddled back to the cluster of cameras and equipment, muttering: "I had to contribute a bloody footprint. Tromping around in the goddamn mud isn't in my contract. You'd think they'd at least get me some decent help."

He stopped. "All right everybody, fun's over. Let's take it from the top."

"What?" Doyle bellowed.

"What?" said Holmes.

The director looked the author up and down. "You got something better to do?"

A. Conan Doyle toed a taped marker on the ground and considered the alternatives. "Ah, er, no, I don't suppose I do."

"Alright, let's see if we can do it right this time."

"What?" Holmes exclaimed, "What's he talking about, Watson?"

"Shut up, Holmes."

"You-know-who is waiting for the rushes, and we wouldn't want to keep him waiting."

TO BE OR NOT

The warm sun glinted down on the murky waters of the pond. Water bugs skated across its placid surface, causing ripples. There was the soft drone of insects and the faint tickle of water from some abomination of a cupid that pissed eternally through a cement member, followed by the lap of minute waves.

Perry Percival opened his eyes and looked around. This was just as he had envisioned his retirement would be. Lush gardens. Sleepy sun. Far from the madding crowd. It was the sort of place he would have chosen if he'd been given a choice.

"But I have that within which passes show. These but the trappings and the suits of woe," he said quoting Shakespeare, and grunted.

This place reeked of upper crust dignity and opulence that the scrawny little boy from east London — which he had once been — could never have imagined; but which the adult actor had come to expect. In his time, Percival had been haled the greatest, and he'd played all the best parts from Richard III to Romeo and, later, Montague. His voice had been his claim to fame — his looks weren't much — but his voice was deep and booming. With the kind of timbre and resonance that carried to the very depths of the theatre and instilled presence into any part.

And Percival avoided the punter, the little people, as he had come to think of them. He disdained them as less than insects, and if he didn't dare to examine his past too closely because therein he would find his roots. Instead, Perry Percival (born Sam Jacuweizt) separated himself from them, believing himself a cut above.

He fed on them, lapping up their praise and applause like a cat does cream. He both loved his fans and hated them. He shunned them, as he courted them, espousing certain ideals because they were popular, peculiar or otherwise would get him some publicity.

Like reincarnation. Now that was a laugh!

And Percival swallowed with a gulp and then blew his

exasperation through too-loose lips.

Out on a limb? How about stuck on a lily pad? And the performer wondered what would Shirley McLain think if she could see him now?

As an actor, Percival appreciated irony. In the theatre, you had to develop a fine sense of irony in order to survive. The ridiculous and the sublime are synonymous, but this...

This was too perfect. It took everything he believed, or thought he had believed, and stood it on its collective head. And it did it by giving him everything he'd ever wanted. The posh garden. The solitude.

Percival glared at the serene scene. A fly buzzed past, and he resisted the impulse to swat at it. His stomach grumbled, and the one-time actor hunkered down beside the pond. Too lazy to move. Instead he dosed, chasing past glory and present failures.

Fat, red Koi rose to the surface of the pond and for a moment he hated them. He shouldn't really. They were stuck here just as much as he was stuck here, in this mockery of an idyll.

Another fly swooped down, diving in a kamikaze path, and he couldn't stop himself.

Slurp! His long tongue detached itself from the back of his throat, flicking outward. A direct hit, and it stuck, its buzz descending in the vibrato of death.

Slurp! It disappeared down his throat and he belched indelicately.

Percival stretched first one long leg and then the other. Some would have said that he had attained nirvana, and many would have thought he should be glad to have had his beliefs confirmed, but Perry wasn't so sure. No one told him that his memories would survive intact, and he never paused to realise you could take a step down instead of up.

What would have happened, he wondered, if he had believed in Darwinism? Would he have found himself the missing link? All said and done, reincarnation wasn't all that it was cracked up to be.

What did it matter now? He was alone with the bugs, the insects. No adoring crowds, no appreciative ear, no applause.

And Perry Percival opened his mouth to shriek his protest at eternity. "Rrrrribbit!"

Then the former Thespian gave his best theatrical sigh. Who,

221

he thought, could have it worse than I?

*

A spider's web trembled above Percival's warty head, waving back and forth under the breath of wind created by the whir of flies' wings. The spider opened a multilensed eye and peered down at the pond. The black widow sidled over to frown at the frog on the lily pad, as a second fly circled past. She crouched down, ready to pounce.

The mellifluous croak rattled the web, and she heard the anguish contained therein. If she could have, she would have smiled, glad at least to have got a ring-side seat.

Serves him right, the pompous old windbag.

The fly buzzed closer. The hairy legs bent. Just a few more inches now...

The next instant, a great tongue lashed out, snapping up the fly just before it would have become entangled in her wed.

The spider hopped up and down excitedly.

Damn, thought Sondra McIntyre, one-time agent to the great Perry Percival, What the hell happened to my ten percent?

THE KING'S PLATE

"Harry!"

The broad back stiffened at the shrill tone, but he did not deign to acknowledge it by turning toward the sound.

"Harry!" This time, the voice was deeper, softer, seductive. It emanated from directly behind him.

Just then two hands intruded upon his field of vision, and he flinched. The fingers twitched as they reached eagerly between the folds of his gown. A harsh, guttural voice clicked endearments into his ear, with hard 'g' and nasal diphthong of German.

"Get off, woman," Harry growled and pushed the hands away.

"Do not deny me, husband."

"Nay, you are but sister to me. Remember?"

"Harry, my poor Harry."

The note of sympathy pierced him more than any criticism ever could. He sagged to lean wearily against the mantelpiece.

Yet another voice, louder and more querulous, penetrated the despair which enveloped him.

"Harry! Harry! Why don't you ever listen to me?"

"Leave me in peace," he said.

"Peace he says!"

A twitter ran throughout the room. Henry the Eighth swirled around to glower at his assembled wives, and grimaced at the sight of Ann Boleyn and Catherine Howard's heads sitting upon a silver plate.

At the opposite end of the table, the shrunken and shrivelled, form of Catherine of Aragon bowed in eternal prayer and her fingers fondled the Rosary beads.

"The man who rules using his yard as a gauge," she said, "should not ask for peace."

"Silence, woman, I am king."

"Not any more. Death is the great leveller, don't you know?" the head of Ann Boleyn sneered.

"Hold your tongue, harlot."

223

"What are going to do, Harry?" The skull bounced around on the plate with an ominous clatter. "Chop off my head?"

Catherine Howard giggled, and the conversation so briefly interrupted by his rebellious display began anew.

"... selfish..."

"... fat... repugnant..."

"... and that sore. Stinks with its putrefaction... I, for one, am tired of dressing it..."

"... does not know how to please a woman... now Thomas Culpepper... there's a man for you, a courtly lover..."

"... how many men wield their member to cleft the church in twain..." Catherine of Aragon added her gentle rebuke to the endless litany of grievances.

Henry cradled his head in his hands, wishing now that he had been a monk or a priest rather than a king.

"Oh, God," he groaned.

This was followed by an annoying buzz. A computerised voice intoned. "We are sorry. We are busy helping other customers. You can wait. There are four-and-a-half billion callers in front of you. Or you can hang up and call back sometime in the next millennium."

The women's voices speaking in unison carried over the recording.

"Harry! Harry! Are you listening to me? Look at me when I'm talking to you."

AN AFTERTHOUGHT

"Bloody hell!"

A fist slammed the side of the VDU. The clerk leered wanly at the woman fidgeting on the other side of the desk.

"Computer's on the fritz. I guess we'll have to do this the old fashioned way." He took a thick cylinder of paper from underneath the desk, grabbed an end and then dropped the roll. It unrolled and unrolled and unrolled and unrolled and...

"Palmer, Palmer. Palmer..."

The woman turned back to the desk.

... unrolled.

"Palmer..." The gnarled finger swept down the scroll.

"Ah yes, here it is." The digit halted above the appropriate entry. "Palmer, Jessica, errwrah —"

He glanced up and gaped at her from under a single raised eyebrow. A smile slid across the warty face.

"Oh, it's you. We've been waiting for you."

ABOUT THE AUTHOR

Jessica Palmer has had 28 books published, both fiction and nonfiction. Her novels – horror, fantasy and science fiction – were released by Pocket Books in the United States and Scholastic in the United Kingdom. She has written two textbooks about Native American history, which were published by McFarland, and an encyclopedia of natural history released by Harper Collins' label Element Books and later by Thorson in the UK.

Palmer has also written ten science-and-technology manuals on the topics of explosives and radiation. These were distributed globally. It was this work that brought her to Great Britain in 1988.

The daughter of a professional clown, Palmer refers to her switch to writing fiction as an exercise in damage limitation. She taught classes and conducted workshops on creative writing and publishing at North Shropshire College in Whitchurch, Stanmore College and the Islington Arts Factory in London.

As a journalist, Palmer won awards in New Mexico and Texas for writing features, public service and breaking news – the most recent in 2013. Palmer has also written satirical columns for newspapers, including "A Slice of Life" and "How to Make Love to your Personal Computer."

Her two loves are writing and animals. She started a nonprofit in Kansas for wildlife rescue and has held a wildlife rehabilitation permit since 2002.

Parallel Universe Publications

A SAUCERFUL OF SECRETS by Andrew Darlington
ISBN: 978-0-9935742-0-7

THE WINTER HUNT AND OTHER STORIES
by Steve Lockley & Paul Lewis
ISBN: 978-0-9932888-9-0

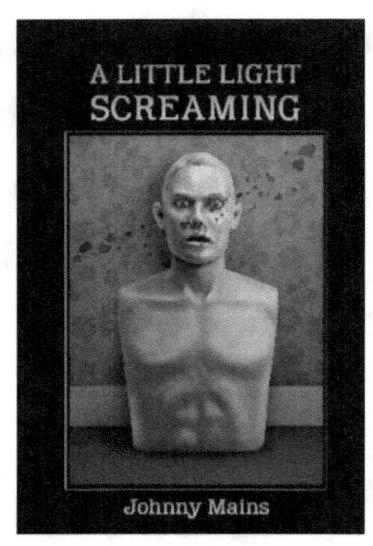

A LITTLE LIGHT SCREAMING by Johnny Mains
ISBN: 978-0-9932888-5-2

ENGLAND 'B': 90 MINUTES OF HELL by Richard Staines
ISBN: 978-0-9932888-7-6

AND NOBODY LIVED HAPPILY EVER AFTER by Kate Farrell
ISBN: 978-0-9932888-8-3

FISHHEAD; THE DARKER TALES OF IRVIN S. COBB
ISBN: 978-0-9932888-6-9

KITCHEN SINK GOTHIC: Selected by David and Linden Riley
ISBN: 978-0-9932888-3-8

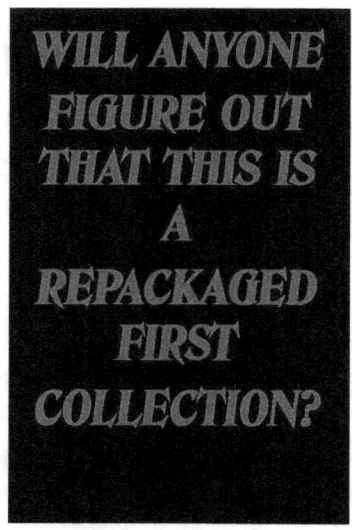

**WILL ANYONE FIGURE OUT THAT THIS IS A REPACKAGED FIRST
COLLECTION?** by Johnny Mains
ISBN: 978-0-9574535-7-9

BLACK CEREMONIES by Charles Black
ISBN: 978-0-9574535-5-5

HIS OWN MAD DEMONS:
DARK TALES FROM DAVID A. RILEY
ISBN: 978-0-9574535-8-6

THEIR CRAMPED DARK WORLD by David A. Riley
ISBN: 978-0-9574535-9-3

THE HEAVEN MAKER AND OTHER GRUESOME TALES
by Craig Herbertson
ISBN: 978-0-9932888-2-1

GOBLIN MIRE by David A. Riley
ISBN: 978-0-9574535-4-8

THINGS THAT GO BUMP IN THE NIGHT
selected by Douglas Draa and David A. Riley
ISBN: 978-0-9574535-6-2

CLASSIC WEIRD selected David A. Riley
ISBN: 978-0-9574535-3-1

MOLOCH'S CHILDREN by David A. Riley
ISBN: 978-0-9932888-1-4

Check our website:
http://paralleluniversepublications.blogspot.co.uk/

www.ingramcontent.com/pod-product-compliance
Lightning Source LLC
Chambersburg PA
CBHW071323250626
47159CB00004B/1441